STATE OF TIME

**VIRGIL JONES MYSTERY THRILLER SERIES
BOOK 20**

THOMAS SCOTT

Copyright © 2024 by Thomas Scott. All rights reserved. No part of this book may be reproduced in any form or by any electronic or mechanical means, including photocopying, recording, or by any information storage and retrieval system without written permission from both the publisher and copyright owner of this book.

This book is a work of fiction. No artificial intelligence (commonly referred to as: AI) was used in the conceptualization, creation, or production of this book. Names, characters, places, governmental institutions, venues, and all incidents or events are either the product of the author's imagination or are used fictitiously. Any resemblance to actual persons, living or dead, businesses, companies, events, locales, venues, or government organizations is entirely coincidental.

For information contact: ThomasScottBooks.com

*For Debra Hizer-Johnson,
and her late husband, Christopher Patrick Johnson*

— **Also by Thomas Scott** —

The Virgil Jones Series In Order

State of Anger - Book 1
State of Betrayal - Book 2
State of Control - Book 3
State of Deception - Book 4
State of Exile - Book 5
State of Freedom - Book 6
State of Genesis - Book 7
State of Humanity - Book 8
State of Impact - Book 9
State of Justice - Book 10
State of Killers - Book 11
State of Life - Book 12
State of Mind - Book 13
State of Need - Book 14
State of One - Book 15
State of Play - Book 16
State of Qualms - Book 17
State of Remains - Book 18
State of Suspense - Book 19
State of Time - Book 20
State of Unity - Book 21

The Jack Bellows Series In Order

Wayward Strangers - Book 1
Brave Strangers - Book 2

Visit **ThomasScottBooks.com** for further information regarding future release dates, and more.

Time /tīm/

The continued sequence of existence and events that occurs in an *apparently* irreversible succession from the past, through the present, and into the future.

"Da story da story, no matter when it get told."
—Delroy Rouche

"Time isn't really real."
—Mason Jones

"Fat chance, Mister. You're stuck with me until the end of time."
—Sandy Jones

CHAPTER ONE

Despite all the good things still with them in their lives…the rescue, the healing, and the continuity of nearly all that mattered, the past was somehow without color, as if everything was made solely of black and white that blended together into varying shades of gray; a bleakness where the future was benign, lost to those who looked at it with any sort of hope or a prophetic eye that might hold answers to questions not yet posed.

The casket was covered with an American flag, and Sandy knew her dreams of a brighter future had just died, any promise of normalcy forever lost. Uniformed men, many of whom she knew and considered family—she'd actually shared meals with them at her home—

stood at attention, tears streaming down their faces, their jaws quivering with such intensity that Sandy could actually hear their teeth clicking together.

The preacher held a bible in his hands but he didn't look at the written passages when he spoke, the words coming from memory instead of the printed page. Once finished with his prayers, he looked directly at Sandy and spoke of heroism, dedication to family, and the fearlessness that was part of the one man Sandy had loved more than anyone else in her entire life.

She wept openly, her own tears dotting her dress, her head down, her shoes resting atop the fake green carpet made to resemble grass. Though nearly everyone in attendance was there for her and what was left of her family, Sandy felt utterly alone, the people around her like wax figures, ones that would, she knew, eventually melt their way out of her life. In her moment of desolation, she thought if it was possible, she'd rip the flag away and let it fall to the ground, then crawl inside the casket to be with the man she couldn't imagine living without.

She wiped the tears from her face and looked up, not at the flag-draped coffin before her, but at the dull gray sky. When she looked back down, Sandy let her gaze come to rest…not on the casket that held her father's remains, but on the boy he'd given his life for when he rescued him from the fire.

The boy's name was Virgil Jones, and while no one knew it at the moment—and wouldn't for decades to come—in his death, Sandy's father, Andrew Small, had given them all what they needed. It was a gift...one that would, over time, change the outcome of countless lives in ways no one could yet imagine.

A MURDER OF CROWS TOOK FLIGHT AMIDST THE SORROW of the day, the flap of their wings like laundry snapping in a stiff afternoon breeze. Virgil and his mother, Elizabeth, along with his grandfather, Jack Bellows, all turned and watched the birds fly off. There were so many that for just a moment the sky seemed to fade from gray to black, the day somehow turning darker than it already was. When Virgil looked back, it didn't escape him that other than his mom and his grandpa, the only other person who seemed to take notice of the crows was the daughter of the man who'd saved him from the fire. He didn't know her first name, but he caught the lack of expression on her face when their eyes met. To Virgil, she looked like a china doll that hadn't yet been graced with a painted brush.

Virgil reached up and covered the bandage on his jawline with his hand before looking away in shame.

Virgil's father, Mason Jones—a sheriff's deputy with Marion County—didn't attend the funeral of the man who had saved his son. He rationalized his absence by telling his wife and father-in-law that he was required to work that day, and there simply wasn't room in the roster for him to take any personal time off. But the truth of the matter was this: Another man had given his life to save Mason's only son, and while Mason had always been the type of person that others looked up to and admired for the kind of man he was, he simply couldn't face the fact that someone else had died in his place.

Bottom line? As Fire Battalion Station Chief Andrew Small was memorialized and laid to rest, Virgil Jones wasn't the only one looking away in shame. Mason was as well. They just went about it in different ways, as fathers and sons are often wont to do.

And then, as if time wasn't real, Virgil was back inside himself, the man on the opposite side of his desk wearing a quizzical smile on his face.

Virgil pulled an envelope from his desk drawer and slid it over to Jim Wilson, the newest member of the Major Crimes Unit, of which Virgil was in charge. The MCU had just wrapped up a case and shut down a major illegal drug manufacturing operation—the case itself cracked wide open by one of Virgil's senior detectives, Tom Rosencrantz. But the whole thing had come with a cost when Rosencrantz himself had been captured, beaten, and almost killed. Rosencrantz would survive, but in the meantime, Wilson—a former Elkhart County sheriff's deputy who'd worked the case with the MCU—would serve as a temporary replacement for the next six months or so while Rosencrantz healed.

After Wilson opened the envelope, he pulled out a gold Indiana State Police badge that had the words *Major Crimes Unit* front and center.

Virgil looked at Wilson and said, "You're a hell of a cop. Welcome to the family, kid."

But Wilson's smile began to fade, his head tilting slightly to the left. "Excuse me, sir? I mean, uh, Jonesy…are you okay? You look a little pale, or something."

Virgil sat back in his chair without really meaning

to, and after a moment, he rubbed his face with both hands, then said, "Uh, yeah. I'm fine. Haven't been sleeping very well lately, and I was just thinking about something that happened a long time ago. It sort of hit me right out of the blue."

"I know we don't really know each other all that well—at least not yet—but is it something you want to talk about?"

Virgil let a natural smile form. "No, but thanks, Jim."

"You bet. It has been a long couple of days," Wilson said. "Probably chalk it up to stress, huh?" When Virgil didn't respond, Wilson looked around the office for a beat, and said, "So, where would you like me to start? Hey, Jonesy…did you hear me?"

But time had sailed away again, and when it did, Virgil went with it.

Jacob Avery walked over to Virgil's bunk and shook him awake. Virgil wasn't pleased. They'd been out all night on patrol, keeping an eye out for any of the Iraqi Republican Guards, who occasionally, but not often, tried to close in on their camp. "Ah, Christ, Ave, I just fell asleep. What the hell is it?"

"For starters, don't kill the messenger. The CO wants you and Wheeler in his office. Said to double-time it."

Virgil and his adopted brother, Murton Wheeler, were nearing the tail end of their tour in the gulf, and Avery had been with them the entire time as part of their recon unit. They'd all formed an unlikely bond with each other, the bond coming from a mistake that Avery's father had made before his son, Jacob, was ever born. Mason had arrested Joe Avery after he'd managed to kill three men in the span of less than ten minutes. Some tried to call the whole thing an accident, but one of the men who ended up dead was a cop, so Avery's old man got the chair. Given all that, Virgil and Murton thought Jacob Avery might give them problems while they served together in the Army, but as it turned out they became friends during their time in the service.

Virgil rubbed the sleep and sand out of his eyes and said, "Did he say what he wanted? The CO?"

"Yeah, he did," Avery said. "And I just told you. He wants you and Wheeler in his office…like two minutes ago. Get moving, will you? The guy's got some sort of hard-on for me as it is, and I'm hoping you won't make it worse by draggin' ass."

"Where's Murt?"

Murton cleared his throat, then kicked Virgil's bunk

from the other side. "I'm standing right here. As usual, I'm waiting on you. Let's go already, huh?"

Virgil and Murton hurried over to the command post operations center, gave their CO a casual salute, then Virgil said, "Ave said you wanted to see us, sir?"

Their commanding officer had a telephone receiver in his hand and it was pressed tight to his chest. Instead of answering Virgil, he reached up and ran his free hand across the top of his buzz cut, then put the phone to his ear. "I'm sorry for the wait, sir. They're here now. Yes, sir, I understand. They're in good hands, I give you my word. One moment, please."

The CO stood from behind his desk, handed Virgil the receiver, then said, "I'll give you some privacy. I'm sorry about this, boys…I truly am." Then he walked out of the office.

Virgil and Murton looked at each other, both young men thinking the same thing. Murton visibly swallowed and said, "Mom?"

It was a valid concern. Both of them knew their mother was sick with cancer, but the last time Virgil had spoken with his father, he'd been told that Elizabeth had a fighting chance.

Virgil put the phone up to his ear and held it at an angle so Murton—who'd moved in close to his brother—could hear what was said. "Hello?"

The static on the line was so bad that Virgil could barely hear who was on the other end.

"Virgil? Is that you? It's your father. Can you hear me?"

"Just barely," Virgil said. "Speak up if you can. What's wrong? Is it Mom?"

"Is Murton with you, Son?"

"I'm right here," Murton said. "What's going on?"

"Your mother and I have been trying to reach you boys for over a week."

"It's the Iraqis, Dad," Virgil said, his relief evident at the mention of his mother. "They don't put up much of a fight, but they sure know how to sabotage things. They've got the oil wells lit up as far as the eye can see. The sky is black as night, even during the day. They also manage to cut the phone lines on a regular basis. I'm surprised you were able to get through at all. Are you and Mom okay?"

Mason paused before he answered, and Virgil could feel the relief slipping away. "No, Son. We're not. There's no easy way to say this, so I'm just going to come out with it. It's your Grandpa Jack, boys. He died last week of congestive heart failure. I'm so sorry to have to tell you like this, but we couldn't reach you. His funeral was yesterday. Hello? Virg, Murt? Did you hear me?"

"I heard you," Virgil said. He sort of snapped it at Wilson without meaning to, because in the moment he wasn't quite sure who he was speaking with. He raised his hands, palms out, then sort of chuckled and said, "Sorry. I might be more tired than I realize. Why don't you, uh, get with Sarah and get started on the paperwork. As a new employee of the state police, there are about a billion forms to fill out. You'll be partnered with Ross until Rosencrantz comes back, and as you know, once that happens, you'll be transferred over to Jon Mok's unit as part of the SWAT team. So, when you're done with the paper, track down Ross and he'll get you set up with your weapons and other gear. Sound good?"

"You bet," Wilson said.

"Listen, do me favor?"

"Sure."

"Send Murt in, will you?"

Wilson said he would, and a few minutes later Murton walked into his brother's office. "What's up?"

"Mind covering for me today?" Virgil said.

"Of course not. You got something going?"

Virgil rubbed his eyes with the heels of both hands. "No, I think I'm just tired. I'm going to go home and take it easy for the day...do a little yard work, or something. Maybe entertain the fish for a while."

"Are you sleeping okay?"

"It's that obvious, huh?"

"In case you've forgotten, I'm familiar with the effects."

"I haven't forgotten," Virgil said. "But this isn't that. I'm not having the same dream every night. In fact, I don't think I'm dreaming at all. Wait, let me rephrase that. I know I'm not dreaming because I'm not getting enough sleep to even make it to that stage."

Murton turned the corners of his mouth down. "Well, there's nothing wrong with a little 'me' time every once in a while. Go home and take a nap. We've got everything covered here."

"I might just do that," Virgil said.

"But, if you're going to do yard work, feel free to mower on over to my place." Then, with a whiff of skepticism: "You're not secretly meeting with gate installers, are you?"

Virgil and Murton both lived out in the country, just south of Indianapolis, on the same plot of land...their houses located at the tag end of a three-mile gravel road, their yards separated by a fishing pond and a helicopter landing pad that had been installed at the behest of Virgil's friend, Hewitt (Mac) McConnell. Mac was not only a friend, but Virgil's business partner, and the former governor of Indiana.

Virgil's wife, Sandy, had been the governor for a short period of time after Mac stepped down to run Said, Inc., and since neither Virgil nor Sandy wanted to move out of their home and into the governor's mansion, a deal was made to turn their gravel road into a private drive. So now Virgil and Sandy, along with Murton and his wife, Becky—who worked as a researcher and computer guru for the Major Crimes Unit—had what was arguably the longest driveway in the entire Midwest. And all that meant Virgil wanted a gate for security purposes. Unfortunately, Murton didn't. He thought there were too many potential problems to justify the whole thing, and he and Virgil had been going back and forth about it for months. So far the women had managed to stay out of the whole thing…though they were secretly calling it The Great Gate Debate.

Despite how he felt, Virgil let out a little chuckle. "No, I'm not meeting with any of the gate companies. But you'll be the third to know if I do." He stood from behind his desk and said, "Anyway, thanks for covering. I'll catch you later tonight…or tomorrow morning."

Murton—who knew his brother better than anyone else in the world—heard the false note of the chuckle and the tone of voice Virgil had used. He turned in his chair as Virgil walked toward the door. "Hey, Jonesman?"

"Yeah?"

"Everything okay?"

CHAPTER TWO

Virgil took more than the afternoon. He took the week, though it didn't seem to make any difference. The sleep, it just wouldn't come. If he had to put a number to it, he thought his nightly average was somewhere in the neighborhood of two hours, tops.

But no matter, Virgil told himself it was time to get back to work. He'd just parked his Range Rover in the MCU lot, and didn't even make it to the entrance before his phone buzzed in his pocket. He thought about ignoring the damned thing because he was almost inside anyway, but Virgil had a wife he dearly loved and two young boys who seemed to be growing up much faster than he wanted them to. So as a faithful family man, Virgil knew he needed to at least check the screen to see who was, in all likelihood, about to change his plans for the day…or ruin them altogether.

He let his shoulders slump without really meaning to when he saw who was calling, and though he desperately wanted to let the call go to voicemail, he knew if he did it would simply be the equivalent of kicking the can down the road. Besides, if he didn't answer, Murton would end up getting the call. So with that thought firmly embedded in his brain, he tried to drop some cheer into his voice as he hit the Answer button. He wasn't sure if he pulled it off or not.

"Good morning, Cora. I'm guessing you're calling to congratulate me and the rest of the squad on a job well done. Another illegal drug and money-laundering operation out of business thanks to the hard work and dedication of the Major Crimes Unit detectives."

He and Cora LaRue—the current governor and Virgil's direct boss—hadn't actually spoken to each other since the MCU had cleared the illegal drug manufacturing case. Cora let out a snort—her version of a laugh—and simply said, "Hardly. If you'd have done your job as well as you seem to think you did, we wouldn't be talking right now."

That got Virgil's attention in a hurry. "I'm afraid I don't know what you're talking about." He pulled the outer door of the MCU open and stepped inside. When he glanced up at the second level of the facility, he saw Murton leaning against the railing, sipping a cup of coffee.

"I'm not surprised. Where's Chucklehead?"

"You're speaking of Murton?"

Virgil heard Cora let out a sigh. "No, sharp stuff. Bozo the Clown. Of course I'm speaking of Wheeler. Where is he?"

"He's right upstairs. Why? What'd he do?"

Murton saw Virgil looking at him, and since he was close enough, he also heard what his brother had just said. He hip-checked himself off the railing and made his way over to the stairs.

"It's not what he did, Jonesy. It's what he didn't do. And he's not alone in it either. It's also what you didn't do. In fact, no one in your squad did."

Virgil loved Cora. As a boss, he knew he could do much worse, but sometimes having a conversation with the woman—governor or not—was a little like trying to pull your own teeth with a pair of tweezers.

"You didn't get the case notes from the Shelby County incident?"

"Yes, yes, I got the case notes. Hairdo finally sent them over and I went through them earlier this morning."

"By Hairdo, I assume you're speaking of our operations manager, Sarah Palmer."

"That'd be the one."

Virgil didn't intend it, but a little annoyance crept into his next statement. "So what, exactly, is the problem?"

"Lose the attitude, Slick." Then Cora lowered her voice a notch and said, "The problem is I've got a DEA agent sitting in my anteroom right now who thinks he's God's gift to the federal government. Want to know who else is here? Don't bother answering…I'll just tell you. It's our two former governors, and a lawyer by the name of J. Allen Turkis."

"Sandy's there?"

"What'd I just say? I want you and Wheeler to signal-10 your butts over here right now. I need some backup. An explanation might go a long way as well. Are you copying me on this, Detective?"

Cora ended the call, and Virgil could feel his brother standing behind him on the stairs.

"What was that all about?" Murton said.

Virgil shrugged. "I'm not exactly sure." Then he let

out a little humorless laugh and said, "Let me try that answer again. I have no idea."

"Run it for me," Murton said.

Virgil stuck the phone back in his pocket. "In the car. She approved lights and siren. Said she wanted backup."

"I guess you're driving, then."

"Yup. Let's go."

As they were walking out of the building, they naturally passed Sarah's horseshoe-shaped desk in the center of the operations area. Virgil took ten seconds to stop and ask her a question. "Any problems with the paper on Shelby County that you sent over to Cora? All the T's dotted and I's crossed?"

Sarah smiled, then shook her head, her long red hair swishing back and forth as she did. "No problems that I'm aware of…other than you just mixed up your alphabet. May I ask why?"

Virgil turned his palms up. "Not sure. At least not yet. Don't sweat it, Sarah. Murt and I are being called onto the carpet, but we'll figure it out."

"Anything I can do?"

Murton gave her a wink. "Let you know."

Once they were on their way—Virgil didn't bother with the lights and siren—he told Murton about the phone conversation. "Cora told me that Mac, Sandy, Turkis, and a DEA agent are all waiting for us at the statehouse. She says we missed something down in Shelby County on our last operation."

Murton looked at nothing for a few minutes, and Virgil let him. "If we did, I'm not seeing it, Jonesy. All the bad actors got taken out at the compound, the DEA got their pill presses and dies back, and other than the paperwork—which Sarah just told us was in order—I can't imagine what it might be."

"Same here," Virgil said. "Cora described the DEA agent as being God's gift to the federal government, by the way."

"Blackwell?"

"Sounds like our guy."

Murton looked out the side window for a moment, then said, "If this is about what went down at the compound, why would Mac, Sandy, and Turkis be there?"

Virgil reached up and rubbed his temples. "You got any aspirin? I'm starting to get a headache."

Murton nodded. "Yeah, in my squad car. But since we're in your Range Rover, you're on your own. You don't carry any?"

"I usually don't need them." Then out of nowhere: "Cora called you Chucklehead when I was on the phone with her."

Murton smiled. "Did she?"

"Yeah, but I think she said it with love."

"How can you tell?" Murton said.

"It's like she's trying to find a nickname that sticks," Virgil said. "I'm starting to think she's closing in on it."

Murton laughed. "Yeah, she'll figure it out eventually. So, anyway…Mac, Sandy, and Turkis? The only thing I can think of is that the old Salter properties—and that includes the compound, as you well know—are now owned by Mac."

Virgil nodded. "That was my thought too."

Murton turned and faced his brother. "Why did you just use the word, 'was'?"

"Because I think there must be more at play, Murt. I'm sure Blackwell will let us know whatever is on his mind…if it is Blackwell. And Turkis being there makes sense because he's Mac's attorney and half the case we either just did or didn't close was wrapped around the money-laundering problem coming out of Said, Inc."

"So that leaves Small," Murton said.

Virgil nodded. "Yeah…and us."

When Virgil and Murton walked into the anteroom outside of the governor's office, things went bad right from the jump. They found Agent Blackwell sitting alone, with Sandy, Mac, Cora, and Turkis nowhere in sight.

Blackwell stood from his chair and got right in Virgil's face. "It's about time," Blackwell said. "LaRue told me you'd be right over…nearly an hour ago."

Virgil stayed calm, looked Blackwell in the eye, and said, "That's *Governor* LaRue. How about showing a little respect?"

"How about addressing my last statement?"

"Traffic," Virgil said. "What can you do?"

"Isn't your vehicle equipped with lights and siren?"

Murton stepped up closer to Blackwell and said, "Ask you a question?"

Blackwell turned and said, "What?" He practically hissed it.

Murton gave him a fake smile. "This is, by my count, the third time we've had some sort of interaction with you."

"That's not a question," Blackwell said.

Murton picked an imaginary piece of lint from his own shirtsleeve then said, "No, but this is: Were you born with a stick up your ass, or do you have to reinsert it on a daily basis? I'm guessing the latter. If I'm right, your monthly lube bill must be outrageous."

Blackwell was so mad he started to vibrate, then out of nowhere he wound up and took a swing at Murton. But Murton wasn't the type of man to let just anyone get the drop on him. He saw the swing coming about two seconds before Blackwell himself knew he was going to throw a punch.

Virgil stepped back because he saw the punch coming as well. It wasn't that he didn't want to help his brother. He simply knew it wouldn't be necessary.

Murton reached up with his left hand, and when Blackwell's right fist hit his palm, it sounded like a firecracker. Then Murton wrapped his fingers around Blackwell's hand and began to squeeze, his fake smile still firmly in place. He kept squeezing until he saw Blackwell's shoulder start to droop, his eyes crinkling at their edges, his face going pale.

Then he squeezed just a bit harder, following his attacker as he went down on one knee. Virgil stepped over, took Blackwell's weapon from his shoulder holster, and tucked it into the back of his belt. Then Murton finally let go.

Once he was finally able to speak, Blackwell said, "That's assault on a federal agent. I'll have you both up on federal charges before the day is out. Give me back my weapon."

Virgil laughed…a mean, guttural grunt, and said, "I'll hang on to your gun for now. You can pick it up from the statehouse security guards before you leave. As for your federal charges, I don't think so. You're a disgrace to your own agency, Blackwell. As a sworn officer of the state and witness to the events that just transpired, here's what I saw: You took a swing at my partner, who, as you know, is also an officer of the state. He defended himself, and for the safety of all parties involved, I disarmed you. It's not that complicated. It also wasn't very hard, either."

Blackwell was massaging his hand. "Say whatever you want, asshole. It's my word against yours. And my words have the weight of the federal government behind them."

Virgil tipped his head to the side and gave Blackwell a thoughtful nod. "That may very well be." Then he pointed at the camera tucked in the corner of the ceiling and said, "But my words have the weight of the state's video surveillance system. It's monitored twenty-four hours a day. I'm sure someone will be along shortly to show you out. In fact, they should be here any second." Then he leaned in close until they were almost nose to nose. "Now answer my partner's question. Born with it, or daily basis?"

Blackwell never got a chance to answer—not that Virgil thought he would have anyway—because just then a uniformed statehouse security guard came through the door. The guard smiled, then said, "Jonesy, Murt. How's it going?"

Virgil stood up straight, and said, "Hey, Bill. Haven't seen you in a while."

The guard named Bill laughed through his nose and said, "Well you would if you'd stop into your own bar once or twice a year. I'm only there paying your rent and electric bill about every other night and twice on the weekends." Then the playfulness went out of his voice. He tipped his chin at Blackwell, and said, "I saw the whole thing. What's with this asshole?"

Blackwell stepped forward and moved into the guard's line of sight. "Who are you calling asshole?"

The guard spun Blackwell around, slapped a set of cuffs on him, then pushed him down in the chair. "Shut up. We're talking about you, but that doesn't mean we're talking to you."

"The aforementioned asshole is an agent with the

DEA," Murton said. Then he looked around, covered his upper lip with the edge of his palm, and said, "I hope no one is holding."

"I'm clean," Bill said.

Then, just for fun, Virgil said, "Kind of surprised at your response time. Thought you'd have been quicker."

Bill bobbed his head around in a circle. "Well, I would have been, but when I was watching the monitor I saw it was you and Murt. Knew if I came running right away, I'd have missed the whole damn show."

"You could have watched the replay," Virgil said.

"Ah, with you guys it's the live performance that counts. Anyway, what do you want me to do with this idiot?"

Virgil pulled out Blackwell's gun, took ten seconds to strip it down to its basic components, then handed the gun parts to the guard and said, "Escort him from the building and make sure he doesn't come back in. If he does, arrest him, put him down in holding, and I'll deal with it later."

Bill made a snick noise with his cheek and tongue. "Gotcha. You check him for other weapons?"

Murton laughed. "He's got a pretty mean stick he carries around. Not sure you'd want to go after it though."

Bill gave Murton a frown. "Why not?"

"It's pretty well hidden. You'd have to do a strip search."

Bill caught on right away. "No thanks." Then to Blackwell: "All right, Stiffy. On your feet. Time to go. Murt, Jones-man, take 'er easy."

"You too, Bill," Virgil said. The guard was no sooner out of the room when the door to Cora's office popped open, and Mac was standing there, a bemused look on his face.

"We saw the entire thing on Cora's monitor. I don't know how many times I've said this in the past, but I'll say it again: You guys are worth the price of admission, and I mean every single time. Step on in, will you? The governor is waiting, and let me tell you, she is not what any reasonable outdoorsy type of person would call a happy camper."

CHAPTER THREE

Virgil and Murton walked into Cora's office and found Sandy smiling, Turkis trying to hide one of his own, and Cora with a scowl firmly fixed in place.

Cora joined Mac and the others at her corner conference table, motioned for Virgil and Murton to have a seat, then said, "Does everything always have to be so dramatic with the two of you?"

Virgil gave his wife a quick kiss on the cheek, sat down, then turned to his boss. "As dramatics go, that was nothing. Besides, Blackwell made the play, not us. He tried to swing on Murton. What were we supposed to do? Stand there and take it?"

Cora waved him off, jerked her thumb at the screen on the wall and said, "Yeah, yeah, we saw the whole thing on the monitor."

Murton pulled out a chair and examined his fingernails like he didn't have a care in the world. "Why was Blackwell out there by himself, anyway?"

"You're not here to ask questions, Wheeler," Cora said. "You're here to answer them." Then she softened just a bit and said, "But since it's not an entirely unreasonable request for information, I'll tell you. The man was so full of himself, Mr. Turkis told him to wait outside."

"I'm surprised he listened," Virgil said.

"I can be rather persuasive when need be," Turkis said.

"That might be something of an understatement," Cora said before turning to face Virgil. "What took you guys so long to get here?"

Virgil repeated the same statement he'd made to Blackwell. "Traffic. What can you do?" Then before Cora could respond, Virgil looked at Turkis, and said, "Forget what I said about the poker table, Allen. I can see you're trying not to smile. It looks like you may have a little bit of a tell after all."

"That's because until just a few moments ago I've never actually seen the two of you in action. It was rather…amusing." Then Turkis's smile went away, and he said, "But I'll sit across the felt from you whenever you'd like to give it a go."

Virgil chuffed. "No thanks. Why was Blackwell here?"

"He dropped a load of fecal matter on Mac's desk, and now we've got to deal with it," Cora said.

When Virgil spoke, it was mostly to the entire group, "So, what seems to be the problem?"

"In a minute, Jonesy," Cora said. "But first, most everyone in this room wants to hear your version of what happened out at the Salter compound in Shelby County."

"You mean former Salter compound," Mac said.

Virgil ignored Mac's comment and gave Cora a frown…not to antagonize her, but because he didn't understand. His next statement said as much. "Why? And what do you mean by our *version*? It's all in the reports. You told me on the phone you have them, you've read them, and I checked with Sarah before we left the MCU. She told me everything was in order."

Turkis cleared his throat, looked at Cora, and said, "May I?"

"It's one of the reasons you're here, Mr. Turkis," Cora said. "Be my guest."

Turkis turned to Virgil and Murton. "I'm sure your paperwork is in order, Detectives. That really isn't the issue. But certain information has come to light, said information having been delivered by the federal government's delightful Agent Blackwell. Our lovely governor here is simply doing her level best not to break any rules."

"What rules aren't we trying to break?" Murton said.

"The ones where the sitting governor of our state divulges highly sensitive operational information to private citizens such as myself and our two former governors, here. Your reports and the information they contain are a result of your work product on behalf of the state. If Governor LaRue were to disclose their contents to us, she'd be breaking any number of laws. I'm sure any lawyer worth their salt could make it all go away on her behalf, but who needs that sort of grief in their life?"

"Okay, I understand about Cora," Virgil said. "But how does that get us off the hook?"

"We've already had that conversation, Detective."

Virgil thought about it for a few seconds, then said, "You're speaking of the fact that you are Mac's corporate lawyer, and because my wife and I are both partnered with the holding company he controls, you are, in fact, our attorney as well."

"That's right."

"So if I tell you what happened at the compound, I'm speaking with my lawyer."

"Correct," Turkis said. "And there is nothing illegal about that."

"That all makes perfect sense," Sandy said. "As private citizens, we're allowed to tell the governor anything we want…and we have informed her of Blackwell's, um, threats, I suppose you could say. But Cora herself is covered because she didn't tell us anything. And since you're the lawyer in the room for myself, my husband, and Mac, we're all good. But what about Murton?"

Murton smiled. "I love you, Small."

"A fair question," Turkis said. "But since Detective Wheeler was a part of the operation—not to mention a part of your family—it seems logical that we'd need at least one other person connected to the operation to corroborate any statements made regarding the events that took place. As second-in-command of the Major Crimes Unit, Detective Wheeler is the rational choice."

Cora actually laughed. "You don't often hear that."

Turkis gave her a kind smile and said, "I'm sure I wouldn't know. And Madam Governor, you'll forgive me, but would you please allow us a bit of privacy?"

"You're putting me out of my own office?"

"It's for your protection, Cora," Mac said. Then he looked at Sandy, let his voice go flat, and finished with, "Besides, you get used to it."

Sandy gave Mac a wink.

Cora stood from her seat, walked over to her desk, and pressed a button on her phone.

"Yes, Ma'am?" Baker said. Emily Baker—a former fighter pilot turned state cop—was Cora's personal security guard and detail driver.

"Meet me at the elevator. You and I are taking an early lunch break."

"Yes, Ma'am. Destination?"

"I'll let you pick. Two minutes." Then she looked at Virgil and Sandy. "I'm thinking of swinging by your place tonight. Any objections?"

"Cora, you're always welcome at our home," Virgil said. "You know that. How about we plan on dinner?" Virgil looked at Sandy. "Seven?"

"Works for me," Sandy said. Then back to Cora: "Bring Baker as well. We'll have a little cookout."

Cora narrowed her eyes. "Who's doing the cooking out?" She was looking at Virgil when she spoke.

Turkis tried to hide his smile again. He'd heard all about Virgil's grilled chicken episodes from Mac.

"Yeah, yeah. We'll skip the chicken. How's Wagyu beef sound?"

Mac let a look of mock horror show on his face. "Wagyu beef? I hope you're not talking about the Kobe variety. That stuff goes for upwards of five hundred bucks a pound. Perhaps we should reevaluate our split on the sonic drilling units."

Virgil laughed. "Not gonna happen, Mac. Besides, I didn't hear you complaining when you drank all my Pappy last time you were out."

Mac smiled at his friend. "Well, if you've room for one more, I believe I'm free this evening as well."

Murton got in on the action. "Wagyu beef, huh? You know, Becky and I don't have any plans this evening, and as you know, we live within walking distance…"

ONCE CORA WAS GONE, TURKIS GOT RIGHT DOWN TO the nut-cutting, as lawyers often do. He looked at Virgil and Murton, and said, "I have some information to share with you, courtesy of Agent Blackwell, but before I do, I'd like to hear everything that happened at the compound. Please don't leave anything out."

Virgil turned his palms up and said, "Well, I—" And that's as far as he got before Murton interrupted him.

"Is this conversation being recorded?"

Turkis shook his head. "No, it is not. I have an

excellent memory, Detective. And please try to remember, we're all on the same side here."

Murton gave Turkis a rueful look. "Sorry, force of habit. Recordings haven't always served me well."

Turkis nodded as though he knew what Murton was talking about. "I'm sure." Then back to Virgil: "Detective?"

Virgil gave his brother a dry look and said, "Well, what I was about to say was you should start with Murt. He arrived at the compound before I did. Agent Stronghill was with him."

Turkis turned to Murton and raised his eyebrows.

Murton leaned back in his chair and interlaced his fingers on top of his head. Then he closed his eyes and told the story.

"The intel came in at the last minute. They had Rosencrantz and we all knew it, but there were two different locations to check. We were out of time and had to split the squad. It was my idea. Rosie was either dead or dying, so we simply didn't have a choice. Mac had given us permission to enter, so Virgil and the rest of the squad went over to the main house and conducted a quick search. While they were doing that, Tony and I made our way over to the compound, then went in on foot from the rear of the property…"

After Murton had finished his recollection of events—he told the story all the way to the end, including the death of Deputy Reynolds—Turkis turned to Virgil and said, "Do you have anything to add, Jonesy?"

Virgil shook his head. Murton hadn't told the part where Ross and Wilson were hiding in the woods and ready to take a shot at Reynolds. "No. Murt hit the highlights. And to be honest, other than the brief gunfight once the chopper set down inside the compound, I was focused on getting Rosencrantz out. You have to understand, the entire thing was nothing more than an emergency extraction on our part."

Turkis kept his face blank, his eyes focused and unblinking. "I see. Let me ask you this, if I may: Had it been possible to extract Detective Rosencrantz from the compound without having to resort to, mm, extreme measures, let's say, would you have done that?"

"You're asking if we could have been a bit more judicious with our ammunition?" Virgil said, rather dryly.

"In a manner of speaking."

"Let me be clear, Allen," Virgil said, his lack of sleep letting some annoyance creep into his voice. "We don't take out the bad actors for fun, nor do we use them for target practice. Does that answer your question?"

"No, I'm afraid it does not."

Murton could sense the direction of the conversation, so he interjected his own thoughts. "I'd like to add something to my previous statement. Prior to Tony and I going to the compound—this was while we were still at the Martin residence—Virgil gave me a very specific set of instructions. He told me…and this might not be word for word, but he said that if Detective Rosencrantz was at the main house, he'd let me and Tony know the second they had him. If that was the case, I had orders to walk away from the compound, which I absolutely would have done. Virgil made it very clear that our mission objective in the moment was the successful rescue of our fellow detective, and nothing more."

"And yet over a dozen men were killed," Turkis said. He kept his voice neutral and calm. Unfortunately, Virgil didn't.

"A few minutes ago you stated we're all on the same side, Allen. I'm beginning to wonder if that was a factual statement. What would you have us do? We were outnumbered and surrounded inside a fortified compound with enemy combatants coming from virtually every angle. When they opened fire on us, we did what we have always done, and what we'll continue to do. We take care of our own. How about you start doing the same?"

Mac cleared his throat, and Virgil felt Sandy's hand on his thigh as she gave him a squeeze. The message was clear. Virgil took a deep breath, got his tone in check, then continued with: "We didn't have a choice, Allen. It's as simple as that. We take no joy from our actions, but when the choice comes down to kill or be killed, we'll take the former every single time. I don't have any trouble with that at all. Want to know why? Because tactics aside, I'm on the right side of the law and I get to go home to my wife and family."

Murton knew Virgil was about to get wound up again, so he tapped the tip of his index finger on the table and said, "There's something I don't understand."

Turkis turned his attention to Murton. "What is that, Detective?"

The dichotomy between the words Murton used and the tone of his voice was so apparent, Virgil saw Turkis swallow when his brother spoke.

"What the fuck are we doing here?"

CHAPTER FOUR

Mac knew how to command the room when it was necessary, and he felt like he was in his element and on his home turf. The fact that everyone was sitting in his former office didn't hurt, either. He spoke with authority, but kept his voice calm, his volume low. "Detectives, please, listen to me. What Allen said is true. We are on the same side. How about everybody take a breath and think about that for two seconds?"

When no one spoke, Sandy jumped into the game. She'd recently taken a board seat at Said, Inc., the company that Mac now ran at the behest of Patty Stronghill, Rick Said's only living heir. "Virgil? Murton? We know this isn't fair, but we needed to hear your version of events before anyone discloses what else happened out at the compound...and in fact, is still happening. But please, hear me when I say this: Mac and Allen's statements are true. We are all on the same side. The information we have came in just this morning, so we're as shocked as you are."

Murton decided to lighten the moment. He looked at Sandy and said, "Well, Small, we've shown you ours. How about you do the same?" He wiggled his eyebrows at her when he spoke, and that took the tension out of the room. That, and the fact that Sandy leaned over and punched her brother-in-law in the shoulder.

Murton slowly turned and looked at Sandy. "That's assault on a state police officer."

Sandy smiled, patted the back of his hand and said, "No, that was a love tap from a family member." Then to Turkis: "Allen, I think Murton is correct. We've heard their version of what happened. It's time to show our cards, though I will admit, we don't have much of a hand."

Virgil looked at his wife and said, "What the hell are we missing?"

Sandy gave his thigh another squeeze and said, "Allen?"

Turkis looked directly at Virgil and Murton. "I hope you'll forgive me for being so blunt earlier. I never intended for either of you to feel like this was an interrogation, or even a deposition. But the hard reality is this: Everyone at this table—even the governor herself if we don't play our cards just so—could be in for a very long and expensive legal battle."

"Care to delineate that a bit?" Virgil said.

"In our discussion with Agent Blackwell, he informed us of a few things, which taken individually are troublesome enough, but taken as a whole could end up being devastating to a great number of people."

Virgil wanted to roll his wrist, but managed to catch himself before he did. "What kind of things?"

Turkis held up a finger. "Just one more question, if you will. Did either of you—or any member of the Major Crimes Unit—return to the compound after you rescued Detective Rosencrantz?"

"No," Murton said. "There wasn't any reason to do so. The entire compound was blocked off as a crime scene, and nearly every single deputy with the Shelby County Sheriff's Department was there, along with Blackwell and his team. Why do you ask?"

Turkis let out a little chuckle. "Mainly because I'm a corporate lawyer. That's my way of saying I'm not intimately familiar with the nuances of law enforcement as it relates to procedural matters."

"Most people aren't," Virgil said. "The truth is, Allen, half the time after a crime is committed, even the cops aren't allowed inside the crime scene area until the technicians have done their job."

"Yes, of course," Turkis said. "I am aware of that much. Are you suggesting that had you wanted or needed to go back to the compound, you would have been denied access?"

Virgil shook his head. "In this case, no."

"Why not?"

"Because everyone who died at the scene after we showed up did so as a result of my unit's response to their actions."

"In other words, you killed them all. Would that be an accurate statement?"

"I thought the interrogation was over," Murton said.

"I simply need to be clear on this point before we move forward."

Virgil let out an exasperated sigh. "We've been through this already, Allen. Yes, we killed them all. It happened when they started shooting at us. If they'd have dropped their weapons and surrendered, they would still be alive."

"That's the first of our four problems," Turkis said.

Virgil was trying not to be defensive, but he couldn't help it. "I'll tell you this: Even though it was a long time ago, I remember my training from the police academy. Want to know one of the things they teach? If someone shoots at you, you're allowed to shoot back. So how, exactly, is that a problem? The superintendent of the ISP has already evaluated and cleared our actions as justified."

"I've no doubt, Jonesy. But you asked the wrong question. One of the problems isn't that you and your team killed them all. It's the fact that you *think* you did."

"Meaning?" Murton said.

Turkis leaned forward slightly and said, "Meaning two of them got away."

VIRGIL LAUGHED...MOSTLY OUT OF CONFUSION. "That's not possible, Allen. After we got Rosencrantz on the chopper, Cool—the ISP's chief pilot—flew him straight to the Shelbyville hospital. Murton and Ross went with them. Myself, along with Detectives Mayo and Ortiz, and former Elkhart County deputy Jim Wilson—who now works for the Major Crimes Unit—checked every single victim. They were all dead. I don't have an exact recollection of how long it took Sheriff Henderson and his men to arrive on scene, but it wasn't long, and the first thing they did was check the victims as well. Every single one of those guys was gone."

"I don't doubt you, Jonesy," Turkis said. "And I certainly don't mean to offend, but your thinking on the matter at hand is a bit lateral, and this is a multi-dimensional problem. The two men who got away were gone before you and your people ever got to the compound."

"How do you know that?" Murton said.

"That's the second part of our four problems," Turkis said. "According to Agent Blackwell, the DEA had a confidential informant inside the operation. The informant kept notes on everything that was happening at the facility…from the time the crew got their hands on the pill presses and dies, right up through their first shipment of drugs. I don't know if the informant was part of the inner circle like Jordan, Hamilton, Reynolds, or Graham, but he had a roster of every single person involved in the operation."

Virgil and Murton touched eyes for a fraction of a second. "You're saying we killed a federal CI?" Murton said. "Because even if you are, again, they dealt the play, not us. The DEA's man should have dropped his weapon and surrendered."

"Based on what you told me earlier, Murton, the man never got the chance."

Murton dropped his chin to his chest. He knew what was coming next.

"That's right, Detective," Turkis said. "The man had an arrow sticking out of his back. Agent Blackwell informed us that according to the Shelby County crime scene technicians, the CI never fired his weapon."

THIS TIME IT WAS MURTON WHO STARTED TO LOSE HIS composure. He pointed a finger at Turkis and said, "The man was acting on my—"

Virgil stopped his brother. "Murt."

Murton looked at Virgil and said, "Why not, Jonesy? According to the lawyer in the room, we're all on the same side." He looked at Turkis and said, "Isn't that right?"

"It is," Turkis said. "I assure you. I'm simply trying to give you the lay of the land. If we all end up in court, what you're feeling right now will be nothing against what you'll face on the stand. Please continue."

"Tony was acting on my orders," Murton said. "He and I were alone, outnumbered, outgunned, and we knew—or at the very least suspected—that in all likelihood our fellow detective was either dead or dying inside that compound. We did what we had to do to get him out. I'd do it again right this very second if I had to, and I wouldn't change a goddamned thing."

"Of that, I have no doubt," Turkis said. "But let me ask you this: Since when does a federal Bureau of Indian Affairs agent take orders from a state detective, and further, what would compel him to do so?"

"I misspoke," Murton said. "I did not give him an order, but of the two of us, I was in charge. We assessed the situation at hand, and given our limited resources at the time—remember, the rest of the squad hadn't yet arrived—we decided to gain entry at the compound by whatever means necessary. The statement Virgil made earlier…about the police academy? I never went there. My training came out of Quantico. And one of the things they teach is that if a fellow law enforcement official, or even a member of the public at large is facing an imminent threat, you're allowed to take lethal action in defense of another. As for the second part of your question…what would compel him to do so? Loyalty and friendship comes to mind, though there doesn't seem to be too much of that floating around the room right now."

Mac cleared his throat. "Murt?"

Murton answered through his teeth. *"What?"*

"I believe you've made your point."

But Murton wasn't quite finished. "Have I, though? Because it sounds like we're all sitting around playing pass the hanky and no one wants to end up with a handful of snot. Do you think I'm going to let a guy like Blackwell try to hang Tony out to dry because he was helping us get to Rosencrantz? Don't bother answering, because I'm not letting that happen. If it weren't for Tony's specific actions, Rosie would be dead right now." Then he shot Turkis a look, and finished with, "That's a fact."

Sandy leaned forward and forced Murton to look her in the eye. "I love you, Murton Wheeler, and I give you my word, no one is trying to hang anyone out to dry. What we're trying to do is mitigate any damage going forward."

Murton nodded without speaking. He was so mad his ears were red.

Virgil looked at Turkis and said, "A few minutes ago you told us that the DEA's CI kept notes…right up through their first shipment of drugs. Do I have that right?"

"You do."

"Then I take it that's the third part of the problem?"

"That's correct," Turkis said. "No one seems to know where this alleged notebook is, or even if it actually exists. Mac and I believe that if you can persuade the governor to let the Major Crimes Unit look into its whereabouts, it may help to ease the tension between the DEA and all other parties involved…if you can find it, that is."

Murton finally got his wheels back under him. He looked at Turkis and said, "And you believe that the CI's notebook has the names of the two remaining players, and possibly where the drugs are located?"

"That's right."

"What amount of drugs are we talking about?" Virgil said.

"According to Blackwell's CI, the shipment that went out was nearly one hundred pounds of fake oxy pills. We're not yet sure if they were laced with xylazine hydrochloride or not."

Virgil ran his hands through his hair. "Christ, that's a lot of drugs."

"Indeed, it is," Mac said. "The DEA puts it at just over a half-million pills."

"Convincing Cora that the MCU should try to track down that much weight won't be the problem," Virgil said. "The MCU is operating on a selective basis, which means that unless we're told by the governor to steer clear, we can take a hard run at it. The question is, why would we?"

"I was under the impression your unit handles major crimes, as the name implies," Turkis said. "Is there something I'm missing?"

"Not exactly," Virgil said. "But looking for fugitives from the law is a job for the US Marshals. They can track down the other two members of the crew. It's what they do. As for the drugs, that's the DEA's job. It's exactly the kind of thing they're tasked with at the federal level. I'm surprised they'd even want our help."

Mac popped his lips and said, "As a point of fact, they don't want your help."

"Good," Murton said. "Problem solved."

"Not quite, Detective," Turkis said. "There's one more piece of the pie, and I think it's big enough that you'll want to help take a bite out of crime, as it were."

Virgil looked at his former boss and said, "You mentioned that the DEA doesn't want our help, but you also said it would help ease the tension between all parties involved. What sort of tension are we talking about? Because a dead CI, as tragic as that is, doesn't seem to be the entire story."

"That's because it isn't," Mac said. "The DEA is trying to take control of both the compound and the main property formerly owned by the Salters under the asset forfeiture laws…properties, as you know, I now control."

"So what?" Virgil said. He tipped his head at Turkis. "That's what lawyers are for."

"I don't think you understand, Jonesy," Mac said. "I don't own those properties as part of my personal holdings. Said, Inc. does. And since the company itself owns them, and the DEA can demonstrate that Jordan and his crew were using Said, Inc. to launder their drug money, they're going to try to seize the entire corporation and all its holdings. Allen tells me they might be able to pull it off."

Virgil, nobody's idiot, put the rest of the pieces together in a hurry. "That's the main reason Cora isn't in the room right now, isn't it? The holding company and the state are tied together in multiple ways…the mobile voting, the sonic drilling operation, and the Cultural Center in Shelby County. If Said, Inc. goes down, the state itself would be in big trouble."

"As would the governor," Turkis said. "Because if I'm not mistaken, she ordered the Major Crimes Unit to originally handle the case, which, up until this very morning, you thought was over."

"And if that doesn't get you motivated," Mac said, "consider this: Patty Stronghill is the woman who not only runs the Cultural Center, she's the majority shareholder in the company that is currently at risk."

Murton let out a humorless chuckle. "Yeah, we're pretty much up to speed on all that, Mac."

"Are you, though? Because her husband, Tony Stronghill, killed a federal informant out at that compound. We're not just talking about money and property here, guys. If the DEA has their way, Tony could end up in jail, and Allen tells me Patty herself wouldn't be immune from prosecution either, as an accessory after the fact. I know I'm not your boss anymore, but you've got a number of people who really need your help."

CHAPTER FIVE

Once the meeting was over, Virgil and Murton headed back to the MCU facility. Neither man spoke much during the drive over, each lost in his own thoughts regarding the case they were, in all likelihood, about to reopen.

At one point Murton sent out a quick text, then turned to his brother and said, "Want me to get with Patty and see if she and Tony can come up tonight?"

Virgil nodded. "Not a bad idea. At the very least, we've got to let them know what's going on."

Murton pulled his phone back out, punched in Patty's number, and when she answered, he said, "Hey, Pickle Chick. How's life in the state's most exciting county these days?"

"Hey, Murt. It's good to hear your voice. And for the record, Shelby County might be exciting for you guys, but lately it's the same-o, same-o for me. I just came from the hospital…went over and saw Tom."

"And that, young lady is why we love you. How's he doing?"

"He says he's doing well, but I can tell he's hurting."

"Rosie is one of the toughest guys I've ever met. He'll get through it."

Patty let out a little laugh. "He must be tough, because they're letting him out late this afternoon."

"Are they? That seems a little soon."

"That's what I thought," Patty said. "But the docs want to get him out because they don't want him to catch any superbugs or whatever the medical profession is calling them these days. They've got his drains out, his stitches are holding, and he's basically just hanging out at the hospital for no actual medical reason. The insurance company is starting to make some noise, so I guess everyone collectively decided that he could recuperate at his house just as well as he could in the hospital."

"Makes sense. How's he getting home?"

"He's going to stay at Carla's place. I guess Ross is

coming down at the end of the day to help him get settled in."

"Gotcha. Listen, Jonesy wanted me to call and ask if you and Tony are free for dinner this evening at his place. Going to have a little cookout."

"Yeah, I think we can make it. But, uh, if you don't mind me asking, who's working the grill?"

"Jonesy is. But don't worry. We're not having chicken. Tonight it's Wagyu beef."

Patty suddenly sounded excited. "Holy cow. And I didn't mean to just make a bad pun there, but if you guys are grilling up Wagyu beef, count us in."

"Dinner is at seven. Show up a little early, huh? We've got some things to talk about."

"Anything I need to know right now?"

"Naw…it'll keep. See you soon."

Virgil turned in to the MCU parking lot just as Murton finished the call with Patty. "You know, despite what everyone thinks, my grilled chicken is actually improving. I've been taking some of Robert's advice, and I think it's working out. I made some just the other night."

"Uh huh," Murton said. He was completely underwhelmed. "How bad was it?"

"I think the thing to focus on is the word *improvement*. I am getting better."

"Is Larry the Dog still turning it down?"

"I'm not sure that's where we should set the bar. He's got a pretty refined palate for a golden retriever."

"Jonesy, I once saw Larry the Dog eat a piece of wedding cake that had been dropped in the grass and stepped on. He ate more dirt than cake."

"Well, whatever. It won't be a problem tonight."

Murton let that go and said, "Patty says Rosie is getting out later today."

"Yeah, I kinda put that together while you were speaking with her. How's he getting back up here?"

"He's not. I guess he's going to stay at Carla's while he recuperates. Ross is going to go down this afternoon to spring him, get him back over there and all set up."

Virgil was quiet for a few seconds, and Murton caught it. "What?"

Virgil killed the engine on the Range Rover, then said, "I was just wondering if that's a good idea, or not."

"Ross helping his partner?"

"No, no. I'm talking about him going back to Carla's place. That's where he was attacked by Reynolds. There could be some lingering feelings he might need to work through."

"Maybe so, but you know Rosie. He'll get past it.

What I told Patty is true. He's one of the toughest guys I've ever met."

"Yeah, I guess so," Virgil said. "Speaking of tough guys, you kind of lost your mashed potatoes there for a minute in the meeting. It sort of surprised me."

"Well, you weren't exactly what anyone would describe as the voice of reason."

"That's because I'm not sleeping very well, and running on empty. Besides, I didn't say…what was it? That we're all sitting around playing pass the hanky and no one wants to end up with a handful of snot." When Murton didn't respond, Virgil said, "What?"

Murton popped the passenger door and gave his brother a big toothy grin. "Nothing. Nobody's perfect, Jones-man. When you're right, you're right."

ONCE VIRGIL AND MURTON WERE INSIDE, THEY stopped at Sarah's desk and asked if there was anything they needed to know.

Sarah had a serious look on her face, one she didn't often let others see. "Mayo and Ortiz are in the conference room going through all the paper we have on Jordan and his crew. Ross and Wilson are in there with them."

Virgil tipped his head to the side. "How did you know I'd want them to do that?"

Sarah brightened just a bit and said, "Murton sent me a text while you guys were on the way back from your meeting."

Virgil turned and looked at his brother.

"What? Why not get the ball rolling?"

"Good idea," Virgil said. "How about you go join them? I'll be right in."

Murton said he would, then headed down the hall. Once he was out of earshot, Virgil turned back to Sarah and said, "Want to tell me what's bothering you? Is something going on between you and Ross?"

Sarah and Ross had been dating and living together for over a year now.

"I'm fine," Sarah said. "It's you I'm worried about."

Virgil gave her a friendly frown. "Why are you worried about me?"

"Because your favorite DEA agent is upstairs waiting in your office."

Virgil let his chin drop to his chest. "That guy...I'm telling you, he's wound a little tight. I don't know how he gets anything done."

"Who says he does?" Then Sarah cleared her throat and let her eyes slide over Virgil's shoulder toward the second level.

When Virgil turned, he saw Blackwell staring down at him from the hallway. He turned back to Sarah, lowered his voice, and said, "I'll handle it. But listen, if he comes sailing over the railing, your report will read that you witnessed a suicide attempt by a federal agent, who, for reasons unknown by anyone present, decided that life simply wasn't worth living anymore."

Sarah finally smiled. "I'll start typing it up right now."

When Virgil walked into his office he was ready for a battle. But to his surprise, Agent Blackwell was standing with his palms out, his expression indicative of a man who knew he'd already colored well outside the lines. Virgil didn't even get a chance to speak.

"Detective Jones, please…let me say for the record, and to you personally, my behavior has been beneath me. The amount of pressure I'm under is not something I'd wish on my second ex-wife. My first either, for that matter. From our initial encounter on the phone, to my arrival in Elkhart…and then earlier today, I've behaved in a manner that is completely unacceptable. On behalf of myself and the agency I represent, I'd like to offer my most sincere apology. I hope you'll accept. I'm also hoping we can start over." He stuck out his hand to shake, and Virgil noticed it was wrapped tight with gauze.

"You sure you want to do that?" Virgil said.

"Apologize?"

Virgil smiled. "No. Shake hands."

Blackwell dropped his hand and said, "Thank God, and no I don't. Your partner has quite the grip. In any event, I'm sorry to stop in unannounced, but I was hoping to have a word with you regarding our mutual problem."

Virgil pointed at one of the chairs that fronted his desk, and said, "I accept your apology. But for the record, based on the things Mr. Turkis has told me, I'm not sure you and I should actually be speaking without any sort of representation…at least on my part."

Blackwell waved Virgil's words away. "It's not hard to know why you'd feel that way, but you have to understand something: The DEA's position on the asset forfeiture laws as they relate to the holding company controlled by your former governor aren't coming from me personally. It's simply how the DEA operates."

Virgil almost felt sorry for the guy. In truth, he knew what Blackwell was telling him was factual, no different from the things Virgil himself sometimes had to do as part of his job. "May I see your phone, Agent Blackwell?"

"You think I'm recording our conversation?"

"It never hurts to be thorough," Virgil said.

Blackwell gave Virgil a grin, pulled out his phone, and set it on the desk. Then he pushed two buttons at the same time and held the phone so Virgil could see it powering off. "How's that for a show of good faith?"

Virgil turned the corners of his mouth down. "It's the equivalent of a hitman going to confession and talking about everything except the real reason he's there."

Blackwell sighed, then took out his other phone, turned that off as well, then sat back. "Satisfied?"

Virgil nodded. "That'll do." Then: "I probably shouldn't be saying this…and I'll deny it to anyone if it ever comes up, but I understand how the DEA operates, and the fact of the matter is you may—and the key word there is *may*—have an arguable position for seizing the compound owned by Said, Inc. As for the rest of the company, your claim doesn't hold water."

"I'm not saying it does, Detective. I'm saying that the higher-ups—the people I answer to—think it might."

Virgil wasn't playing. "The people who think they have all the power usually end up on the wrong side of things, Agent Blackwell. I'd put my money on Mac and his team any day of the week. In fact, as a minority stakeholder in the company, I'm doing just that."

"I'm aware, Detective. That's why I'm here."

"Explain that," Virgil said. "And why did you say we have a mutual problem?"

"I've been told—quite unofficially, of course—that if you and your team were to somehow manage to retrieve the drugs, and capture the two men who have them, the DEA would be very grateful. So grateful, in fact, I think you might discover that all your other problems go away."

"You're extorting me?"

"Absolutely not. If anything, I'm here to eat a little crow. I'm also trying to answer your question while asking for a little off-the-books inter-agency cooperation."

Virgil tipped his head back and thought about it for a few seconds. Then he looked at Blackwell and said, "Why did you say off-the-books? What's your angle in all this?"

Blackwell deflated just a bit. "I'm six months away from having my twenty-five in. I've also made some mistakes along the way. If I can't find those drugs and the two guys who have them, I'll not only lose my job, but my pension as well."

"Why didn't you tell me you had a CI inside the operation?"

"Because it wasn't official. I was running my own op."

That surprised Virgil and he said so. "Why?"

"Because my supervisor thinks I'm an idiot. Lately I'm beginning to think he may be right. My job for the last two years has been sitting at a desk and filing status reports on vacant buildings all across the Midwest. It makes me feel like a real estate agent with a badge and a gun. I thought if I could make something happen, I might be able to regain a little goodwill within the department. Bottom line, I didn't want to go out a loser."

"I'll need to speak with your supervisor."

"You can't do that."

"Why not?" Virgil said.

"Because as far as my supervisor goes, I'm not even supposed to be here. My job was to recover the presses and dies. I've done that. They never knew I had someone on the inside."

Virgil's next question wasn't really relevant, but he asked it anyway. "Where are the presses and dies?"

"Where do you think? I'm in enough trouble as it is. They're right back where they were stolen from…at the facility up in Elkhart County."

Virgil shook his head. "That makes exactly zero sense, Blackwell."

"Maybe to you, but my job of late is to make sure that the property is secure, and the equipment is where it is supposed to be until such time that the DEA decides to auction it off or destroy it. That means I'm back to sitting at a desk. If you do this, you'll be doing it on your own."

Virgil said, "We'll see." Then he stood…an indication that the meeting was over. He handed Blackwell his phones and said, "I'll speak with my boss…and Mr. Turkis. If they tell me to do it, we will. If they tell me to steer clear, we'll do that as well. It's the best I can offer. Either way, I'll let you know by tomorrow."

Blackwell took out a card and wrote a number on the back before handing it to Virgil. "That's my personal cell. If you find anything, please call me. Day or night."

Virgil set the card on his desk, and tipped his head at the door. "Just so we're clear, Blackwell, I haven't agreed to anything yet. But I will be in touch, either way. I'll also let you show yourself out." When Blackwell didn't move, Virgil said, "Agent?"

Blackwell's face reddened just a bit. "You didn't happen to bring my weapon back with you, by chance?

I'll have about twenty-five pages of forms to fill out if you didn't."

"Your weapon is still at the statehouse, but I'll make a call and see that you get it back. I wonder how many forms you would have had to fill out if my partner had arrested you."

Blackwell was backing out of the office. "I don't want to think about it…really…I'll be waiting to hear from you."

CHAPTER SIX

Once Blackwell was out of his hair, Virgil sat down at his desk, hit the intercom button and said, "Hey, Sarah?"

"Yes, Jonesy?"

"Could you have Ross come up here for a moment?"

"Sure, let me go get him," Sarah said.

"Also, bring me a couple of aspirin or whatever we have. I started the day with a headache, and Blackwell seems to have made it worse."

"Be right there," Sarah said.

Two minutes later, Ross walked in carrying a bottle of Advil. "Sarah said you wanted these. I brought you a water as well. Didn't know if you had any up here or not."

"Thanks, Ross. Have a seat. Murt fill you guys in on what's happening?"

"We've been given the basics. Sounds like that Blackwell idiot is trying to run everyone out of town so he can plant his own flag."

Virgil held up a wait-a-minute finger, chased four Advil with half a bottle of water, then said, "He just left…Blackwell. Believe it or not, he came with hat in hand and offered an apology. It was actually a pretty good one, too, although I'm not sure I believe his entire story. But based on what he told me, he doesn't have much say in the matter. It's all coming from higher up in the chain."

"Doesn't that sort of make it worse?"

"Maybe," Virgil said. "But the higher up the chain, the more political things become, and Mac is a master politician. Bottom line, Blackwell says that if we can get the drugs back…along with the two guys who took them, the whole thing would probably go away."

"We gonna do it?"

Virgil shrugged. "Not up to me…and not why I wanted to speak with you, either."

"Gotcha. What's up?"

"Get the door, will you? We need to have a little talk."

"You bet," Ross said. Then, as he turned toward the

door, time took hold of Virgil, and he went away again…

———

He was standing in the kitchen with his mom, and helping her do the dishes, when they heard a loud crash in the front room of the house. When they made their way to the living room, they discovered the entire picture window had been shattered. A large rock was on the floor in the middle of the room, and Murton was on his hands and knees in the front yard, trying to rip out the grass seed Mason had just planted.

Large pieces of jagged glass were everywhere in the living room, and Elizabeth told Virgil not to move. Virgil thought the statement his mother had just made was sort of silly, because he didn't think he could move just then if he wanted to. His best friend in the whole world had just thrown a rock through their window and was now trying to vandalize their new front lawn.

The sky was pitch black, the streetlights gave off a dull yellowish glow that left swarms of moths fluttering about near the light and all the way down close to the sidewalk in an ever-widening cone. Mason had heard the window shatter as well, and he came around the corner from the side yard, sat down in the grass, and held Murton tight until he'd cried himself out. Then they had a little talk…

Ross was waving his hand in front of Virgil's face. "Hey, Boss-man…anybody home? You said you wanted to have a little talk."

Virgil blinked a few times, then rubbed his face with both hands. "Uh, yeah, sorry. I was thinking about something else."

"You looked like you were practicing to be a mannequin. Murt said you've been having trouble sleeping. You feeling okay?"

"Yeah…off and on. I'm simply tired…right down to my core. Anyway, listen, Patty told Murt that Rosie is checking out of the hospital later this afternoon."

"Yup. As a matter of fact I was going to ask you if I could take a little lost time and go down to help him out. Make sure he gets settled in and all that."

"Absolutely," Virgil said. "But I'd like you to do a bit more, if you don't mind."

"Like what?"

"I'm sort of concerned about him going back to Carla's place. It might be harder than he thinks, if he's even thought about it at all."

"You mean because that's where he got hit?"

Virgil nodded. "I do."

"How can I help?" Ross said.

"First, I don't want you to leave later. I'd like you to go as soon as possible. Take Wilson with you—we need to get Rosie's squad car back to him anyway—and then go straight to Carla's and clean the place up. We were staged out of there when everything went down at the compound, and we sort of left a little mess. So if you guys could put the place back together, I'd appreciate it, and I know Rosie would too."

"Sure, that's no problem. I was going to stock him up on groceries, anyway. Didn't want him trying to drive all over the countryside until he's ready."

Virgil tipped a finger at him. "Good. Do that. Get him some grub, square the place away, get rid of that burnt tire in the backyard, and then—I guess this will be up to him more than you guys—but maybe you should bag out there for a night. You know, just sort of hang with him…make sure he can get around okay, and all that."

"We're operating from the same playbook, Boss-man."

Virgil nodded. "Good. What's with the look?"

"Sorry," Ross said. "No look. But I am wondering

about everything Murton just told us. It sounds like we've got a few things to address around here."

"We do. But we don't have the green light yet, so you won't be missing anything. Murt and I are getting back together with Mac and Cora this evening, so hopefully I'll know by tomorrow if we're operating or not. Don't worry. If we are, I'll keep you in the loop. Since you'll probably be gone, Sarah and Liv are welcome to stay with me and Sandy."

"Thanks, Boss. I'll let her know."

"Do that, and let me know once you've got Rosie settled, will you?"

"Absolutely," Ross said. "See you in a day or so."

Ross walked out of the office, then less than five minutes later he was back. He gave Virgil a dull look and said, "I just heard."

Virgil was lost. "Heard what?"

"What you're having for dinner tonight at your place. Sarah is already drooling."

Virgil gave Ross a fake smile. "Well, you'd be welcome to attend, but you're doing a kind and thoughtful thing for your partner and friend in his time of need."

Ross shook his head. "Yeah, well, Wag-*yu*, Bossman, if you know what I mean."

"Hey, Ross, c'mon, man…"

Virgil went downstairs and walked into the conference room. He looked at Murton and said, "Ross tells me you've got everyone up to speed."

"I went over the basics," Murton said. "Where is he? Ross?"

Virgil answered his brother's question by looking at Wilson. "Go get with your partner. You guys are headed down to Shelby County. Might be there for the day, or maybe more. He'll fill you in."

Wilson stood from his chair and said, "You got it, Boss."

Then, Virgil stopped him. "Hey, Jim, hold on a second. Go get Ross and have him step back in, will you? I'm getting ahead of myself here."

"Sure. Two minutes."

Once Ross and Wilson were back in the room, Virgil looked at his entire squad—Becky was there as well—and said, "Okay, you all know what the situation is, but I don't want to have to keep repeating this, so I wanted to tell everyone at once."

"Tell us what?" Mayo said.

"That the landscape might have just changed. When Murt and I met with Mac, Turkis, and Sandy, they made it very clear that the DEA is going to make a run at not only the old Salter properties, but the entire holding company that Mac runs."

"Yeah, Murt already told us that," Ortiz said.

"I know," Virgil said. "But what he didn't tell you is this: I just came out of a brief meeting with Agent Blackwell in my office, and he informed me that if we can locate the missing shipment of drugs that left the compound prior to our arrival—along with the two men who took them, the DEA would be grateful enough that Mac's problem—which is directly tied to everything else—will, in all likelihood, go away."

"And you believe him?" Becky said.

Virgil looked away from the group for a few seconds as he considered the question. "To be honest, I'm not sure I do. He's been shooting from the hip for a little too long. The confidential informant he had inside Jordan's crew wasn't approved by Blackwell's superiors. He was running his own private op, and when the CI got killed, Blackwell knew his end of the operation was about to come crashing down on top of his head. That's why he was so upset. Bottom line: I'm not sure if we should believe him or not, but he's changed his tune in a big way—at least for now—and if he's being straight with me, it could be the singular thing that cleans up the whole mess...for Mac, the state, the cultural center, Tony…all of it."

"Except you don't entirely believe him," Mayo said.

Virgil shrugged. "Right. Sort of."

Ortiz looked at Virgil and said, "Murton told us that Cora was excused from her own meeting."

"Couldn't be helped," Virgil said. "She needed the deniability. But with Blackwell's offer on the table, we'll have to bring her into the circle. I'll handle that tonight. Once that happens, I'm fairly certain we'll get the green light to start working the case…again. Our real problem, though, is this: We've been under the assumption that the whole thing was wrapped up. It's not. That means those drugs—and the two guys who took them—could be anywhere. They're not going to be easy to find."

"Who's the CI?" Becky said. "Do we have that information? It might be a good place to start."

"I don't know, Becks," Virgil said.

Becky gave Virgil a look. "The man was just here and you didn't ask him?"

"No, I didn't."

"Mind telling us why?" Murton said, his expression one of surprise.

Virgil tugged on his earlobe and said, "We've been given the authority to choose our own cases. But that authority comes with a caveat. If we're told to back off and leave it alone, that's what we'll have to do. This thing is getting heavy on the politics already, and it'll probably get worse before it gets better. Blackwell has put an offer on the table. The problem is, I don't know if it's genuine or not. On one hand he's trying to distance himself from the whole thing, but on the other he's making promises I don't believe he has the authority to offer."

Becky gave her eyes a little half roll and said, "Let me guess…you want me to get into the DEA's system and find out who the informant was. Do I have that right?"

Virgil gave her an evil grin and said, "Not exactly."

Ross got Virgil's attention. "I don't mean to interrupt, but if you want me and Wilson to get going, we should probably get going."

Murton rubbed his face with both hands. "Jonesy, don't."

But Virgil couldn't help himself. He looked at Ross and said, "You just used the same two words twice in the same sentence."

Ross barked out a laugh. "So did you."

Virgil ignored his own gaffe. He looked at Becky and said, "I'll answer your question in just a second." Then to Ross: "What I said earlier in my office still stands. But I want you and Wilson to ride down to Shelby County together."

Ross, who could often be very direct, looked at his boss and said, "Why? You told me yourself that we need to get Rosie's squad car down to him."

"We do, but Mayo and Ortiz are going to do that."

"Why?" Ross said again.

"Because I want them to do something else, as well."

CHAPTER SEVEN

Virgil looked at each of his detectives one by one, then said, "I know you all know this—and Jim, you might be the singular exception—but we've had our share of problems whenever one of us gets sent out alone to do their job. It's happened to me...Ron Miles comes to mind, even though Ed Henderson was with him when he was killed. And most recently, look at what happened to Rosie. I sent him to nose around in a place called Boggstown to look at an empty lot and interview a guy. *One guy*. And you all know how that turned out. He ended up fighting for his life. I don't want that to happen again. If he hadn't been alone, I'm certain the whole thing would have turned out differently."

"So what does that have to do with me and Ortiz?" Mayo said.

"I want you guys to pack your bags and go down to Shelby County. Get with Sheriff Henderson, sit down in a room, and go through his files…every single scrap of paper he and his department have regarding what happened out at that compound. Go through the crime scene reports, the individual deputies' statements, all of it. They'll have more information than we do because they are the ones who have the records from the bank where Jordan worked, and any other evidence that may have been pulled out of the Salter residence. Look for the notebook Blackwell's CI had. It's probably there. We need to find out who these guys are and what vehicle they used to move the drugs. Once we have that, put out a statewide BOLO. In short, I want you guys to get down there and *detect*. Don't come back until you have some answers. And please, stay together and watch your backs, okay?"

"We can do that," Ortiz said. "And we will. I assume we're taking Rosie's squad car down to him?"

"That's right. Drop it at Carla Martin's place, then get with Henderson. I'll let him know you're coming."

Mayo and Ortiz said they were on it, and left the room.

Virgil looked at Ross and Wilson. "Any questions?"

Ross shook his head. "No, but I do have an observation."

"Let's hear it," Virgil said.

"Earlier you said we haven't been given the green light to reopen this case, but it looks like we're moving forward anyway."

Virgil turned his palms up. "I'm operating under the assumption it's going to happen. In fact, I'm all but certain it will. Why not get ahead of the game?"

"Look, Boss-man, I don't have any problem hanging with Rosie for a day or two. In fact, there's nothing I'd rather do than help him out. But what about after that?"

"That depends on what Mayo and Ortiz find," Virgil said. "If they can get us headed in the right direction, all our efforts will be focused on getting those drugs back, and hopefully catch the last two guys from Jordan's crew. That is our singular focus right now. So, stay in touch. I'm hoping that sometime within the next twenty-four to forty-eight hours, we'll be rolling."

Ross stood, looked at Wilson, then tipped his head toward the door. As they were leaving the room, Ross looked at Virgil, and with just a whiff of sarcasm, said, "Enjoy your dinner."

Wilson looked at Ross. "What's up with dinner?"

"I'll tell you in the car."

"What's the matter with right now?" Wilson said.

"Because I know what they're having, I'm pretty sure you'd kill for it, and I've seen you shoot. Let's go, huh? You can thank me…or hate me…later."

ONCE EVERYONE ELSE WAS OUT OF THE ROOM, BECKY moved over and sat down next to Murton. Then she looked at Virgil and said, "So, into the DEA's system or not?"

"Yes. How long will that take?"

Murton leaned over and touched the side of his head against Becky's shoulder. "You knew he was going to ask."

Becky didn't seem to mind. "No more than a day. I'd say eight to nine hours, tops."

Virgil was surprised, and said so. "Jeez, that's pretty good, Becks. I thought you were going to tell me a week, or some damned thing."

Becky gave Virgil a fake smile. "Okay, it'll probably take a week."

"Becky?"

"Yes, Virgie?"

"Is it really just a day?"

Becky decided to let her brother-in-law off the

hook. "Yeah, I was in once before when we were dealing with that Witlock idiot, so I never completely backed out. Most of the hard work is done."

If Virgil had been let off the hook, he didn't realize it and decided to swim back around for another nibble. "If most of the hard work is done, why is it going to take so long?"

Becky made a motorboat noise with her lips and said, "Thirty seconds ago you were pleased that it would happen so fast, and now you're giving me a hard time about how long it will take?"

"No, I'm just trying to understand," Virgil said.

"Okay, let me put it in terms you'll be able to grasp. When I was in before, I had to go slow and lay all the groundwork. You don't go poking around in a federal database with a sledgehammer if you want to stay out of jail…which I do. You have to sneak in quietly and cover your tracks as you go. You also have to watch your back when you leave, and lock the door behind you."

Murton let his head roll toward his brother in a lazy fashion, and said, "What my lovely wife is trying to say is this: The door is still there, but she can't just walk up and kick it down. What she has to do is essentially pick the lock." Then he rolled his head back at Becky and said, "Do I have that right, m'love?"

"Close enough," Becky said. Then to Virgil: "Although I'm not sure what I'm going to be looking for once I'm in. You and Murt both said that Blackwell was running his CI off the books. If that's the case, he's not going to be listed in the DEA's database."

Virgil shook his head. "I may or may not agree with you. The truth is, I'm hoping you don't find him."

"I'm not sure I'm following your logic, Jonesy," Murton said.

"Me either," Becky added.

"It's simple. Blackwell let it be known that he was running an off-the-books op, and his informant was killed at the compound when we got Rosencrantz out. He also said that the informant kept notes on everything he could regarding the operation. That notebook is out there, and I'm guessing that Ed Henderson has it, and probably doesn't know what it means. That's why I sent Mayo and Ortiz down there to look at his files."

"Then why bother to get inside the DEA's system?" Becky said.

"Because if you can find a record with the DEA that shows Blackwell had someone on the inside, we'll know he's yanking our collective chain, and we'll have to work around that. If you don't, we might be able to trust him and everything he told me earlier, up in my office."

Murton thought about that for a few seconds, then said, "What if the informant is in the system from a prior op, and Blackwell decided to use him anyway?"

Virgil drew his lips into a tight line. "That'd be unfortunate because then we wouldn't actually know if Blackwell is being truthful or not. It wouldn't help us, but it wouldn't really hurt us either, because we're not sure if we can trust him anyway. But at least we'd know who the CI is."

Becky stood and gave Murton a kiss, and Virgil got a friendly punch on the shoulder. "Okay, I'll get started first thing tomorrow morning."

Virgil glanced at the clock on the wall. "Little early for quitting time. Why not get started now?"

"Ask you something?" Becky said.

"Sure."

"You know how I'm always running this sequence or that once I'm in a system somewhere?"

"Yeah," Virgil said. "What of it?"

"Those are all mostly automated. Once I'm in, I'll be able to do that with the DEA as well."

"Still doesn't address why you're not going to get started now."

"Because running the sequence and getting inside the system are two different animals. The sequence practically runs itself. Getting in, though, is something that has to be done all at once. If I started right now, I'd end up working way past quitting time, and I don't want to miss dinner tonight."

"So, you can't start it, then, uh, I don't know, hit the Pause button or whatever?" Virgil said.

Becky looked at Murton and shook her head. "I can't believe we're having this conversation." Then to Virgil: "Jonesy, this isn't a video game. There is no Pause button. The analogy that Murt used is a good one. I've got to go back in and pick the lock. An electronic lock with a lot of security measures in place, all designed to prevent people like me from getting in."

"Yeah, I get that," Virgil said. "But still, it seems like—"

"Jonesy?" Becky said.

"Yeah?"

"Have you ever picked a lock?"

"Of course I have. I'm actually pretty good at it."

Murton laughed. "That's because you've got a lock rake in the back of the Rover."

Becky laughed as well. "This isn't that. It has to be done carefully and quietly. And like I said, all at once. See you tonight for dinner. I can't wait."

ONCE THEY WERE ON THEIR WAY DOWN TO SHELBY County, Wilson looked over at Ross and said, "Ask you something?"

"You bet."

"Look, I know I'm the new guy, and this job is really just a stepping stone to get with Mok's crew. That's my way of saying I don't want to speak out of turn."

"That's not a question," Ross said.

"I know. I'm sort of working my way up to it."

Ross was driving, but he took a half second to glance at Wilson. Once he had his eyes back on the road, he said, "When you discovered it was Reynolds who attacked Rosie, you followed your gut and came to me with the information. Not only that, but you were prepared to go all the way with it. We were in position and ready to take the shot when Stronghill stopped us. Want to know what all that means to me? I'll tell you: It means I can trust you. It also means that for the next six months, or however long it takes Rosie to heal, you and I are partners. People think I'm too direct sometimes. Maybe they're right. But I can get as well as I give. You don't have to work your way up to anything with me. What's the question?"

Wilson turned and looked out the side window for a few seconds, then said, "Have you noticed anything odd with Jonesy lately? I don't know him well enough to tell if I'm imagining it or not."

Ross remained quiet for a very long time. It went on for so long that Wilson thought maybe his new partner wasn't going to answer him. When Ross did answer, Wilson almost wished he hadn't asked the question to begin with.

"You're not imagining anything. I've noticed it too."

"It's like he just goes blank or something," Wilson said. "Do you think one of us should talk to him about it?"

Ross kept his eyes on the road. "No, I don't."

"Mind telling me why?"

Ross raked his teeth across his bottom lip. This was new territory for him. He'd never had to break in the new guy all by himself. "You told me your old man lives up near Kokomo, right?"

"Yeah."

"Are you guys close?" Ross said.

Wilson smiled. "Yeah, we are. He's a good man."

"So is Jonesy."

"Not sure I'm making the connection, here, Ross."

"Look, there's more to the story—and I'll tell you the whole thing at some point—but when I was still in grade school, I lost my dad. He was a vice cop. A few of the guys he was after showed up at our house one afternoon and took him out. He was still alive when I got to him, and I tried to save his life but couldn't do it. I was just a kid."

"Jeez, I'm sorry to hear that, man."

"Long time ago now," Ross said. "Over twenty years, although sometimes it feels like it was just yesterday."

"How does that connect to Jonesy?"

Ross still wasn't quite sure how to answer. "Look, here's one thing I know about Jonesy, and I know it right down to my core: He's slow to trust. Sometimes painfully slow. But once you've earned that trust, he's there for you every single time...no matter the cost to himself."

"Like he was when we were about to take down Reynolds?" Wilson said.

"Yeah, that's a pretty good example. Reynolds was going to die one way or another. You and I knew that… and so did Jonesy. But he didn't want us to take the fall, so he sent Mok and his team in, and they did the job for us."

"Why did you ask me about my father?" Wilson said.

"Because after everything I went through with my own dad when I was a kid, and then all the things I've been through ever since I joined this unit, Jonesy has been like a father to me. That feeling didn't just materialize out of thin air, either. I had to earn it…the hard way. We've had our moments. I almost quit on him once."

"That's good information, and I'm glad to hear it—not the quitting part—but it doesn't really answer my question."

"Maybe because I just wanted to know if you and your dad had a good relationship."

"What is it you're not telling me?"

"Only the things that aren't mine to share."

Wilson thought about that for a few seconds, then said, "So your official answer is he hasn't been sleeping very well lately…emphasis on the word, 'official.' But the unofficial answer is that the stories about Jonesy and his dad are true."

Ross let a small grin tug at the corner of his mouth. "You might turn out to be a pretty good detective."

CHAPTER EIGHT

Mayo and Ortiz arrived in Shelby County, dumped Rosencrantz's squad car at Carla's house, then sent Ross a text to let him know where to find the keys. After that, they headed over to the sheriff's office to start going through the paperwork and other evidence that Henderson and his people had gathered from the compound and the main residence where Jordan had lived.

It went bad right from the jump.

They walked in the door of the county law enforcement center and introduced themselves to a fiery redhead who had a hairdo that looked like a substitute for a wasp nest. Mayo had no sooner gotten their names out before Betty was on them like a feral cat that hadn't eaten in a week.

Betty gave both men a nasty scowl and said, "No one informed me that state detectives were coming by today. Let me guess: You two clowns work with that bozo, Jones. Am I right? Every time he or one of his people walk into this office, no good ever comes from it. In fact, people usually end up dying. Good people."

"Were any of their deaths suicide, by chance?" Mayo said.

"Don't you dare sass me. Just because you've got a state badge hanging around your neck doesn't mean you get to talk down to me."

Mayo pulled his chin in tight. "*I'm* talking down to *you*?"

Betty ignored his comment and said, "Mayo? What kind of ridiculous name is that? Thanks to you, I'll now have to come up with something else to put on my cheeseburger." Mayo opened his mouth to answer, but he never got a chance because Betty turned to Ortiz without skipping a beat, and said, "And you…if your partner is named Mayo, you look like yours ought to be Crisco. You've got enough product in your hair that I'd stay clear of any open flames, I was you. I hope you're not a smoker. I should probably pick up the phone and put the fire department on high alert."

Mayo and Ortiz looked at each other, neither man knowing exactly what to say. Fortunately, Sheriff

Henderson's office door was slightly ajar and he'd heard Betty's opening salvo. He ran out to rescue Mayo and Ortiz before either of them got hurt…or scarred for life. Henderson wasn't concerned about Betty, although he secretly wished one of the men might overreact and take matters into his own hands, thus relieving him of what he'd once described to Virgil as his abject tale of woe.

"Betty, I've been expecting these gentlemen. Jonesy called me on my cell not long ago. I didn't get a chance to inform you."

"Why not?" Betty said. "Wait, don't answer. I already know. You made it to level two on *Words with Friends,* am I right?"

Henderson let out a sigh and said, "Betty, how about we turn it down to thirteen on the attitude meter?"

"Don't tell me. I'm not the one making a fuss. Hot Sauce and the Condiment King walked in here like they own the joint. You know I don't abide that kind of behavior on official county property."

Henderson knew the best way to put an end to it all was to simply capitulate. "Of course. Like I said, Jonesy just called. Anyway, maybe a fresh pot of coffee would go a long way right about now."

Betty made a rude noise with her lips. "Do not patronize me, Sheriff. And speaking of Jonesy…it's more like Moansy, if you ask me. And another thing: If I wanted to play barista for Mr. Miracle Whip and his sidekick, Taco Bell, here, I'd apply for a job at Starbucks. This ain't the fifties no more, and I'm nobody's secretary-slash-waitress. What's next? I have to sit on someone's lap and take dictation?" Then, as if her own words held no meaning, she turned to Mayo and Ortiz, and said, "You take it black, or you want the works?"

Henderson rubbed his forehead, then gave Mayo and Ortiz an apologetic smile. He tipped his head at Betty and said, "She has an unusually candid sense of humor. It takes a little getting used to."

Mayo looked at Betty and said, "I don't think we'll need any coffee, but thank you anyway."

"Well, I wish people around here would learn to make up their own minds every now and again. First it's make the coffee, then it's we don't want any coffee. I've got better things to do than listen to this nonsense." Then she huffed down the hall, turned the corner, and was out of sight.

Ortiz looked at Henderson and said, "Good grief. How long ago did that one escape from the zoo?"

Henderson suddenly had a look of panic on his face. He waved his hands in front of himself and said, "Not out here. Christ, I've got enough trouble as it is. The woman either has the hearing of a bat, or she's got the entire reception area bugged. C'mon, let's step into my office."

Henderson took a seat behind his desk, motioned Mayo and Ortiz to a couple of chairs opposite himself, and said, "Sorry about all that."

"Is she always so cranky, or just having a bad day?" Mayo said.

Henderson let out a humorless laugh. "Believe it or not, that was nothing. I've seen her make grown men cry. I'm talking about men who are in uniform…and armed."

"Why do you keep her around?" Ortiz said.

Henderson gave them a lazy shrug. "She is a giant pain in the ass, I'll give you that. But she's been here forever, and I'll tell you something else: She's actually very good at her job. She keeps the place up and running."

"I'm surprised she doesn't have people running screaming from the building," Ortiz said.

"That has happened," Henderson said. "No joke. By the way, did you know she worked for the Major Crimes Unit for a short period of time?"

"Now I know you're fucking with us," Mayo said.

"Jonesy wouldn't hire that woman in a million years, and on the off chance he did, I'd take the under on how long it took before he shot her."

Henderson held up his right hand. "On my honor. It was after sheriffs Ben Holden and Ron Miles both died. I don't think you guys were around for all that."

"We weren't," Ortiz said. "We hadn't been hired by the state yet."

Henderson shook his head. "The whole goddamned thing was tragic. Holden was getting on in age and had some health issues. His knees were shot to hell, and he'd been hiding some kind of heart condition from everyone. Bottom line, he had a heart attack right as we were wrapping up a case, Miles was in an unusual position to take over in his absence, so that's what happened. Then Ron got shot down right in front of me, and Holden had a stroke at the hospital. Lost two sheriffs back-to-back. Anyway, Betty was pretty busted up about the whole thing—hell, we all were—and she ended up quitting."

"How does that get her to the MCU?" Mayo said.

"Shortly after she left here, Jonesy lost his departmental manager, or whatever her title was, and I guess things got sort of messy within the Major Crimes Unit. So he gave her a shot. It didn't work out, though."

Mayo laughed. "I'm not surprised. I can't believe he didn't lock her away and toss the key in the river."

"Ah, things are a little different down here than up in the city," Henderson said. "She sort of grows on you, and like I said, she *is* good at what she does." Then with the bullshit out of the way: "Jonesy told me you guys want to see the files from everything that happened out at the compound."

"Along with all your case notes and whatever you've got in the evidence room, if you don't mind," Mayo said.

"I don't mind at all," Henderson said. "Though Jonesy was a little vague on the specifics when I asked why. He said you guys would fill me in."

Ortiz sort of waved him off, not as a dismissal, but as an indicator of his own thought processes regarding the job at hand. "It's the DEA. They're making a stink over the fact that Jordan was secretly laundering money through Mac's holding company—"

Henderson tipped a finger at him, and interrupted. "You mean Patty's holding company there, I think."

Ortiz turned his palms up. "Ah, you know, six of one…anyway, they're using the asset forfeiture laws against him and are trying to take a run at the whole enchilada. It's going to get political because the state is tied up with both the company and the cultural center."

"So what does any of that have to do with me?"

"Nothing really," Mayo said. "Other than the fact that ninety percent of it happened in your county. There's nothing for you to worry about, Ed. Mac and Cora are going to tackle the politics—most of which will be behind the scenes, anyway—but Jonesy wants us to look at all your evidence because apparently we didn't get the whole crew out at the compound."

Henderson let his eyelids droop. "Sure looked like you did." Then he leaned forward slightly and let a little irritation creep into his voice. "Even got one after the fact, as I recall. I'm still sort of wondering why I never got notified that the state was going to roll through with their SWAT team and take out one of my own men."

Mayo wasn't interested in dancing around Henderson's attitude. "How about it on the tone, Sheriff? I know it's considered common decency to do so, but like it or not, the state isn't obligated to notify you of our actions. Besides, a dirty cop is a dirty cop. Sorry it was one of yours. We wanted to handle it before Reynolds knew we were coming."

"Mission accomplished," Henderson said. "The man was gunned down in his own front yard."

Mayo leaned forward himself. "By his own actions. You know damn good and well that had Reynolds surrendered he'd be in jail right now instead of the cemetery."

Henderson looked at nothing for a few seconds, then said, "You're right." He ran his hands through his hair. "I'm not mad at you guys, your department, Mok and his crew, or even the state. I'm really mad at myself. I worked with Reynolds for years and never knew he was bad."

"Don't beat yourself up, Ed," Ortiz said. "You've lost Holden, Miles, and Carla…all in the span of what? Less than two years? It's not like you'd have had time to notice."

"Carla noticed, though, didn't she? Sometimes I don't think I'm cut out for this job."

Mayo didn't want to be cruel, but he also didn't want to be someone else's confessor. He looked Henderson in the eye, and said, "So, the files?"

Ross turned in to a supermarket parking lot in Shelbyville, found an empty spot, and killed the engine on his squad car. Then he just sat for a minute staring at the entrance of the store.

"What's the matter?" Wilson said. "Did you forget your wallet, or something?"

Ross chuckled, then said, "No, but I just realized I don't know what to buy."

"What's Rosie like to eat?"

"Junk mostly. I don't know how he keeps the weight off. If you can microwave it, deep-fry it, or order it over the phone, he's all in. The problem is this: I'm pretty sure what he likes isn't part of the equation. He lost his spleen, dude. His liver is still healing as well."

"So what's the plan?"

Ross pulled out his phone, then scrolled through his contacts list. When he found the number he needed, he put his thumb over the Call button, but didn't press it right away. Instead, he looked at Wilson and said, "Tell me again the words Jonesy used when he hired you."

"He told me I was a hell of a cop."

"After that."

"He said, 'Welcome to the family, kid.'" Then: "Why do you ask?"

"Because if the person I'm going to call answers her phone, you're about to get another lesson on what that phrase means."

"Well, not to put too fine a point on it, but when we were in the tree line waiting to take Reynolds out, I sort of got the message."

"That's why I used the word, 'another.'" Then Ross

hit the Call button and put the phone on speaker so Wilson could hear the conversation. When the woman answered, she simply said, "Evans."

Dr. Julia Evans was Cool's girlfriend, an ortho doc with dusty red hair, and an unusually playful personality for a surgeon. She and Cool had met a number of years ago when she had to pin Cool's leg back together after the Freedom incident. They'd been dating ever since.

"Hey, Doc. Ross here. How's it going?"

"It's going well, thank you. I'm standing in front of a surgical sink with a nurse holding a phone to my ear as I scrub." Then, "Ouch, okay, okay. I'd like to revise my last statement: I meant to say *surgical nurse practitioner*. Anyway, you've got about ninety seconds before I start cutting. I've got to put some bones back together. I only answered because I saw it was you. What's up? Rosie okay?"

"Yeah, he's good. As a matter of fact, I'm getting ready to spring him in just a little while. But before I do, I need your professional advice on something."

"Sixty seconds, now, handsome."

"Gotcha. And thank you. I'm sitting in the grocery store parking lot as we speak. I'm going to stock Rosie up on some grub, but given what he's been through, I'm not sure what I should get."

"You're one of the good ones, Ross. Don't ever let anyone tell you different. Okay, Rosie: His organs are still healing, and they will be for quite a while. Get him non-processed, soft foods that are low on sodium. Organics if you can find them. Stuff like applesauce, rice, jello, clear broth, yogurt, tofu would be good, plenty of juice…like that."

"Tofu? Christ, Julia, I'm trying to help him, not have him kill me."

Over the phone they heard a voice in the background: *The anesthesiologist is tapping his watch.*

They heard Evans quietly say, "Finishing now. I'll be right there." Then back into the phone: "He'll thank you later. I promise. Gotta go, Ross. Love ya." And Evans was gone.

Ross stuck the phone back in his pocket, then looked at Wilson and said, "That's what Jonesy was talking about when he hired you. It had very little to do with Reynolds or what we were about to do. What you just heard? What that woman said? That's what Jonesy meant when he said welcome to the family. Bank on it." Then, almost as if he'd gotten too personal, Ross popped his door, and said, "Come on, let's go get some fuckin' tofu."

Wilson felt like he was floating on air.

CHAPTER NINE

THE REMAINING MEMBERS OF JORDAN'S CREW—brothers by the names of Kevin and Jake Crow, were sitting in a motel room in the southern part of the state, not far from one of the river crossings that would take them into Kentucky. When Jake's cell phone rang, he snatched it up, put it on speaker so his brother could hear, and said, "Please tell me you've got this whole thing figured out."

"Not just yet, but the wheels are in motion."

"I'd like for our wheels to be in motion, if you get my drift," Jake said.

"I'm doing everything I can to mitigate any further disruptions."

Kevin looked at his brother, shook his head, and said, "Mitigate further disruptions?" Then into the phone: "Listen, asshole. We were supposed to be out of the state weeks ago, but instead we're sitting down here in butt-fuck nowhere at a fleabag motel, peeking through the curtains every five minutes. This is the fifth move we've made over the last eighteen days. And if that isn't enough for you, we're driving around in a box truck packed with enough product to get us sent away for life. How about you stop playing games and *make* something happen."

"I am not, as you say, playing games. And ease up on the vulgarities, already. I told you I have a plan, but until and unless certain pieces come together, there isn't anything we can do."

"Yeah," Kevin said. "It's the 'unless' part that bothers me."

"You're overthinking it. Kentucky can't keep the police presence in place at the river crossings for much longer. It's far too expensive."

"And we've told you that going across the Ohio River isn't the only way into the state," Jake said. "We could go in through Illinois. Hell, we could even cut down through Missouri and come up from Tennessee."

"You could, but you're not going to. It's too risky. This isn't your deal…it's mine. That means you both do what I say if you want your cut…and your freedom."

Jake was about to go off again, but Kevin stopped

him. Then he took the phone off speaker, held it to his ear, and said, "Look, you better figure this thing out one way or another, and soon, because if you don't, Jake and I are going to take our chances. Maybe we'll get caught, and maybe we won't. If we do, that's on us. But if we don't, then you'll be shit out of luck, and we'll keep *your* cut. Are you hearing me on this?"

"Nice try. There's only one thing wrong with your thought process. I'm the one who has the buyer. What are you going to do? Open up a lemonade stand and peddle the load off two or three pills at a time? I'm in constant contact with our buyer, and together we're going to figure this thing out. Sit tight. We're almost there."

Kevin killed the connection, then tossed the phone on the bed. Jake looked at his brother and said, "What are we going to do?"

Kevin didn't like it, but he knew they were stuck. "We're going to do what the man just told me. For now, we sit tight."

Ross and Wilson got the groceries, spent a couple of hours putting Carla's house back in order, got rid of the burnt tire in the backyard, then drove over to the hospital to get Rosencrantz. When they got to his room, they discovered he wasn't there.

"Maybe he's doing some physical therapy, or something," Wilson said.

Ross nodded. "Probably. Let's go find out."

They walked out of the room and headed for the nurse's station. Once there, the nurse at the desk informed them that Rosencrantz was almost ready to go.

"Where is he?" Ross said.

"The attending physician wanted to get one more scan to make sure everything is still holding together on the inside. They went down about an hour ago, so it won't be long now."

"Sounds like he wanted to get one more line item on the bill," Ross said.

The nurse actually smiled. "I'll tell you something: A lot of people think that, but it really isn't true. Those tests are expensive…and they have to be justified. If they're not, the insurance company won't pay, which means the hospital has to absorb the cost."

"How often does that happen?" Ross said.

The nurse put some thought into her answer. "It's not what I'd call frequent, but it does happen often enough that the doctors are very careful about what gets ordered and what doesn't."

"Ever go after the patient if insurance doesn't pay?" Wilson said.

"Not usually. By the time it's all said and done, it costs more to pay the lawyers and collection agencies than it does to just write the whole thing off." Then she looked over Wilson's shoulder and tipped her chin in the air. "Here comes the doctor now. He'll be able to tell you when Detective Rosencrantz will be ready."

Ross and Wilson turned around just as the doctor made it to the nurse's station. The doctor handed a chart to the nurse, downloaded a bunch of medical jargon on her that neither Wilson nor Ross understood, then turned and gave both men a smile. "Your friend is on his way to his room. He should be up any moment. The scan was clear and I've already signed the release, so all he has to do is get changed and he'll be a free man."

"Sounds like you're letting him out of prison," Wilson said.

The doctor gave him a polite little chuckle and said, "Yes, I suppose it does. If I had to venture a guess, I imagine Detective Rosencrantz probably feels like he *has* been in prison." Then with no segue whatsoever: "Are one of you gentleman Detective Ross, by chance?"

"That's me," Ross said.

"Ah, wonderful." He reached into his pocket and

pulled out an envelope and handed it to Ross. "I received a call from a Dr. Julia Evans up in Indianapolis. I've never met the woman, but she seems rather nice…especially for a surgeon. In any event, she said to give you this list of my recommendations on dietary restrictions for Detective Rosencrantz during the initial portion of his rehabilitation." He looked at both men, smiled, and said, "Your friend is a lucky man. He's going to be just fine." Then he wished them well before walking away.

Ross wiggled the envelope at Wilson and said, "See? I'd bet you any amount of money that the first thing Julia did when she got out of surgery was make a call to that doctor on Rosie's behalf. That's not just being a good friend…that's family."

Before Wilson had a chance to respond, the nurse cleared her throat and said, "You better let me see that envelope."

Ross gave her a friendly frown. "Why?"

"Because everyone thinks it's a joke, but it's actually true."

Ross kept his frown in place. "I don't think I'm following you."

"The only people who can read that doctor's handwriting are nurses and pharmacists, and sometimes we get quite a few calls from the pharmacy, if you get my drift."

"You should see my boss's handwriting," Ross said. "It's like trying to decipher a petroglyph."

The nurse leaned forward slightly, and said, "So, you're a betting man?"

"Why do you ask?"

"Well," the nurse said, "you just offered to make a bet with your friend. I'm willing to do the same."

Ross decided to play along. "Okay, what's the bet?"

"Twenty bucks says that you can't make out one single word on that list."

Ross looked at Wilson, who shrugged and said, "I'm in for ten."

"You'd take money from a nurse?" Ross said.

The nurse rolled her eyes and reached into her pocket. She pulled out a twenty dollar bill, slapped it on the counter and said, "C'mon, what's it going to be, ladies?"

Ross gave the nurse a dry look, tore open the envelope, examined it for exactly two seconds, then pulled out his wallet and set ten bucks on the counter. He looked at Wilson and said, "C'mon, big spender…you said you were in for half."

"I haven't even seen the list yet," Wilson said.

"Trust me, it doesn't matter. Pay the lady."

Wilson put his money next to Ross's, but he wasn't ready to give up. "Still want to see the list." There was forty dollars on the counter, but the nurse hadn't yet touched the money.

Ross handed the paper to him, and Wilson gave it a long look. Then he glanced at the nurse and said, "All we need is one word, right?"

"That was the bet."

Wilson turned to Ross and said, "We're good."

Ross stepped closer. "What have you got?"

Wilson pointed at one of the items halfway down the list. "Right there. It clearly says jello."

"Mind if I see that?" the nurse asked.

"Help yourself," Wilson said. When he handed the paper to her she simply laughed.

"What's so funny?" Ross said.

The nurse took all the money from the counter, slipped it into her pocket and said, "Nice try. That doesn't say jello. It says avocado. Give me five minutes and I'll type this out for you and get it printed. Feel free to wait in Detective Rosencrantz's room. I'll bring it in."

Once Wilson and Ross were gone, the doctor reappeared from around the corner and held out his hand. "That will be ten genuine American dollars, please."

"I think I need a bigger cut," the nurse said. "I'm the one who's selling it. All you have to do is hand over a list of gibberish."

"Yes, that may be true, but without my gibberish, you wouldn't get your half, would you?" The doctor still had his hand out, palm up. He wiggled his fingers, and said, "Let's have it."

The nurse forked over ten dollars, then said, "Okay, fine, but you better make a new list. This one is starting to look a little used up."

By the time Ross and Wilson made it back to Rosencrantz's room, he was dressed and ready to go. He stood carefully—and slowly—from the edge of the bed and gave both men a smile. "How do I look?"

Ross gave Rosencrantz the once-over, and said, "Do you want the truth, or the feel-good answer?"

"C'mon Ross. How long have we been friends? You should know by now that I want the feel-good answer."

"Okay," Ross said. "You look like hammered crap."

"I'm glad I didn't ask for the truth. I think it's the food they serve in here."

"Wait until you see what you're supposed to eat for the next two months," Wilson said.

"No jokes from the new guy," Rosencrantz said.

"Who said I was joking?"

Rosencrantz looked at Ross, tipped his head at Wilson, and said, "I kinda like him."

The nurse walked into the room, handed the printed list to Ross, then looked at Rosencrantz and said, "An orderly will be here in a few minutes with a wheelchair to escort you out."

Rosencrantz shook his head. "Nope. No way. I came in here on a stretcher. At least that's what they told me. I'm walking out on my own two feet."

The nurse held her ground. "Can't allow it. There's too much liability. If you fall and crack your head open, we could get sued. You're our responsibility until you reach the other side of the front door, and that means you have to take the chair."

"That's one way of looking at it," Rosencrantz said.

The nurse put her hands on her hips and tilted her head to one side. "What's the other?"

Rosencrantz stepped over, leaned down and whispered in her ear. When he was finished, the nurse looked at him and said, "You'd do that to me after everything I've done for you?"

"Yep. And I wouldn't lose a wink of sleep."

"That's mean."

"That's life," Rosencrantz said.

The nurse wasn't quite ready to let it go. "I've seen you naked. I might even have pictures."

Rosencrantz laughed. "And you'll get to carry those fond memories with you for the rest of your life."

The nurse finally gave up and laughed right along with him. "Yeah, that, or see a shrink." Then she gave her patient a gentle hug and said, "Please don't take this the wrong way, but I hope I never see you again." Then she turned and walked out of the room.

Once she was gone, Rosencrantz looked at Wilson and Ross, gave them a big smile and said, "I think she digs me."

Ross let out a snort. "Or maybe she's a horse lover. Who's to say?"

"That's not funny," Rosencrantz said.

"Yeah, okay. No more teeth jokes, because they actually do look pretty nice. But here's what I heard from the woman, and she practically said it all in the same breath: She never wants to see you again because once was enough. Also, she's seen you naked, and now she has to see a shrink. I'm guessing they'll consider her damaged for life and suggest an application for disability is in order, based on emotional and mental distress."

Rosencrantz smiled. "I can tell you've missed me."

"I never miss," Ross said. "And by the way, what did you just whisper to her?"

"I told her that if I didn't walk out of here on my own two feet, I'd tell the hospital administrators what else she's done besides see me naked." He wiggled his eyebrows at them when he spoke.

Ross waved him off. "Right." He pointed at Wilson and said, "You might be able to sell your bullshit 'the hot nurse did me' story to the new guy here, but I'm not buying."

But if Ross thought he'd just bested his senior partner, he was wrong. "Let me see that list," Rosencrantz said.

"Why?"

Rosencrantz laughed again. "She might have seen me naked, but nothing else happened in that regard. Besides, do you think I'm the only patient who has dietary restrictions after leaving the hospital? I don't know how long that pretty little nurse and her doctor friend have been running that handwriting scam, but they've been doing it ever since I got here. You two were just played like it was your first time down at the pool hall." Then: "C'mon. Are you guys busting me out, or what? I could really use a cheeseburger."

CHAPTER TEN

Henderson walked Mayo and Ortiz down to the basement and into the evidence cage. He showed them where the boxes were that contained the files and everything else they needed to see, then helped carry it all over to an eight-foot table along the side wall. Once everything was in place, Henderson said, "I've got kind of a busy afternoon. Do you guys need my help going through any of this stuff?"

"I think we're good," Mayo said. "Might have some questions along the way, but for right now we just sort of need to lay everything out and see what we're working with."

"I'll leave you to it then," Henderson said. He pointed to the far corner of the room. "Copy machine is over there if you need it." He started toward the door.

"Good enough," Ortiz said. "And listen, do you have any Chain of Custody forms down here? If there's any relevant evidence, we'll probably want to take it with us."

Henderson stopped and turned around. "What are you talking about?"

"I just told you," Ortiz said. "Evidence…you know, the stuff that your crime scene people collected after the fact."

"The only things my crime scene people collected were a bunch of guns, five bloody arrows, and quite a few shell casings. According to their report, most of the casings belonged to the Major Crimes Unit. And we all know where the arrows came from, don't we?"

"Do we have a problem, here, Sheriff?" Ortiz said.

When Henderson spoke, his lips barely moved. "Not at all."

"Then what is it?" Mayo said, his tone not quite inside the lines of civility.

Henderson's face visibly reddened. He took a deep breath, then walked back over to the table, pulled out a folding chair and sat down. Mayo and Ortiz did the same. They all sat in silence for a few minutes, then Henderson said, "Before Ben Holden became sheriff, he ran a dry-cleaning company. He did it for years. When he got elected, the first thing he did was put one of those big jackpot flashers on top of his own personal vehicle. It was a wood-paneled station wagon, of all things, and if you saw him drive past, it looked like there was a dirty laundry emergency somewhere because he never bothered to remove the business logo from the car doors. He was a grumpy old bastard, but I loved the hell out of him. He hired me, he was a good boss, and a very good sheriff. Ron Miles would have been just as good—maybe even better—if he hadn't gotten gunned down right in front of me."

Mayo softened up and said, "You'll forgive me for saying so, Ed, but you've already told us most of this."

"I know I did. What I'm wondering is whether or not you heard me."

"What are you talking about?"

"After Ben died, I was in charge for a very short period of time. Then, in the middle of the night, Miles got sworn in and I was back to my regular duties."

"And you're upset about that?" Ortiz said.

"That question right there is why I don't think you're hearing me. Holden and Miles died within hours of each other, and just like that I'm back in the big chair. Then Carla comes along, the county holds a special election, she flat kicked my ass, and I was out again. The upshot of the whole thing is this: I was glad she won. No disrespect to Ben, or Ron, but she was the best of the bunch. She had her finger on the pulse of this county in ways I didn't think were possible. Carla Martin knew something was going on down here, and for some reason, she decided to keep it to herself."

"I don't really think it was a matter of trust," Ortiz said. "Rosie didn't even know."

"Same song, different dance," Henderson said. "My point is this: According to you guys, this thing isn't over yet. That means if Rosie hadn't found Carla's file, Jordan and his band of merry idiots—and that includes my deputy, Reynolds, by the way—would still be getting away with what they were doing…right under my damn nose. I can tell you for a fact I'd be clueless about the whole thing."

"So why the animosity?" Mayo said. "The MCU is on your side."

Henderson stood and gently pushed his chair back in place with both hands, then stood up straight, his arms hanging limp at his sides, almost as if he were in front of a firing squad. "It's not animosity. It's shame. Tom Rosencrantz—a very good friend of mine—almost died because of my incompetence. The only reason I have this job is because the people I previously reported to keep dying. Try making it through your day with that on your mind."

Murton turned to his brother and said, "So how do you want to handle all this?" They were sitting in Virgil's office and talking about the drugs, the two unknown men, Blackwell, and the DEA.

"At the moment, there isn't much we can do, other than what we've already set in motion, which, admittedly, isn't much. What I told everyone else is true. I think after tonight we'll have a better idea on how to proceed."

"Good," Murton said. "Then do me a favor, will you?"

"Sure," Virgil said. "What is it?"

"Go home. You look like death warmed over. Try to get some rest before tonight, huh?"

"Ah, that isn't going to help, Murt. As tired as I am, if I go home and take a nap, it'll mess up my sleep tonight."

Murton shook his head. "Says the guy who's so damned tired he looks like he's auditioning for a part on *The Walking Dead*. You're barely functioning as it is, Jones-man. Go back to your place and relax."

"You giving the orders now?"

"If I have to. Look, it was your idea to begin with. If you don't want to try to sleep, then do what you said you were going to." Then with a little light in his eyes: "I think it had something to do with mowing my lawn, if I'm not mistaken."

Virgil smiled, and the smile turned into a yawn. "Well, you're mistaken-adjacent, but I guess you're probably right."

"If you've been paying attention, you'll notice it has been known to happen with great regularity."

"Don't push it," Virgil said. "I'm going. Since we're asking each other for favors, do one for me?"

"You bet," Murton said.

"Give Robert a call and tell him I'm on my way over to the bar, will you?"

"Why are you going there?"

"Gotta pick up the Wagyu beef for tonight," Virgil said. "Robert's been aging it for nearly two months."

Murton's eyes lit up again. "I'll call him right now. After all, that's what brothers are for."

Virgil stood, slapped Murton on the shoulder, and headed for the door.

On the way over to the bar, Virgil spent the drive time thinking about the meeting at Cora's office, and the ramifications of Said, Inc. being chopped to pieces by a government agency for no other reason than the fact that they could. Virgil knew the asset forfeiture laws really weren't the issue. In fact, he had no qualms about the laws themselves. The problem was the people who used them to justify a means to an end. The laws weren't put in place to destroy a legitimate company like the one his friend had built from the ground up. They were meant to be used against the people who operated outside the rule of law. He thought it through about ten different ways until he realized two things: One, he was so tired his thought process wasn't really getting him anywhere, and two, he'd just missed his turn.

He went around the block, got stuck for a few minutes in a literal mini traffic jam—a Mini Cooper with a flat tire was partially blocking the intersection—then pulled into the bar's back lot, parked his Range Rover, and headed toward the rear entrance. Virgil didn't like going in through the front door. He had his reasons, and they were valid.

Years ago, after Virgil's mother passed away, his father decided he wanted to open a bar. The idea was sound, because as the former sheriff of Marion County, Mason had plenty of friends who were law enforcement officers, so the sauce was already cooked into the goose. Virgil liked the idea, so he went in for half with his father, and together they got the place up and running. Mason worked it full-time, and Virgil filled in as often as he could when he wasn't chasing down criminals for the state. They named the bar Jonesy's Place, and made a modest go of it as a local cop hangout.

Shortly after purchasing the bar and while on vacation, Virgil met and became fast friends with two Jamaican men, Delroy Rouche and Robert Whyte, who ran their own roadside bar and grill in Jamaica, in the small town of Lucea, which sat near the halfway point between the resort towns of Montego Bay and Negril. Delroy served the drinks and befriended the customers, while Robert handled the cooking.

Both Delroy and Robert eventually came to the states to work for Virgil and Mason, and in doing so, they soon turned Jonesy's Place into one of the hottest bars and restaurants in the entire city. Then time and fate intertwined, and at the tail end of one of Virgil's earliest cases as the lead detective for the MCU, Mason was shot and killed inside the bar by a deranged woman who was seeking revenge against Virgil over the death of her husband. The bullet was meant for Virgil, but hit Mason instead.

Weeks later when Virgil was finally able to meet with their family lawyer, he learned that his father's will stipulated that three other people were to receive Mason's ownership share of the establishment: Delroy and Robert were among them...as was Murton.

And then, no matter how devastating the loss of Mason was to Virgil and others, life went on as it tends to do for the living. The name of the bar was eventually changed to Jonesy's Rastabarian, and it was, by almost every measure, a huge success. Yet still, years later, Virgil grieved. He often thought in some ways it defined his life...a silhouette between what was, and what could have been.

As he made his way into the kitchen to speak with Robert about the beef for the evening's meal, he saw the sous chefs and wait staff hard at work preparing for the bar's dinner rush, but Robert was nowhere in sight. Virgil knew his employees had a tough enough job as it was, so he didn't disturb them. In fact, they were so busy, none of them seemed to even notice Virgil's presence. He closed his eyes for a moment and let his other senses take over...the aroma of the food and the sounds of tinkling glassware and cutlery reminding him of the many times he'd been to Jamaica.

Then someone said, "Excuse me," when they walked by, and Virgil knew he was in the way, so he walked into the bar area to ask Delroy if he knew where Robert was. As he pushed through the swinging door,

Virgil saw something that so surprised him, he stopped dead in his tracks, the door slapping him on the shoulder as it swung back the other way.

His wife was sitting at the bar. She was leaning forward slightly, deep in conversation, her forearms resting across the smooth, polished mahogany. Despite the fact it was a bit unusual for Sandy to be at the bar by herself late in the afternoon, that wasn't what gave Virgil pause. It was the man on the other side of the railing.

The man wasn't Delroy, or any of the other bartenders he employed.

Sandy was speaking with Virgil's father, Mason.

THE LATE AFTERNOON HAPPY HOUR CROWD WAS JUST getting started, and it was loud enough that Sandy was leaning across the bar, her feet on the railing, her butt barely touching the stool. She'd just said something to Mason, and Virgil thought whatever it was must have been funny because Mason tipped his head back and laughed. It was the kind of laugh that Virgil hadn't heard from his father in a very long time. Then Mason took the towel he always kept slung over his shoulder and gave Sandy a friendly, gentle swat on her hands.

Mason turned to reach for something—Virgil didn't know what—and that's when the two men saw each other. Mason smiled and waved at his son, and Sandy naturally looked at whoever had caught Mason's eye. When she saw Virgil, she hopped off the stool, walked over and gave her husband a kiss.

"Hi there, boyfriend. What are you doing here at this hour?"

Virgil still had his eyes on his father when he answered. "I was about to ask you the same thing."

"Give me two minutes and I'll tell you." Sandy said. "I've got to use the bathroom. Go sit and relax. You look like you're ready to drop. I'll be right back."

Virgil watched Sandy go into the bathroom, then turned and slowly walked over to the bar. He took the same seat where his wife had been sitting, and as soon as he did, Mason set a mug of Red Stripe beer in front of his son, and said, "Hey Virg. Remember all those times I tried to tell you that time isn't real?"

Virgil visibly swallowed, his eyes sliding away without speaking.

"I can see you're at a loss for words," Mason said. "So, let me ask the question this way: Believe me now?"

CHAPTER ELEVEN

When Virgil picked up his mug, he was trembling so much he had to use both hands in order not to spill the beer.

"You don't look so well."

"Lack of sleep will have that effect," Virgil said.

"Give me a minute, will you?" Mason said. "I've got to step into the cooler and grab more ice."

"I'm not going anywhere," Virgil said.

"I hope not. You're not here often enough as it is."

Virgil rubbed his face with both hands, then watched the door of the walk-in cooler as it swung shut. A few seconds later Sandy walked over and sat down next to her husband.

"It's not polite to steal a lady's chair, you know." Then, "Hey, Virgil, are you okay?"

"I'm not sure. Who were you just speaking with?"

Sandy tipped her head to the side. "What do you mean? Didn't you see us?"

Virgil stood up and said, "Would you excuse me for a moment?"

"Where are you going?"

"To help with the ice. I'll be right back." Then, with little forethought, he grabbed Sandy's wrist. "How about you come with me?"

"Sure," Sandy said. "But ease up on the grip, tough guy. You're going to give a girl a bruise."

"Sorry," Virgil said. Then he took his wife by the hand and together they made their way into the walk-in cooler behind the bar.

The cooler wasn't overly large, but it was a maze of stacked beer cases, soft drinks, kegs for the tap, and various kitchen supplies that needed to be kept chilled for Robert and his sous chefs. The ice machine was at the far end of the cooler, and though they couldn't yet see it, Virgil heard someone scooping ice into a five-gallon bucket. When they turned the corner, Virgil looked at the man's back and said, "What are you doing here?"

"Ha. I practically live here, mon," Delroy said. Then he turned and faced Virgil. "Besides, didn't you just hear me? Delroy say he had to get some ice."

Virgil spun around and grabbed his wife by the arms. He had such a strong grip that Sandy was standing on her toes, her shoulders up close to her ears. "Who were you talking to when you were sitting at the bar?"

"Virgil, stop. Let go. You're scaring me. What's wrong?"

Virgil dropped his hands to his sides, then started backing out of the cooler. "I don't know. I don't know. I'm sorry. I'm not myself."

Sandy followed her husband out of the cooler, then gently took his hand and led him over to a corner table that had a *Reserved* sign on it. "Sit down, Virg. I'll be right back. Do not move."

When she got to the bar, Delroy looked at Sandy, his face full of concern. "Everyting irie? Virgil, he look exhausted, him."

"He hasn't been sleeping very well, Delroy. You know what that's like."

Delroy had once gone through a bout of sleeplessness shortly after his baby daughter, Aayla had been born. His long-time lover, Huma Moon, was Virgil and Sandy's live-in nanny and housekeeper. Delroy, Huma, and Aayla all lived with them in a separate wing of the house.

"Do I ever, me. I wouldn't wish dat on anyone. Especially not Virgil."

"Could I get three fingers of Pappy…neat? In fact, make it two glasses."

"Coming right up, you. Go. Sit. Delroy bring it right over, me."

Once they had their drinks, Sandy looked at her husband and said, "Virgil, I know you've not been sleeping well, but I think it's time you talked to Bell." Doc Bell was their family physician.

Virgil tried to wave it off. "I don't need to see Bell, sweetheart. I just need to get some rest."

But Sandy wasn't playing. "Virgil Jones, you listen to me, and listen good. I'm your wife, and this isn't a negotiation. I'm going to have Bell come out and give you a look." Then she pushed his glass forward, and said, "Drink up. You at least need to relax. I can see the veins throbbing in your neck."

Virgil took a small sip of his drink, then said, "You never answered me. What are you doing here?"

Sandy reached out and took hold of her husband's hand. "Trying to be an attentive wife, and a good hostess for tonight's dinner party."

Virgil gave her hand a squeeze. "You're more than an attentive wife. You're the woman of my dreams. I'm sorry about what happened in the cooler…the way I grabbed you. But how does being a good hostess equate with you being at the bar?"

"I'll tell you in a second," Sandy said. "But let me ask you the same question. Why are you here?"

"I came by to pick up the meat for tonight."

"Me too. Except Robert beat you to it. I sort of helped him. That's why I'm here, Virg. I know we have to talk a little shop this evening, but I also wanted to take some of the pressure off of you. Robert is going to handle the grilling for us tonight. You don't have to do anything. Now, drink up, big boy."

"I can't," Virgil said. "I have to drive."

"No, you don't. I've got a town car waiting outside as we speak."

"What about the Range Rover?" Virgil said.

Then, as if the universe itself might have been listening in on their conversation, Robert walked up to the table and said, "Da meat is packed up and ready to go. I'm going to get it loaded in my car, den I see you at da house, no?"

"Thanks, Robert," Sandy said. "Hang on just a second, though." Then she held out her hand to Virgil, palm up. "Keys."

Virgil reached into his pocket and handed over the keys to his Rover. Sandy gave them to Robert and said, "Take Virgil's ride, will you? I'll make sure you have a way back at the end of the evening."

Robert laughed. "Yeah, mon. I be happy to. Maybe I make it an emergency run, no?"

Virgil looked up at his friend and business partner. "Robert, you're one of the most sought-after chefs in the entire Midwest."

"I know dat, me. What of it?"

"You're a professional, right?"

"Of course."

"So am I. How about we leave the emergency runs to the people authorized to make them?"

"Sure, mon, sure. Dat no problem. Robert just kidding. Though you might want to have a word with Becky, you."

Once Robert was on his way, Virgil looked at his wife and said, "Ask you something?"

"Anything," Sandy said.

"When I walked into the bar, you were speaking with someone. Who was it?"

Instead of answering, Sandy pulled out her phone and made a call. "Bell? It's Sandy. Got any dinner plans this evening? Good." She told him what time, then added, "Come a little early, will you? And bring one of those banana bags."

Since Sandy was a board member and full-time employee of Said, Inc., she took every advantage her position had to offer. Among them, a hired driver who picked her up each day for work, and brought her back home—along with anywhere else she needed to go. Mac didn't care one bit, because he and Sandy had worked well together when running the state, and he knew she was worth her weight in gold.

Sandy's driver—a kindly gentleman named Arlo Gonzalez—held the door for them, and once everyone was settled, he started the car and headed for Virgil and Sandy's house. Virgil was sort of squirming around in the back seat—he'd never been a good passenger—and Sandy noticed. She leaned forward and said, "Arlo?"

"Yes, ma'am?"

"Would you excuse us, please?"

"Of course, ma'am." The words were no sooner out of his mouth when the privacy screen that separated the front of the vehicle from the rear was raised.

Once the barrier was up, Virgil looked at his wife and said, "So this is how the other half lives, huh?"

Sandy made a rude noise with her lips. "Virgil, you are the other half."

"I hope you mean that in a good way."

"You know I do. At the very least, you're my other half, which makes you the luckiest guy on the planet."

"Now that is something I already knew. Although I do try to remember that I'm simply a humble public servant…with a gun." Virgil tipped his chin at the privacy screen. "What's with the barrier?"

Sandy began to wiggle out of her dress. "There's a reason it's called a privacy screen." Then, "C'mon, off with the Jockeys. This isn't a one-horse race. Not today, anyway."

And Virgil said, "Hey…"

Arlo got them home, and Sandy asked if he'd be willing to come back later in the evening to pick up Robert.

"I'm at your disposal, ma'am." Then he turned and winked at Virgil.

As the car was driving away, Virgil looked at Sandy and said, "How private is that privacy screen?"

Sandy gave him a shrug. "I don't know. Private enough, I guess."

"I wouldn't be so sure. Arlo gave me a wink like he knew what we were doing."

"Forget about that, Virgil. How do you feel now?"

Virgil laughed. "Like a humbled public servant."

Sandy laughed right along with him. "One who seems to be out of ammunition." Then she checked her watch, and said, "C'mon, let's go get cleaned up for the main event."

Virgil chuffed. "Uh, not to split hairs or anything like that, but I'd say the main event just happened."

Sandy gave her husband a long, lingering kiss, and was about to poke a little fun at him, but then thought better of it. "You got that right."

Virgil—who'd never been one to let much slip past him—knew his wife had just pulled her punch at the last second. For some reason, it made him sad.

Sandy caught the look on her husband's face. "Hey, Virg, what is it?"

Virgil looked out at the road and saw Murton's squad car drive by. Murton must have seen them standing in the driveway because he burped his siren as he went past.

"Virgil?"

"I was thinking about something earlier, and I'd like to ask you about it."

"Sure," Sandy said.

"It might not be easy to talk about."

Sandy took hold of Virgil's hand. "We've done easy,

and we've done hard. I know it, and so do you. Let's hear it."

"I know it was a long time ago, but on the day your dad was buried, you and I both saw the same thing. I know we did because I saw you watching. Do you remember?"

If the question bothered her, Sandy gave no indication. She closed her eyes in thought for nearly a full minute. When she opened them, she looked at Virgil and said, "A murder of crows took flight. Is that what you're talking about?"

"I am."

"Why were you thinking about that?"

I wish I knew, Virgil thought. "I don't know. I've nearly lost you so many times I can't hardly stand to think about it."

Sandy kissed him again. "Then don't."

"I couldn't live without you, Sandy. I won't ever have to, will I?"

This time Sandy didn't pull her punch, though Virgil secretly wished she would have. "Fat chance, Mister. You're stuck with me until the end of time."

They both went inside to shower and get ready for their guests, and because Virgil knew it would take his wife longer to get ready, he told her to go first. "I'm going to spend a few minutes with the boys before I get cleaned up."

Virgil and Sandy had two boys: Their eldest son, Jonas Donatti, who they adopted a number of years ago after his parents had both been killed; and their youngest son, Wyatt, who everyone secretly called their miracle baby. "That's a good idea," Sandy said. "Go throw the ball around with them, or something."

Virgil made his way into the kitchen and was about to go out to the backyard—his sons were already out there—when Huma walked in. She was moving fast, getting the rest of the preparations going for their guests. She wore a long white apron that covered her dress, and had her shock-white dreads tied up in some sort of funky knot. "Hey, Jonesy. Robert is on the back deck getting the grill set up. The meat is in the fridge, and I'm in charge of everyting else."

Virgil smiled, then walked over and gave her a hug. "What was that for?" Huma said.

"I need a reason?"

"Of course not. I just like to hear you say it."

Virgil slipped out of his jacket and tossed it over

one of the kitchen chairs. "You're the best, Huma. And you're sounding more and more like Delroy."

"Now that's a compliment. And tank you."

Virgil looked at her and said, "Listen, I was going to go out and play around with the boys for a few minutes until Sandy is done showering, but is there anything I can do to help you…or Robert?"

"We've got it covered, Jonesy."

"You sure?"

Huma gave him a warm smile and said, "Yes. Now if you really want to help, you'll get yourself a beer from the fridge, go outside, and get out of my way."

Virgil was being excused from his own kitchen, and knew it. But the truth was, he didn't mind. Huma had a job to do, so why not let her do it? He grabbed a Red Stripe, gave Huma a lopsided smile and said, "You're the boss." Then he headed for the door.

"Jonesy?"

Virgil stopped and turned back. "Yes?"

"I don't mean to speak out of turn, but if you're going to go play with the boys…" Huma let her statement hang, hoping she wouldn't have to actually say the words.

But Virgil didn't get the message, and said so. "If I'm going to play with the boys…what?"

"Your guns, Jonesy."

Virgil shook his head, slipped out of his shoulder rig, then headed for the gun safe in the bedroom. Along the way, he thought, *Christ, I'm tired.*

CHAPTER TWELVE

Bell showed up just as Virgil finished getting dressed. Sandy led him back to the bedroom, and when Bell saw his friend sitting on the bed pulling his boots on, he said, "How's the world's worst patient doing?"

"I'm not in the mood Bell," Virgil said. "Though it is good to see you."

Doc Bell had been with Virgil and his family for years, and during that time, he'd saved Sandy and Wyatt's lives, and Virgil's, on more than one occasion.

"You too, my friend. Thanks for having me over for dinner this evening."

Virgil knew the real reason Bell was there and tried to skirt the issue. "Anytime, Bell. Let's go out front and I'll fix you a drink."

Bell got serious. "Nice try, Virg. You can leave your boots on if you like, but sit back on the bed and roll up your sleeve. I'm going to give you a quick exam."

"C'mon, Bell. I'm fine. Just a little run-down is all. Give me a few of those sleeping pills you gave Murt when he was having trouble and everything will be all right."

Sandy stepped up next to Bell, and with a little wife in her voice, said, "Virgil Jones, you are going to get an exam. We're not going to discuss it, we're not going to debate it, and we're not taking no for an answer. Now sit back, and do what the man says."

Virgil knew the tone of voice Sandy was using on him meant business, but he tried one more time anyway. He gave her a grin, then said, "Or what?"

Sandy checked the time, and said, "Well, everyone is going to arrive in the next twenty minutes or so, and that includes Cora. As your loving wife—and remember, Cora was my lieutenant when I served as governor, so we have a very good relationship—I could casually mention that you might not be fit for duty. Then she'd order you to get an exam."

Virgil gave his wife the brow. "You'd do that to me?"

Sandy walked over and sat down on the bed next to her husband. "No, Virg, I wouldn't do it to you. I'd do it *for* you. I'd do it for us, and I'd do it for our family. Now be the big boy I know you are and do as the doctor says. Sit back and roll up your sleeve. If Bell brought what I asked, in about a half hour you're going to feel like a new man." Then she stood and walked out of the room.

Bell looked at Virgil and said, "You gotta admit, it's hard to argue her logic."

Virgil shook his head. But he also sat back and rolled up his sleeve.

BELL GAVE VIRGIL A BASIC EXAM, AND WHEN HE WAS finished, he said, "Your blood pressure is higher than I'd like to see, but given what you've told me about what you've been going through, I'm not really very surprised. Tell me more about these waking dreams you've been having. And hold still while I get you hooked up to the banana bag."

Virgil looked at the plastic container and said, "Is that the same stuff you gave Sandy when she didn't feel well?"

"It is. Lots of vitamins, minerals, and a bunch of other stuff that won't mean anything to you, so I'm not going to waste time explaining it."

"I'm not sure I want to do this."

"Why not?"

"Two reasons. Here's the first: The last time I let you hook me up to an IV, I was out for days. Don't think I've forgotten about that."

Bell said, "Uh-huh. I'll say it again, you should have read the fine print on the release form. Besides, it worked, didn't it?" Then he stuck the needle into Virgil's vein. "You told me there were two reasons. What's the other?"

"Just this: That thing looks like a bag of urine."

Bell laughed. "Well, I did just remove someone's catheter shortly before I arrived here. I hope I didn't get the bags mixed up."

"And people tell me I need to work on *my* sense of humor?"

"Relax, Jonesy. I'm kidding, and you know it. Anyway, the waking dreams…?"

"I'm not quite sure how to explain it, Bell. They're not really dreams. They're more like visions, or some damned thing."

"Are you aware of your actual surroundings when they happen?"

Virgil's answer was almost truthful. It wasn't that he wanted to deceive his friend, but he also didn't want to be relieved of duty, or lose his privilege to drive. "Mostly. With the exception of what happened this afternoon, it's like closing your eyes for two seconds and reliving a past experience. It seems longer than it actually is because the memories of those events are still with me."

"But that wasn't the case this afternoon, was it?"

"No. Somehow that was different. I saw Sandy speaking with my dad. It was him, Bell. He was at the bar."

"But it was actually Delroy, wasn't it?"

Virgil knew he had to give Bell the answer he wanted to hear, so that's what he did. "Yes, it was Delroy. Obviously it was Delroy. Look, I'll let you give me the bag of pee, but I really just need a few nights of decent sleep. Once that happens everything will be fine."

"Great," Bell said. "When do I start?"

Virgil didn't understand. "Start what?"

"My new job as a detective with the Major Crimes Unit."

"You're losing me, Bell."

I sure as hell hope not, Bell thought. "Isn't that what we're doing? You're playing doctor right now, so I thought it only fitting that I get to play detective. Will I get one of those cool badges on a chain like the kind you and Murton are always wearing around your necks?"

"I thought you said my blood pressure was a little high."

"It is."

"Then you're not helping," Virgil said.

"Don't worry, Jonesy. I will give you a few pills to get your sleep back on track. And once you're finished with that bag of pee, as you called it, you'll feel much better. We'll talk more later tonight, after dinner."

"Why later?" Virgil said.

"Because I don't want to miss the appetizers that Robert is preparing. He's getting ready to put some shrimp on the grill. C'mon, let's go try it."

Virgil jerked his thumb at the bag that hung from the bedpost. "What about this thing?"

"What about it? Bring it with you. It's a banana bag, not a ball and chain. Just keep it elevated."

Virgil pointed at the dresser and said, "Hand me my badge, will you?"

Bell grabbed the badge and gave it to Virgil. "What are you doing?"

"Following doctor's orders." He unhooked the clasp on the chain that held his badge, then attached it to the bag and hung the whole thing around his neck. "How's this?"

Bell scratched an eyebrow and said, "I'll see you out there."

Ross and Wilson got Rosencrantz back to Carla's place, and when they walked inside, Rosencrantz looked around and said, "I know you guys were staged out of here when everything went down, but I didn't think you were going to trash the place."

"What are you talking about?" Ross said. "We came over here before we went to the hospital to pick you up. We spent two hours putting everything back together."

"It looks like you spent two hours putting everything back in the wrong place."

"You're welcome," Ross said, his voice dry.

"Ah, I'm just fuckin' with ya. It's fine. Listen, give me a minute, will you? I need to step outside and see something."

Ross and Wilson said they would, and watched as their friend and fellow detective walked out the back door.

"Is he doing what I think he's doing?" Wilson said.

"If you think he's out there reliving what happened when Reynolds attacked and kidnapped him, I'd say you're half right."

"What's the other half?"

"Listen, I don't want to offend you, or anything like that, but would you mind hanging inside for a while? Rosie and I have a history. I'd like to check in with him on a personal level."

Wilson understood, and wasn't offended in the least. "Not at all. Go ahead, man. I sort of feel like a third wheel right now anyway."

"You're not," Ross said. "But the fact that you feel like you are tells me what kind of man I'm dealing with. That's my way of saying thank you." Then he followed his partner out the back door.

He found Rosencrantz staring at the spot where the burnt tire had been. Rosencrantz heard Ross coming, but didn't bother to turn around. When he spoke, his words were clipped and tight. "I was an idiot. I fell for Reynolds's act like a rookie right out of the academy. He called me on the phone, told me the house was on fire, and I came rushing over. When I turned in to the drive, I saw all this black smoke billowing from the backyard and I thought it was the house. I saw Reynolds grab a fire extinguisher from his trunk and run to the back. I did the same. When I turned the corner that guy was on me like a feral cat."

"Could have happened to anyone," Ross said.

"Maybe, but it happened to me, and I feel like a dope."

"Why?"

"Because I could have prevented it." Rosencrantz snapped it at him. "I wasn't thinking clearly."

Ross let the snap go and said, "What were you thinking?"

"It doesn't matter now."

Ross moved into his partner's line of sight. "I think it does."

Rosencrantz wasn't mad at his friend, but he was mad, just as Virgil had predicted he might be. "Okay Ross, we'll do it your way. If I'd have been on my game, I would have known it wasn't a coincidence when Reynolds pulled me over and blew my tail on Fiona Vale after she left the bank. But it never occurred to me." He tapped the side of his head with his index finger…hard. "It never even made it into my brain. If it had, I wouldn't have followed the same path that Reynolds did when I thought the house was burning. I'd have gone around the other side. If that had happened, I would have seen him waiting to take me down."

"Look, Rosie, you can't unwind the clock. Neither can I. But there are about a thousand different ways the whole thing could have played out. What matters is this: You're going to be okay."

"Am I? Because it sure doesn't feel like it. When I saw that smoke it made me think the whole house was going to burn down, and I thought…" Rosencrantz let his statement fade away, like he couldn't bring himself to finish the sentence.

"I know what you thought, partner."

"Oh yeah? How's that? Because you've never been through it."

"Maybe not," Ross said. "But I can do the math. And I'll tell you something else…I'd have done the exact same thing you did."

"Why's that?"

"Because this place isn't just a house to you. What you said about Reynolds and Vale? Sell it to yourself however you want, man, but that wasn't part of the equation. The reality is this: Your fiancé and unborn child were brutally murdered, and this was the house where you were going to begin your lives together. It's the last piece of Carla and your baby that you have left, and you didn't want to lose it. Tell me I'm wrong."

"I can't, because you're not." Rosencrantz said. He was quiet for a few minutes, and Ross let his friend have the time he needed. Finally Rosencrantz said, "I made a decision while I was in the hospital. I'm going to keep this house. I'll be moving in permanently as soon as I'm able. The commute is doable, and I just can't let the place go."

"Want to know what I think?" Ross said.

"I don't know why you bother to ask the question. You're going to tell me anyway."

"You're right. I am. I also think it's a good idea."

"Do you think Carla would approve?" Rosencrantz said.

Ross threw his arm around Rosencrantz's shoulders. "I'm certain she already has. She's probably wondering what's taken you so long to decide."

Rosencrantz was quiet again for a long time, then he pointed to a particular spot in the backyard. "I was going to build a swing set right over there. I think now maybe I'll put in a vegetable garden instead."

A single tear ran down his cheek, and after that they didn't talk about it anymore. Rosencrantz wiped the tear away and said, "C'mon, let's go eat an avocado or some fuckin' thing, huh?" Then he turned and started back toward the house. He made it all the way to the door before he noticed that Ross hadn't yet moved.

Rosencrantz walked back over and said, "What is it?"

Ross looked his friend square in the eyes. "I once read something. It said, 'Happiness is a choice we all have the power to make,' and I'll tell you something: I believe that statement to be true. What it didn't say though, was sometimes the choice is easy, and sometimes it's not."

"What's the greater message?" Rosencrantz said.

"You have to ask? We all miss the hell out of Carla, Rosie. Don't think you're ever alone in it because you're not." Then, "Let's go inside. Jim and I have some things we need to tell you."

CHAPTER THIRTEEN

Mayo and Ortiz spent the rest of their day getting the Shelby County files separated and organized, made copies of everything they needed, then boxed up what they'd put together and went to get hotel rooms and something to eat. They got themselves checked in, left the material in Mayo's room, then went out and grabbed a couple of sandwiches to go. Once they were back and had eaten, Ortiz unpacked the box of paperwork and laid it out on the table next to the window. He spent an hour looking through everything, then said, "Are you sure we got all the relevant information from the files?"

Mayo was sitting on the bed trying to figure out how to work the hotel's TV remote. "I'm telling you, I think they make these things more difficult than they need to be. It's like they want you to accidentally watch porn so they can put it on your bill."

"Or, you could forget about that and answer my question," Ortiz said.

"Yeah, we got it all. The only thing we didn't take was the actual physical evidence, because like Henderson said, most of the shell casings were ours. But we got all the paper."

"Let me ask you something," Ortiz said. "What are the chances that Henderson kept something out of the files?"

"You mean on purpose?"

"Yeah…that's exactly what I mean. Jonesy was hoping the notebook was in Henderson's files."

Mayo scratched at the back of his head. "I'd say the chances of that are about as close to zero as you could get."

"So you're saying there's a chance?"

"Let me revise my last statement," Mayo said. "The chances are zero."

"What makes you so sure?"

"Two reasons. No, wait…make that three." He ticked them off his fingers as he answered. "One, he would have absolutely no reason to do so. Everything was over by the time he and his deputies arrived. Two, by all accounts, he's an honest cop, and three, Jonesy trusts him. If he didn't, we wouldn't be looking for a truck full of drugs and the two guys who took them. We'd be looking at Henderson himself. And since that's not the case, my answer remains the same. Zero chance."

"Then what he told us about his ability to do the job properly must be true."

"Why do you say that?"

"Because unless he's holding out on us, he's dragging his feet on the follow-up."

"In what way?" Mayo said.

"Over a dozen men died out at that compound after we showed up. Other than Jordan, Graham, and Hamilton, he still doesn't have positive IDs on any of the other men…including Blackwell's CI."

"Did he put all their prints through the system?"

Ortiz shuffled through the file, then pulled out the paper he wanted. "Yeah, he did. The problem is, ironically enough, he gave them a little too much information."

Mayo got off the bed and took a seat at the table. "What are you talking about?"

Ortiz handed him the paper. "Look at the disclosure he made with the request. He stated that all the victims were dead and the case was closed."

Mayo shook his head in disgust. "With that sort of

declaration on the request, those prints might get looked at sometime shortly after we retire. What the hell was he thinking?"

"I'll tell you something," Ortiz said. "I believe Henderson is a good cop, but that doesn't necessarily make him a good administrator."

"That might be a bit of an understatement," Mayo said. "He's in over his head…at least when it comes to this sort of thing."

"How do you want to handle it?"

Mayo checked the time, then said, "Not much we can do tonight, but first thing in the morning I think we should let Jonesy know what's happening. Maybe he can get Franklin or Parr to push the list to the front of the line. Or at the very least have Becky run them through the state database."

"So we're done for the night?" Ortiz said.

"Looks like it. I've got an idea though."

"What's that?"

"Well, Ross and Wilson are down here. Why not make a run over to Carla's and check on Rosie? We can bring them up to date at the same time."

"Think Rosie's feeling well enough for that?"

Mayo gave his partner a shrug. "If he is, he is. If he's not, we'll leave him be. What's the downside?"

Murton and Becky arrived at Virgil and Sandy's place first, followed almost immediately by Tony and Patty Stronghill. Virgil got everyone set up with drinks and was about to explain the finer points of their mutual problem when Murton said, "I love the new necklace. Let me guess: We're adding another U to our squad's name."

"What are you talking about?" Virgil said.

Murton laughed. "It looks like you've got a bag of urine hanging from your neck, so I thought you were going to change the name to Major Crimes Urination Unit. That makes you the head of the pee-pee police."

"You're a riot, Murt. Anyone ever tell you that?"

"Yeah, pretty much on a daily basis."

"It's not urine," Virgil said. "It's, uh...well, to tell you the truth, I don't know what it is. Some sort of vitamin concoction Bell whipped up. It's the same stuff he gave Sandy when she wasn't feeling well."

"It does sort of look like pee," Becky said.

Bell was standing next to the grill with Robert and heard the whole thing. "It's a banana bag."

Murton turned in his seat and looked that way. "Are you going to try to hypnotize him like you did with me?" Then before Bell could answer: "Maybe you could implant some humor into his subconscious."

Virgil looked down at the bag and saw that it was nearly empty. He also realized that Bell had been right. He was already feeling better.

Mac, Cora, and Baker came around the corner and onto the back deck. Mac clapped Robert on the back as he walked by and said, "That, my friend, looks delicious." Then he saw Virgil and said, "I know you've always been a bit fashion-challenged, as they say, but why are you wearing a bag of urine around your neck?"

They all got a laugh out of that, but the laughter went away in a hurry when Virgil sat down and said, "Does anyone know when Ed and Pam are getting here?"

WHEN TIME CIRCLED BACK AND HAD ITS WAY AGAIN, Virgil was standing on the front porch of his old house. He knew he didn't need to knock, but he did so anyway out of respect. It was almost at the exact same time that Jonas's biological father, Ed Donatti, was fighting for his life with Hector Sigara, the man who'd knocked Becky's teeth out with the butt of a shotgun, then dragged her naked and unconscious down the stairs.

Murton was tied to a chair in the center of the room, and when Augustus Pate fired at the front door, the shock of the blast brought Virgil back.

Everyone was crowded around Virgil in a tight little circle, with Sandy, Bell, and Murton closer than anyone else.

"Virgil, what just happened?" Sandy said.

"What do you mean? All I did was sit down and say I wish Ed and Pam were here. How about everyone step back a little, huh? You're all sort of crowding me. I'm fine."

Murton looked directly at his brother. "That's not what you said, Virgil. I heard every word plain as day. You said, 'Does anyone know *when* Ed and Pam are getting here?'"

Virgil tried to wave it off. "I misspoke. Since when is that the crime of the century?" He stood and said, "Would you all excuse me for a minute? I want Bell to get this line out of my arm. Bell?"

Virgil walked inside the house without another word. Bell and Sandy followed him in.

Murton told Becky he'd be right out, and moved toward the back door as well. He happened to glance at

Cora just before stepping inside and saw her sitting alone, her elbows on the table, her face in her hands.

Bell was all but insistent, and Virgil didn't want to hear it. "I was looking right at you when it happened, Jonesy. That wasn't just someone reliving a memory. You were virtually catatonic there for a few seconds. Now sit still and be quiet so I can get this blood pressure reading."

"Whatever, Bell. You saw what you saw. I simply misspoke, and when I did, I remembered something about Ed. It's not that big of a deal."

Murton moved into his brother's line of sight. "Virgil, the man said to shut up."

"Oh, like that's going to help my blood pressure," Virgil said.

Bell looked at Sandy and said, "Would you and Murt please step out so I can continue? As much as I hate to admit it, neither of you are helping." They were all inside Virgil's home office, and while Sandy didn't like it, she knew Bell was right.

She hooked her hand into the crook of Murton's elbow and said, "C'mon, Murt. Bell makes a good point. Let's wait in the living room."

Bell closed the French doors to the office, got the blood pressure reading, checked Virgil's eyes and his carotid arteries, then started in with the questions.

"What happened outside…would you say that's a fair and accurate example of the kinds of things you've been experiencing?"

Virgil nodded. "Pretty much."

"And how many of these episodes have you had?"

"Four or five, I guess."

"Close your eyes," Bell said.

And Virgil being Virgil, said, "Why?"

"Jonesy, close your eyes."

Virgil sighed, then did as Bell asked. "Now think about this next question carefully. Right before they happen, do you notice anything out of the ordinary?"

"I don't understand the question."

"Do you have any unusual sensations, like a weird taste in your mouth, or an odd sense of smell?"

"No," Virgil said.

"I asked you to think carefully."

Virgil opened his eyes. "Just because I can remember and think fast doesn't mean I'm not telling you the truth, Bell."

"Fair enough. What about physical abnormalities? Are you dizzy, lightheaded…anything like that?"

Virgil actually thought about the question this time before he answered. "No."

"What about ringing in your ears, or blurred vision?"

"Nope, and nope."

"Headaches?"

Virgil didn't want to admit it, but then thought, what good was it to have a doctor if you weren't going to tell the truth. "Yeah, I've had a few lately."

"Define few," Bell said.

"More than usual."

"How bad are they?"

Virgil subconsciously reached up and touched his head. "They're not debilitating, or anything like that. But they are sort of persistent."

"Do you have one right now?"

Virgil shook his head. "No."

"Did you have one right before you asked about Pam and Ed?"

Virgil thought about the question for a few seconds. "Not that I recall."

"That's not good enough, Jonesy. You either did or you didn't. Are you saying you don't remember?"

"I guess I am."

"How do you feel right now…right this second?"

"Hungry."

Bell pushed his John Lennon glasses up on his nose and said, "Virgil, I'm serious."

"So am I. But I gave you the most honest answer I could. I'm starving. If you'd like me to elaborate, that bag of bananas you gave me really helped. I feel pretty good, actually."

Bell shook his head and smiled. "So let's go eat."

They stepped out of the office, and Sandy said, "Bell?"

"He's fine…for now. There are a few things I'd like to talk with you both about later, but I have to do a little research first."

"What kind of research?" Murton said.

"Various tests are available, and given the unique nature of the problem—if it even is a problem—I want to make sure we choose the correct diagnostics."

"There is no problem," Virgil said. "So, how about we skip the diagnostics? I've got about two grand of meat out there that's going to look like my grilled chicken if we don't eat it."

Sandy gave Bell a hug, then gently grabbed Virgil's arm. "Let's go. Our guests are waiting. But hear me when I say this, Virg. We are going to talk about it."

CHAPTER FOURTEEN

When Mayo and Ortiz arrived at Carla's house, Ross answered the door and said, "What are you guys doing here?"

"Hello to you too," Mayo said. "Mind if we come in?"

Ross stepped back and let his fellow detectives inside. "So, what's up?"

Ortiz clapped Ross on the back and said, "In a word? Nothing. It was either hang here for a while with you guys, or sit and watch Mayo try to work a hotel remote. Is Rosie up for the visit?"

"Of course I am," Rosencrantz said. He'd just stepped from the kitchen. "Come on in, guys. You want some tofu?" Then he let his eyelids droop and said, "It's delicious."

"We already ate," Mayo said. "But fuck you, anyway. How are you feeling?"

Rosencrantz laughed and said, "Ah, I'm okay. I've got about two months of misery ahead of me though on my diet, then a few more after that before they'll let me come back to work."

"So enjoy the time off," Ortiz said. "You earned it…the hard way. What's the matter? Were you out of vacation time or something?"

"You've been hanging out with Jonesy too much. That sounds like the kind of joke he'd offer up. Have a seat. Want a beer?"

"Is it non-alcoholic?" Mayo said.

"No, it's Red Stripe."

"Then yes."

Ross grabbed beers for everyone—Rosencrantz had to drink a smoothie that tasted like stale dirt—and they all ended up in the living room. They spent a few minutes tossing a little manure around the way cops often do, then Rosencrantz looked at Mayo and Ortiz, and said, "I know why Ross and Wilson are here, and I'm grateful for their help, but what brings you guys down this way?"

"Maybe we just wanted to come by and see how our fellow detective and friend is doing," Mayo said.

Rosencrantz turned the corners of his mouth down.

"Or you could just give me the whole story, because that's not the only reason you're here."

"How do you know that?" Ortiz said.

"Because I heard what you said about Mayo trying to work the hotel remote. If you were coming down to check on me, you wouldn't bother with hotel rooms. So let's hear it."

Mayo touched eyes with Ross, who gave him a nod. Then he looked at Rosencrantz and said, "There's been some developments in the case where, uh…"

"Where I got my ass handed to me?" Rosencrantz said.

"That's the one. It looks like two of Jordan's crew got out of the compound where you were being held. They made off with a shipment of drugs before any of us ever arrived. Ortiz and I are supposed to find them."

"Have you talked to Ed yet?" Rosencrantz said.

"We have," Ortiz said. "We got copies of all his files from the case back at the hotel. We also had the pleasure of meeting Betty."

Rosencrantz winced. "How'd that go?"

"She treated us like we just dropped a turd in the punch bowl," Mayo said. "I don't think I've ever met a more abrasive woman in my life."

Wilson looked over at Ross. "Didn't you tell me not long ago that you were going to fix me up with a woman named Betty? If I'm not mistaken, you mentioned something to the effect of she has a strong personality."

Rosencrantz looked at Ross. "You didn't."

"It was a joke," Ross said. "He's the new guy. I'm trying to break him in."

Mayo laughed. "Drop the last word of your sentence right there, and I'd say mission accomplished. Ortiz and I had to sneak out the back door when we left Henderson's evidence room. It was either that, or come out shooting."

Rosencrantz got them back on track. "So, the case?"

Mayo and Ortiz exchanged a look, and Ross caught it. "What?"

Mayo took a sip of his beer, turned to Rosencrantz and said, "Look, I know Ed is a friend of yours, and I don't want to disrespect the guy, but he closed this case so fast it was like he was trying to sweep the whole mess under the rug."

Rosencrantz shrugged. "I can't say I blame him. It was his own deputy who attacked me. That's a hard thing to come to terms with…not only for me, but for Ed as well."

"I can understand that part," Mayo said. "But he closed the case prior to getting the IDs back on the rest of Jordan's crew."

Rosencrantz was underwhelmed. "So what? Eventually we'll get the IDs, Ed can stick them in the file, and it won't make one bit of difference."

"Right," Ortiz said. "Except, like we stated, there are still two guys unaccounted for, along with a truckload of drugs."

"Did Ed know that before he closed the case?" Rosencrantz said.

"Not to our knowledge," Mayo said. "In fact, to be fair, I don't know how he could have known. We weren't even aware of the situation until Blackwell informed Jonesy."

Rosencrantz took a long drink of his smoothie, made a disgusting face and said, "So there you go."

"There we go…what?" Mayo said.

Rosencrantz set his glass on the coffee table before he answered. "The type of work we do is very different from what the counties and their sheriffs have to deal with. I should know. I used to live with one. Half the time they handle a bunch of administrative bullshit that I wouldn't wish on anyone because the county council is always crawling up their butts about one thing or another. The other half of the time they're out serving warrants, busting up bar fights or domestic disputes, and doing traffic stops. We don't do any of that crap. If you're looking for mistakes that Ed made based on how we do our jobs, I'm sure you'll find some. But if you look at it from his perspective, you might see it differently."

"Look, Rosie, we get it," Ortiz said. "We really do. Everything you just told us makes perfect sense. But the guy put in a request for prints on every bad actor out at that compound."

"As he should have," Rosencrantz said.

"Right. Except he added a little commentary to the request, and said the case was closed. It'll take forever to get those prints back. Mayo and I thought maybe Jonesy could get DHS to push the request, or at the very least have Becky run them through the state database."

"You're thinking that if you can get the IDs, you'll have a place to start?" Wilson said.

Rosencrantz looked at Wilson and said, "As the new guy, you should let me ask the questions."

"Sorry," Wilson said. "Just trying to help."

Rosencrantz turned back to Mayo and Ortiz. "You're thinking that if you can get the IDs, you'll have a place to start?" Then before they could answer, he turned back to Wilson. "Don't give up so easily. It takes all the joy out of my heart."

"That was our thought," Mayo said, ignoring the back and forth between Wilson and Rosencrantz.

"So do that," Rosencrantz said. "Once you have the intel, you'll be off and running."

Ortiz drained his bottle of beer, let out a little belch and said, "We intend to. But it's still going to take time. Jonesy told us not to come back until we have something. That's my way of saying we're not sure what to do while we're waiting."

"I've got something for you to look into, if you're interested," Rosencrantz said.

Aside from the little scare Virgil had given everyone, the meal went off without a hitch. Everyone had a great time, and after they were finished eating, Huma and Sandy took care of the kids and got them ready for bed. Virgil pulled Tony and Patty aside, quickly brought them up to speed on the situation, then joined everyone else back at the table.

Cora got them started by saying, "Just so we're all on the same page, I heard every word that was said in my office after I stepped out. That means no one has to dance around anything to try to protect me."

"How'd you pull that off?" Virgil said.

"Simple. When I hit the intercom button and spoke

with Baker, I never killed the connection. I sat out in the anteroom and listened to the whole thing."

"Then why are you smiling?" Murton asked. "It wasn't what anyone would describe as a happy event."

"For once, you and I are on the same page, Wheeler. But you're forgetting something. Didn't you hear what Turkis said? He called me lovely. That hasn't happened to me in a very long time."

Murton laughed. "I don't mean to burst your bubble, but if I'm remembering correctly, he also said Blackwell was delightful."

Cora's smile went away. "You know something, Wheeler? If you hadn't saved my life that time in the parking garage, I'd reassign you to the janitorial department."

"Well, you know what they say. Cleanliness is next to godliness."

"Keep it up and you'll be next to a urinal with a scrub brush and a pail." Then, before Murton could keep going, Cora looked at Mac and said, "Do you really think Blackwell has a shot at taking the company?"

Mac glanced at Patty, then said, "Allen tells me that there is precedent. That's the bad news. The good news is that it has never been tried on this scale. I'm not certain the DEA could pull it off, but if they decide to go forward, the fight would be long…and expensive."

Patty leaned in and said, "I don't care how long it takes or how much it costs. My Uncle Rick built that company from the ground up. I will fight this thing until we've spent every last nickel we have in the bank to make them go away. And even if they don't, in the end, what will they have, and what will they accomplish? I'll tell you what: They'll have a bunch of commercial buildings and equipment worth absolutely nothing because we'll mortgage them to the hilt. As far as the company goes, the employees are the real issue, along with the work we do at the cultural center. But none of that matters one single bit if Tony and I go to jail."

"Let's not get ahead of ourselves," Virgil said.

"How can we not?" Tony said. "The facts are the facts. What Agent Blackwell told you is true. I killed five men that night. Not one of them ever fired at me, or anyone else, for that matter."

"What you did was in defense of another," Murton said to Tony. "Blackwell is using scare tactics to get what he wants. And while what you just said is true, the fact remains that we were right. Rosie was being held captive, he was dying, and that makes our actions justified."

"It also makes them lucky," Cora said. "Because according to the case notes, no drugs were ever found on the premises."

"They had the presses and dies," Murton said.

Cora nodded. "As much as I hate to admit it, Wheeler, you're right. They did. And while it may be a federal offense of one kind or another, that in and of itself doesn't justify the deaths of those men…especially the federal confidential informant."

"Let me add a couple of things," Virgil said. "First, I don't completely agree regarding what you said about the CI. The man's death is not on us, Cora. Blackwell should have said something the minute he knew we were working the case. And, luck didn't have anything to do with it."

"Explain that."

"Since Mac, as the CEO of Said, Inc., was in charge of those properties at the time, we had permission to enter and conduct a search…both at the main residence, and at the compound. Once we arrived, they opened fire on us. So that makes it self-defense. Bottom line, we've been cleared on the shootings, so that's off the table. Secondly—Murt and Becky already know this—but Blackwell came to my office after our meeting at the statehouse. He made it clear that if the MCU is willing to, and does, in fact, find the other two men and the drugs, the DEA will go away."

Mac leaned back in his chair and smiled. "There you go. What are you waiting for?"

"Permission comes to mind," Virgil said. "And I can't believe I'm about to say this, but so do optics."

"As for permission, you officially have it," Mac said.

Cora's voice went flat. "It seems someone has forgotten who the current governor is."

Mac let out a little chuckle. "You're right, of course. Force of habit. My apologies. But please tell me they have it…permission."

"Of course they do," Cora said. Then to Virgil: "Tell me about the optics."

"I'm not sure I trust what Blackwell told me in my office. For some reason he's trying to distance himself from all of this—his reasoning has to do with his impending retirement—but it feels like there's more. He said he wants to go out on top and, in his words, not a loser. But he told me he was running his own private op, and if that's the case, why take yourself out of the equation and drop the whole thing in our lap?"

"So he has an ulterior motive behind his request?" Becky said.

"He must," Virgil said. "He's in too deep as it is. Otherwise it doesn't make sense."

"What, exactly are you driving at, Jones-man?" Cora said.

"I think the way to attack this problem shouldn't be focused exclusively on finding the rest of Jordan's crew and the drugs. That's a priority, of course, and I've already got Mayo and Ortiz working that angle. It won't be more than a day…two at the most, before Ross and Wilson will be ready to help them."

"So much for waiting for permission," Cora said.

"Ah, I knew you'd go for it. I could have always pulled them back."

Cora didn't like it, but she knew Virgil was right. "And you and Wheeler? What are you two going to do?"

"That's where the optics come into play," Virgil said.

Cora leaned back and crossed her arms. "I wondered if you were ever going to answer my question."

"Murton and I talked about this earlier. We think it's the only way any of this will work."

"The only way what will work?" Sandy said. She'd just joined the group after getting the boys settled in.

When Virgil finally decided to answer the question, he did so with action as much as words. He and Murton both pulled out their MCU badges and set them on the table in front of Cora. Virgil looked her in the eye and said, "We quit. Effective immediately."

CHAPTER FIFTEEN

Rosencrantz went and found the file Carla had put together when she was running her own private investigation. When he returned to the living room, he sat down in his chair and handed the file to Mayo. "Take a look at that and let me know what you see."

Mayo opened the folder, gave it a casual glance, then said, "I know you don't really have any way of knowing this, so I'll just tell you. Not only have I seen this file, but so has everyone in this room. Jonesy and Murton have seen it as well."

"I know they have," Rosencrantz said. "Ross came to the hospital nearly every single day I was there. He told me even though Carla's list didn't exactly solve the case, it did help you guys find me, and confirmed a number of suspicions after the fact."

Mayo handed the file folder back to Rosencrantz. "That about says it. So how does the file come into play?"

Rosencrantz set the file down next to him and said, "Apparently, after Reynolds attacked me, he destroyed my phone. Ross had Becky fix me up with a new one, and he brought it to me a few days ago. Becky did a complete restore from the latest backup, so I not only had a copy of that file on my phone, I also had the most current daily reports out of the MCU."

"Not seeing your point," Ortiz said.

Rosencrantz gave him a look. "That's because I haven't made it yet. According to what I've been able to piece together, Becky was running the list of initials from Carla's file through her system, but somewhere along the way, she stopped. What I want to know is why?"

"You already know why," Ross said. "The mission objective changed. You practically broke the whole thing wide open all by yourself." Then, simply because they were partners, Ross poked a little fun at his friend. "Although I might have gone about it in a way that didn't end with me getting my ass handed to me."

Rosencrantz ignored the shot and continued with, "I know the mission objective changed. You guys went from chasing a bunch of criminals to rescuing me. I'm grateful beyond words." He picked the folder back up, then flipped to the page that contained the names and initials. He gave it back to Mayo and said, "There is still one set of initials that no one ever looked into, and it's right there on the list."

Mayo looked at the list again and said, "And you want us to have Becky restart the entire process?"

Rosencrantz shook his head. "No, there's no need for that. But I do want you to have her finish it. There's a chance that whoever those initials belong to are one of the guys you're looking for."

Ross looked at Mayo. "Let me see that list."

Mayo handed the file over, and after Ross had examined the list of initials, he looked at Rosencrantz and decided to be gentle instead of direct. "Rosie, go back through the daily reports. This one set of initials? It'd be a waste of time for Becky to try and figure out who it is. We already know. I simply forgot to mention it to you."

"What are you talking about?" Rosencrantz said.

"The initials are AB. When we were up in Elkhart at the Freedom Pharm facility, it became clear that Benjamin Clark—the dead guy that Wilson found—had a father in prison way up in Baraga, Michigan. We were getting ready to fly up and interview him, but we never even made it onto the chopper."

"Why not?"

"Because there was an incident in the prison yard right after Jonesy called and told the warden we were headed his way. Clark's father was killed by the Aryan Brotherhood the second they found out we were coming. That's your AB initials, right there."

Rosencrantz sat back and closed his eyes. "Then that must have been right before I spoke with Becky and told her the whole thing was happening down here, in Shelby County."

"What makes you say that?" Ortiz said.

"Because I'd no sooner gotten off the phone with her when Reynolds called and tricked me into believing that Carla's house was on fire, and we all know what happened after that, don't we?"

"What happened after was the fact that you survived," Ross said.

Rosencrantz stood and put the file away. "So much for my theory. Listen, guys, I'm sort of beat. I'm going to go to bed."

"Ross and I were going to bag out with you for the night," Wilson said. "If you want us to, that is."

"Yep. Knock yourselves out. You know where to find everything."

Ross could tell by the tone of his partner's voice that he was feeling down. "Hey, Rosie?"

"Yeah?"

"It was a good thought. But don't worry, we'll get the rest of it wrapped up. Even if we don't, as far as I'm concerned, it was a successful operation because we got you back."

"Yet some of the guys who are responsible for what happened to me are still out there," Rosencrantz said. "I thought maybe I had a solid lead for you." Then he turned and walked down the hall to his bedroom.

Rosencrantz didn't know it at the time, but he had been correct all along. Carla's file held the piece of information they needed, and while all of them had been looking right at it, they just couldn't see the clue for what it really was.

Tony and Patty excused themselves, said goodbye to everyone, then left to go home. They weren't trying to be rude, but they knew whatever was about to happen with Virgil and Murton was state business. Bell left as well, letting Virgil know that he'd be in touch with either a plan, or a referral for diagnostics. Once they were gone, Cora turned and said, "What the hell do you two think you're doing?"

"It has to be this way, Cora," Virgil said.

"Why?"

"Look, if the MCU finds the rest of Jordan's crew, and the drugs, we're all good…if you believe Blackwell, which I'm not sure I do. I'm telling you, there's more at play here. I can feel it in my gut."

Cora, who used to be a cop herself, knew about gut feelings. "And what does your gut have to do with optics?"

"Like I said earlier, if we locate the men and drugs, everyone's problems go away…probably. Said, Inc. might lose the Salter property, but Mac and Patty can take that hit without blinking."

"That doesn't necessarily mean we'd want to," Mac said.

Virgil nodded. "I understand. I'm simply saying it won't hurt you financially. But if the MCU can't find the crew and the drugs, it's a wash, for both the DEA and the MCU, because let's face it, not every criminal gets caught, and that sort of thing happens all the time. Mac, you and Patty may or may not have a battle on your hands if that's what happens, but there really isn't anything we can do if it shakes out that way."

"How does that get us to you and Wheeler quitting?" Cora said.

Virgil chuckled at the question, but there was no joy in the sound of his laughter. "I'm surprised you have to ask. The entanglements of this case are almost too complex to keep track of. Two of the state's former governors—one of whom is my wife—are running the company built by the man whose niece now holds the controlling interest in that very same company. A niece, I might add, who is in charge of the cultural center whose financing was a joint private-public venture brought about between the state and the Popes' foundation."

"And don't forget that the Popes control the tech for the mobile voting app," Murton said. "The same app that got you elected."

"They also control the tech for the sonic drilling units," Virgil said.

Cora held up her hands. "Yeah, yeah, I get it. And the drilling operation was a joint venture between the state, the Popes, you, and Said."

"Exactly." Virgil said. "And since Murt is my brother, if we start poking around where we don't belong, it's going to look like the state is trying to cover up our actions when a federal informant was killed out at the compound, one that the DEA has—at least for now—complete control over. Tony is on the hook, and he was the one guy who pointed us where we needed to be to save Rosie. I know he's a BIA agent, but he's backed our play every step of the way in multiple cases, some as far back as that time he saved Mac's life at the Salter's."

"Are you sure this is how to play it?"

"There are some conditions."

"How many?" Cora said.

Virgil bit into his lower lip. "Four."

"Let's hear them."

"First, Murt and I will be running everything out of our private investigations office. That gets us off the books, off the record, and gives us room to maneuver as needed, without any official oversight by you or the state."

"It also takes away your backup," Cora said.

"I'm aware," Virgil said. "But I have every faith that if the services of the Major Crimes Unit are required, they'll be there for us."

"What else?" Cora said.

"For this to work, the billing will have to be funneled through Said, Inc."

"Why would you do that?" Mac said. "And funneled through to where?"

"To Nichole and the Pope Foundation," Murton said.

"Why?" Mac said, again.

"Because it's another way to distance both the state and the company you run from what we'll be doing."

"Which is what, exactly?"

Virgil let his eyes slide over to Becky, who caught the slide like a pro shortstop and side-armed it right back to the former governor. "Don't ask questions you don't want the answers to, Mac."

"My goodness, it feels just like old times," Mac said.

Cora got them back on track. She looked at Virgil and said, "What's the third?"

"I'd like to make the notification of who'll be running the MCU in my absence."

"Jonesy, I'm not a micro-manager," Cora said. "You know that. Pick someone, and get it done. What else?"

"When this is all over, no matter how it works out, I'll need you to do something."

"What's that?"

When Virgil told her, Cora gave him a nasty smile, picked up their badges, and stuck them in her purse. "Get to work. I'll think about it." She was looking at Murton when she spoke.

Once everyone was gone except for Murton and Becky, Sandy looked at her husband, and said, "Virgil, why are you guys doing this?"

"I don't see any other choice. Everything we told Mac and Cora is true. We'll either find the rest of Jordan's crew and the drugs, or we won't. But in the meantime, Tony is being used as a pawn by the federal government and I'll do whatever it takes to get him out of this mess."

"And you guys can't do that from within the MCU?" Becky said.

"We could," Murton said. "But Virgil is right. If we do, there are so many entanglements between Patty's company and the state, it will look like a total cover-up. The cultural center could go down, the sonic drilling could be halted, Tony could wind up in prison, and Cora herself could end up getting pushed out of office."

"So, what, exactly are you going to do?" Sandy said.

Murton tipped his head at his sister-in-law. "Isn't it obvious, Small? We're going after the federal government."

Sandy visibly swallowed. "What if you get caught?"

Murton stood, then walked over and kissed the top

of Sandy's head. "Hasn't happened yet." Then he looked at Becky and said, "Let's get Ellie Rae and head home."

Sandy reached up and grabbed Murton's hand. "Leave her be, Murt. She's already asleep. She can spend the night." Then, rather dryly: "Besides, you and Becky might want to have some private time before you have to start planning your conjugal visits."

Virgil and Sandy spent some time alone talking about everything that was happening…not about he and Murton resigning from the Major Crimes Unit, but the other problem Virgil was facing.

"I want you to promise me something."

"Sure," Virgil said. "What is it?"

"Whatever Bell says goes. If he wants you to get a head CT, or an MRI, I need you to agree."

They were still sitting outside, the sky was clear, the temperature mild, and Virgil was staring out across the pond as his wife spoke. He watched as the lights started to blink out one by one over at Murton and Becky's house. He turned, faced his wife, and tried on a smile. "So, you want me to get my head examined?"

"I've been wanting that for years," Sandy said. "But, yes."

"I want to tell you something, and I'd like you to hear me out." Then Virgil lowered his voice as if someone might be listening in on their conversation, even though no one was. "I've had frequent and regular conversations with my father right down there by that cross ever since he died. I know you know that. What I don't know—and neither does anyone else who's aware of it—is how or why that happens."

"I'm not sure I'm making the connection," Sandy said.

"It's simple. What if those conversations had never happened before, and they just started this week? Would you still want me to get an MRI to make sure nothing is wrong with me?"

"Yes, I would."

"Why? You didn't ask me to do that when it first started."

"This is different, Virgil."

"In what way?"

"In that what you have with your dad doesn't happen in a vacuum. It's happened on occasion with Murt…Robert and I have seen him, I'm certain Huma has, and don't forget the night Jonas got to say goodbye to Ed and Pam. You carry that video around on your phone as proof. But what's happening to you now is something else. You're experiencing it on your own, and by yourself. It's different, it scares me, and we are not going to ignore it."

Virgil knew he was beat, and said so. "Okay, I'll take Bell's advice, no matter what. But I'm telling you, he isn't going to find anything. All they really amount to are very vivid memories."

Sandy stood from her chair. "Good. Then there's nothing to worry about, is there?"

Virgil gave her a smile. "There's plenty to worry about, sweetheart. My head just isn't one of them."

When Sandy responded, Virgil couldn't help but laugh. "Keep telling yourself that, Mister." Then she kissed him on the cheek and said, "I'll see you inside. Try not to be too long."

And Virgil thought, *Message received.*

He walked down to the pond and pulled a lawn chair close to his father's cross. After Mason died, Sandy, Murton, and Delroy brought his bloodied shirt and a young willow tree out to Virgil's house. They put the shirt in the hole and planted the tree over it. A tornado later destroyed the tree, so Virgil cut what was left of its trunk into a small cross as a memorial to his father. They'd been having conversations there ever since that day. Virgil didn't understand it, but he no longer found it odd or even mysterious. It was simply a part of his life…one he was grateful for.

But on this night, as he sat by the water's edge, something felt different, though if pressed, Virgil wouldn't be able to explain what it was, save this: He sat next to the cross for nearly an hour, and Mason never showed.

CHAPTER SIXTEEN

THE NEXT DAY, MURTON WALKED ACROSS HIS backyard, went around the edge of the pond, and made his way up Virgil's back deck. A few minutes later, Virgil came out with two cups of coffee, and saw his brother deep in thought. "What are you thinking about?" Virgil said.

Murton took the cup of coffee and said, "I'm thinking that someone died at that compound who shouldn't have, and like it or not, that's partially our fault." Then, "How bad does a good man have to be?"

"It's not a question of good or bad, Murt. It's one of right and wrong. You and Tony did what you had to do as a means to save Rosie. The rest of the squad did as well. I'm not losing any sleep over it."

"Speaking of sleep, how'd you do last night?"

"Not too bad, actually," Virgil said. "I think Bell's magic mango bag did the trick."

Murton ignored his brother's attempt at humor, then said, "You make the call yet?"

"No."

"Why not?"

"I'm wondering if it's the best move."

"It's the only move, Jonesy. Someone has to be in charge of the MCU."

"I was sort of hoping we could skirt the issue. Maybe it won't be for very long."

"Or maybe it'll be permanent. But no matter how long it is, someone has to be in charge over there."

"I'm not disagreeing with you, but Rosie is out for another five to six months at least, so he can't do it. Mayo and Ortiz are still too new, and that only leaves Ross, and he's a little young to be running the show."

"So what are you going to do?"

Virgil took a sip of his coffee, then said, "The same thing I usually do when faced with a difficult decision and there doesn't seem to be a right answer."

"Let me guess," Murton said. "You're going to bend a rule."

Virgil tipped a finger at his brother. "Yup. C'mon, let's roll."

"To the office over the bar?"

Virgil nodded. "Yeah, I want to get Becky started on a few things. But we've got a stop to make on the way."

"Where?" Murton said.

"Where else? The MCU. What good is it to bend a rule if the person you're bending it for doesn't even know it's happening?"

Blackwell took a call from his supervisor, a field agent by the name of Paul Cooper, and the conversation didn't go exactly as Blackwell hoped it might.

"Tell me where we're at," Cooper said. "I'm feeling a little exposed here."

"There's been no change as of yet. I dropped the bomb on the governor and she acted as if the entire matter was of little consequence to her."

"That's because she's insulated about ten different ways. I told you that would be a waste of time."

"It wasn't a waste," Blackwell said. "It was necessary. The state, Said's company, the cultural center, and even the lead detective with the Major Crimes Unit are all tied together."

"And you think I don't know that?" Cooper said. "*I'm* the one who told *you*, once I discovered your little set-up with Jordan and his crew. Did you go back to Jones like I told you to?"

"Of course. I made nice and told him that the DEA would back down if they found the drugs."

"Did he buy your story?" Cooper asked.

"It's not exactly a story, though, is it? It's a no-win situation that you manufactured to get what you want."

"Sell it to yourself however you like. The fact remains that you had a man in place who could have given me exactly what I've been wanting for years, which is control of that field, and as usual, you screwed up again. Stronghill killed our man out at that compound, and Stronghill's wife is now one of the richest women in the state. If I didn't know any better, I'd think you're working against me, not with me."

"Look, Paul, I wasn't there that day in Jones's field when your son died, but he was a rookie who made his own mistakes. His first one was probably taking a job working for that idiot, Ben Holden."

"He had to start somewhere."

"Then it should have been someplace else. Said is gone. So is Roger Salter. They're the ones who were ultimately responsible for what happened to your boy. He died in the line of duty. Why not let it go?"

"I'll let it go when everyone responsible for his death has been dealt with. That means the Stronghills and Jones have to be handled. Now tell me what you're going to do about it."

"I've got a plan for Jones. The less you know the better. As for Stronghill, he's on record for killing five men—one of which was my guy—and I don't see how the state's attorney general can let that go."

"If the drilling doesn't stop, and Stronghill and his wife don't end up behind bars at the very least, you'll be getting a visit when you least expect it, Ethan. Do not disappoint me on this."

"I won't. You have my word. But there's another problem."

"I don't want to hear about other problems."

"Too bad," Blackwell said. "Because this one concerns me, and I need your help. I've got two men sitting downstate with a truckload of product that is going to fund my retirement."

"And this affects me how?" Cooper said.

"We have an agreement, in case you've forgotten. I help you, and you help me. The problem is we can't get across the river. I need you to contact someone with enough juice to make the Kentucky roadblocks go away. The buyer is in place, he has the cash, and he's running out of patience."

"I can't do that and you know it," Cooper said. "And even if I did, how do you think it would look if the DEA tells Kentucky not to bother with trying to catch a truckload of drugs?"

"So, what should I do?"

"Move your product north and offer your buyer a discount if he comes up and gets it."

"That can be done, but why move it north? That just puts it further away."

"The river crossings aren't just being watched by state and county officers…they're being monitored in real time by cameras hooked right into the DEA computer system. Have him cross anywhere he likes coming up, then send him back through Ohio in a different vehicle."

"I'm not sure the buyer will go for that," Blackwell said.

"Then send your guys and hope for the best, because that's all you've got."

"They're not exactly the brightest bulbs in the lantern."

"Why is it I'm not surprised?" Cooper said. "Now get busy, and take care of business. If you do, we both get what we want, and I'll keep my mouth shut with the DEA about your little side business you had going."

"I'll need you to get me a vehicle."

"Believe it or not, I've already anticipated that," Cooper said, his voice full of sarcasm. "I'm at the safe house in Crows Nest, just north of Indy. I assume you know where that is."

"Not off the top of my head, but it's in the database. I'll find it."

"Good. Meet me there and I'll have a van for you to use."

"I'll need a couple of hours," Blackwell said.

"Yes, yes, just don't keep me waiting all day." Then Cooper hung up.

AFTER COOPER ENDED THE CALL, BLACKWELL SAT down, opened his laptop, and pulled up his file on available properties the DEA had confiscated over the years and hadn't yet sold off. He found the one in Crows Nest, then kept searching for another location…this one for a different purpose. But despite his best efforts, none of them were the type of property he needed. He looked for another thirty minutes or so, then decided, why complicate the issue? The more he thought about it, the better his idea sounded. He could move the drugs and take care of Jones, all at the same time. When he finally convinced himself it would work, he picked up the phone and made the call.

"It's me," Blackwell said. "There's been a change of plans."

"What kind of change?" Jake Crow said.

"I want the two of you to move the truck up north. The buyer is going to do the heavy lifting for us."

"Why north?"

"Because you said it yourself. You're peeking out the curtains of a motel room every five minutes. It's too risky. Besides, I don't have any available properties in the southern part of the state."

"When do you want us to make the move?"

"As soon as we hang up."

"Where are we going?" Crow said.

"The last place anyone would think to look."

When he told Crow the location, there was a pause, then Crow said, "You gotta be shittin' me. That seems a little risky."

"That's because you don't know the entire plan. I'll fill you in when you guys arrive. How long will it take to get there?"

"Probably be about three hours. We've got to shower, and grab something to eat before we hit the road."

"That'll work," Blackwell said. "And be careful. You've got our entire futures in the back of that truck."

Murton followed Virgil in his squad car in case they needed to go in different directions later in the day, and after they pulled into the MCU lot, they walked inside a mostly empty building. Their crime scene technicians—Mimi Phillips and Chip Lawless—were sort of wandering around with nothing to do. When they saw Virgil and Murton walk through the door, Mimi—with a voice that sounded like honey straight from the hive—asked if they could take the day.

Virgil looked at her and said, "Mimi, I can't answer that."

"Why not? Nothing is going on right now."

"That's not what I mean. You're asking the wrong person."

Mimi turned and looked at Murton. "Did someone get a promotion?"

"It wasn't me," Murton said. "Give us five minutes, and someone will let you know."

"Who, exactly?" Chip said.

Virgil dropped his chin to his chest for a second, then said, "Guys, please, go restock the crime scene van, or something, will you?"

Chip turned to Mimi and said, "Hear that? We've been reduced to mere stock personnel. I heard Amazon is always hiring. Maybe we should apply. I think the pay is better."

"So are the hours," Mimi said. "I'm going to go polish my resume."

"Guys, please," Virgil said.

Mimi got serious. "What's really going on, Jonesy? Other than us, Sarah is the only one here. Where is everyone?"

"I'll let Sarah fill you in shortly."

Mimi and Chip both gave Virgil a shrug, then walked away.

"You could have just told them yes," Murton said.

Virgil nodded. "I know, but I didn't want to undermine anyone's authority right out of the gate."

Sarah came around the corner, and heard Virgil's statement. "Whose authority?"

Virgil smiled and said, "Yours."

"You *what*?" Sarah said. Her eyes were wide with disbelief.

"It's a tactical move," Murton said. "Jonesy and I need room to maneuver without putting anyone else at risk."

"Okay, that makes sense," Sarah said. "And I'm

going to try to keep my ego out of the equation, even though I know I'm very good at my job, but I do know one thing for certain."

"What's that?" Virgil said.

"I'm the operations manager for the MCU…not an officer of the law."

"The fact that you're the operations manager makes you the perfect choice," Virgil said. "You practically run the place as it is."

"That may be true, Jonesy, but you can't ignore what I just said. You need an actual law enforcement official as the head of the unit. I know that Rosie would be next in line if it wasn't for the fact that he's still recovering."

"That's true," Virgil said, with little enthusiasm… mostly because he knew what was coming next.

Sarah was trying to hide her smile, mainly because she didn't want to overstep. "So if we're going by seniority of available personnel, that leaves Ross."

Virgil tried to counter. "Mayo and Ortiz have more actual experience."

Sarah wasn't backing down. "As police officers, yes. But not that much more, and certainly not enough to justify placing one of them in charge over Ross. Besides, let's say you picked Mayo. How do you think

Ortiz is going to feel about your decision, because you hired both of them at the same time."

Murton looked at his brother and said, "You gotta admit, Jones-man. The woman makes a valid point."

"And I'll tell you something else," Sarah said. "If you pass Ross over, how do you think he's going to feel about it? You're like a father figure to him, Jonesy. If you don't at least give him a shot, you'll be sending the message that you don't value or trust him enough to handle the job. Is that what you want?"

"Of course not."

"Good. Then it's settled."

Virgil gave Sarah a lopsided grin. "Uh, I didn't actually agree."

"No, but you did just put me in charge, and by your own admission you're no longer with the MCU. So that means it's my call. Would you like to inform him, or should I?"

"I'll do it," Virgil said. "And listen, even though Murt and I aren't officially part of the MCU—for now, anyway—I'd still like to keep the intel flowing. We're working the same case, we're just going about it differently. I'll want Becky copied on the daily reports, and she'll do the same for you. Deal?"

Sarah tipped her chin in the air and said, "I'll take it under advisement, Mister Jones." She verbally italicized the word 'mister.' "Now, if there's nothing else, I think it's time someone around here reviewed the discretionary budget. Have a good day, gentlemen."

Murton laughed out loud, looked at his brother and said, "Told ya. I'm out of here. See you at the bar." He gave Sarah a wink, then walked down the hall and out the door.

But Sarah wasn't quite finished. She gave Virgil a hug, then looked him directly in the eye, and said, "Please tell me this is only temporary."

"Believe it or not, that's not up to me," Virgil said. "But try to keep Ross busy enough that he doesn't have time to redecorate my office, huh?"

CHAPTER SEVENTEEN

On his way over to the bar, Virgil decided to call Ross and let him know what was happening. But to his surprise, Rosencrantz answered his partner's phone. "Hey, Jonesy. What's up?"

"Did I misdial?" Virgil said.

"Nope. Ross is in the shower, and when I heard his phone I saw it was you, so I thought I'd answer."

"How are you feeling?"

"Like someone rearranged my internal organs with a garden spade," Rosencrantz said. "But it does feel good to be out of the hospital."

"I'll bet. Listen, are you able to get around okay, and all that?"

"Yeah, I've just got to take it easy for a few months. I'm moving slow, but I am moving. I'm using a cane, for Christ's sake, if you can believe that. Makes me feel like an old man, if you know what I mean."

"I can, and I do." Then with no segue at all, "We've made some changes at the MCU in your absence."

"What kind of changes?"

"That's what I wanted to speak with Ross about. If you don't mind, I'll let him fill you in."

"Or you could just tell me," Rosencrantz said. "Unless one of the changes is that I'm no longer part of the unit."

"Of course you're still part of the unit," Virgil said. "But I need to tell Ross something first, out of respect."

Rosencrantz had plenty of other things on his mind and didn't really care. "No problem. Speaking of respect, I wanted you to know that I'm going to take your advice. As soon as I'm able, I'm going to move into Carla's place. I know I can't go back in time and unwind the clock, but it's all I have left of her. Bottom line, I'm keeping it."

Virgil was pleased. "Ah, that's great, man." Then with the slightest bit of trepidation: "I was a little afraid that after what happened out there with Reynolds, it might push you the other way."

"You know what? It was the exact opposite. I think if it hadn't happened, I'd probably still want to let it go."

"I'm glad to hear it, man. And listen, I'm not a real estate expert, but how will that work, exactly?"

Rosencrantz laughed. "It's simple. I'll rent a truck, then you, Murt, and the rest of the MCU will help me move. I probably shouldn't be doing any heavy lifting for a while."

"Why do I think you're aware of the fact that wasn't what I meant?"

"Because you know and understand my superior intellect, and can recognize it when I'm speaking."

"Well, that's one possibility," Virgil said. "Of many."

"To be honest, I'm not sure how it will work, but once Carla and I knew we were going to spend our lives together, she made me the executor of her will. That means I get to decide what happens to the house. I'm sure I've oversimplified my explanation of the whole thing, but that's what lawyers are for, right? Anyway, the place will end up being mine, one way or another."

"I'm happy for you, Tom. Really. Have Ross give me a call as soon as he's able."

"I would, but as luck would have it, here he comes now. Stop by sometime soon, will you?"

"I sure will. Thanks, Rosie."

"You bet. Hang on."

Virgil heard the phone being handed off, then Ross said, "Hey Boss-man."

Virgil got right to the point, or so he thought. "Are you dressed?"

Ross laughed. "Look, I value our relationship, both personally and professionally, but if trying to picture me naked—"

"Ross?"

"Yeah?"

"Answer the damned question before I change my mind."

"Yeah, I'm dressed. And you sound a little stressed out. What's going on?"

"I wanted to know if you were dressed because I'd like you to step outside."

"Gotcha. Hang on."

Virgil heard Ross tell Rosencrantz that he'd be back in a few minutes. Then into the phone: "Okay, I'm heading out the back door as we speak. What's with the cloak and dagger routine? You said something about changing your mind?"

"I'll tell you in a minute. I asked Rosie if he's able to get around okay, and all that. He told me he was. Do you agree?"

"Yeah, pretty much. He's sort of shuffling everywhere like an old man, which is understandable, but he is moving."

"He told me he's using a cane," Virgil said.

"He is, but not to walk. He's using it to help him in and out of his chair. I think it's the transition between sitting and standing that's the hardest. He's lost a little core muscle mass."

"But he's doing okay?"

"Look, Boss, I'm not a doctor, but if you want my opinion, yeah, he's doing as well as could be expected."

"Good. There's been some changes within the MCU, and Sarah already knows, but out of respect, I wanted you to hear it from me..."

Ross's response was exactly the same as Sarah's. "You *what*?"

"It has to be this way, Ross."

"Why?"

Virgil spent nearly ten minutes explaining everything, then finished with, "And since Rosie is out of commission, from a seniority standpoint, you're next in line. Think you're up for it?"

"Mayo and Ortiz might not like it."

"Ah, they won't care. Besides, I'm hoping it's temporary. Sarah will be in charge of everything else, so all you have to do is keep doing your job, try to be a little more diplomatic if you can when need be, and everything will be fine."

"I'll do whatever you need, Virgil. You know that."

It didn't escape Virgil that Ross had managed to pick up Murton's habit of using his proper name when he wanted to make a point of being heard. "I know you will, kid. I'm proud of you. If I wasn't, we wouldn't be having this conversation."

"I won't let you down. You've got my word. One question, though."

"Let's hear it."

"If you and Murt are running off the books, and the rest of the crew is, uh, coloring inside the lines, how are we going to communicate and coordinate with each other? Because unless I'm missing something already, we're both going to be working the same case, just from different angles."

"You're not missing anything," Virgil said. "Murton and I will be giving all our intel to Becky, who will then pass it on to Sarah. As the operations manager of the MCU, Sarah has agreed to reciprocate in kind. My hope is that together we can figure the whole thing out."

Ross let out a little chuckle. "So the women are in charge now?"

Virgil chuckled right along with him and said, "When were they not? Good luck." Then he hung up.

Ross made a quick call before he went back inside. When Sarah answered her personal phone, she said, "I take it you've talked to Jonesy?"

"I have. If I'm being honest with you, I'm sort of freaked out."

"Ross, you're one of the best at what you do. Why would this freak you out?"

"Because if something goes to shit, I'm the one who'll have to be on the receiving end of Cora's wrath. That woman scares me."

"It's mostly an act. She's a good woman, and you know it."

"I do," Ross said. "It's the mostly part that bothers me."

"Well, I, for one, have all the confidence in the world that you'll do just fine. Besides, you know Jonesy as well as I do. He'll have your back every step of the way."

"Let's hope," Ross said. "Listen, Do me a favor?"

"Sure. What is it?" Sarah said.

"Get in touch with Mayo and Ortiz and tell them to

stay put at the hotel. Wilson and I are going to head that way in just a few minutes."

"I could do that, but then it would be repetitious."

"You already made the call?"

"It seemed like the logical thing to do."

"So you're really running the show?"

"When was I not? Love you, Ross."

After he finished his phone call with Sarah, Ross went inside, and found Rosencrantz stirring a pot of broth. "Your breakfast is almost ready. If I have to eat this crap, you do too."

"I don't eat breakfast," Ross said. "And even if I did, it wouldn't be that." He leaned over and gave the pan a whiff. "What are you making? It smells like a combination of weed killer and BO."

"You bought it for me," Rosencrantz said. "It's a good thing you're my partner, or I might have to arrest you for police brutality."

"Well, I'm not just your partner."

"What are you talking about?" Rosencrantz said.

"I'm hoping your recovery doesn't take as long as expected."

Rosencrantz smiled. "Thanks. Me too. But the look on your face tells me there's more to the story."

"That's because there is. Guess who the new lead detective of the Major Crimes Unit is? Don't bother, I'll tell you. It's me. That means I'm your boss now."

"Ross, I'm about to eat what looks like a bowl of mucus. That means I'm not in the mood for jokes."

"I'm not joking. Jonesy and Murt both quit the MCU."

Rosencrantz dropped his spoon. "They *what*?"

Ross brought Wilson and Rosencrantz up to date on what was happening and why. Once Rosencrantz heard the entire story, he found himself wishing he was able to go right back to work. "Man, it should have been me."

"It would have been you," Ross said. "But since your insides are still knitting themselves back together, I was next in line." Then: "Listen, Wilson and I have to get over to the hotel where Mayo and Ortiz are staying and come up with a plan. We'll check back with you as soon as we're able. Might be a day or two."

Rosencrantz waved them out. "Okay, I get it. Take off already. I'll catch you soon."

They were almost to the door when Rosencrantz called out to his friend. "Hey, Ross?"

Ross stopped, and turned back. "Yeah?"

"Be careful, huh?"

Ross said he would, and then they were gone.

Virgil walked in through the kitchen, said hello to Robert, then Delroy—who was behind the bar—before going upstairs to speak with Murton and Becky. When he walked into the office, Becky smiled and said, "I just realized something this morning."

"What's that?" Virgil said, already suspicious.

"Since you are no longer the lead detective of the MCU, I don't have to take orders from you anymore. You wouldn't believe how well I slept last night."

"Well, not to ruin any sleep you may or may not get tonight, but you still have to take orders from me. Murt and I own the PI firm, and in case you've managed to forget, that's where your paycheck comes from."

"Oh, I haven't forgotten," Becky said, her smile still in place. "But you and your partner—who happens to be my husband—own equal shares. That means I really answer to Murton."

Murton laughed. "News to me."

"It's just an example," Becky said. "We all know who really runs the show around here."

Virgil took a seat on the sofa and said, "Maybe we could discuss the corporate flow chart later. Are you working on access to the DEA's system?"

Becky got serious. "No, I'm not."

Virgil tossed his hands in the air and let them fall back in his lap. "Why the hell not? You told me yesterday that it would take all day, and that once you started you couldn't stop until you were in."

"Murton told me not to."

Virgil turned to his brother. "Murt?"

"Think about it, Jones-man. We no longer have the state backing our play. That means whatever we decide to do, we have to be a little more strategic regarding our thought process."

Virgil let his voice go flat. "Okay, I'll bite. What's the strategy?"

Becky spun her desk chair around in a circle. "I've got the Pope crew working on the DEA's system. That frees me up to do whatever else you guys need. Plus, Nicky and Wu will be able to get it done faster because there are two of them as opposed to one of me."

For once, Virgil didn't push back on someone else's idea. "You know what, Becks? That's a great plan because it does limit our exposure. But I'm a little surprised they went for it."

"You shouldn't be," Murton said. "Financially speaking, they're wrapped up in this as much as anyone."

"That's true enough," Virgil said, as he took out his phone.

"Who are you calling?" Murton said.

"Mayo. I need to ask him something."

Ten seconds later Mayo was on the line. His greeting got right to the point. "I'm sitting here with my partner, along with Wilson, and the new lead detective of the MCU. I don't think I should be talking to you right now."

"Why the hell not?" Virgil said.

"Because I heard you lost your job. I'm not at liberty to discuss any ongoing investigations with private citizens."

"Mayo, save your material for open mic night. I didn't lose my job. Murt and I resigned for political reasons."

"Well, at least now we've got you on record," Mayo said.

"On record with what?"

"Simple. You might be a quitter, but at least you're

not a loser. I think the general consensus had always been the exact opposite." Then he laughed and hung up.

Ten seconds later Becky's phone rang. She answered by saying, "Wheeler and Jones Private Investigations. Oh, yeah, hey, Mayo. What's up? Uh-huh, uh-huh. Oh boy, that's not good. Let me guess, you want me to handle it. Yeah…sure. I'd be happy to. Are they digitized? Ah, that's good. At least they did something right. You can email them to me, or I could send one of my underlings down to pick them up. They're really not doing anything except sitting around waiting on their welfare checks. Makes you wonder sometimes, doesn't it? Yeah, yeah, I hear ya, but slackers gonna slack, if you know what I'm saying. Anyway, send them over, and I'll let you know as soon as I have the results."

Virgil looked at Murton and said, "This was a bad idea."

"I knew that the minute you suggested it."

"How?" Virgil said.

"Simple. Replay the last three words of my previous sentence."

CHAPTER EIGHTEEN

BLACKWELL MADE HIS WAY UP TO CROWS NEST, dumped his car in the Highland Golf and Country Club parking lot, then walked the last six blocks to the safe house where Cooper was waiting. A dark blue Sprinter van was sitting in the driveway. When he knocked on the front door, Cooper answered and said, "What took you so long?"

"I'm trying to keep a low profile. That means I followed the speed limit. Are you going to let me in?"

Cooper pulled the door open all the way, and Blackwell stepped inside. Once the door was closed, Blackwell looked at his supervisor and said, "I take it that van in the drive is my new set of wheels?"

Cooper tossed him the keys. "It is. Where's your car?"

"I dumped it close by. Didn't think you'd want it sitting here."

"Well, at least you're finally thinking for yourself. It might actually be a first."

"Enough with the insults, already. I'm trying to help you, even though I think you should let the whole thing go."

"You wouldn't think that if it had been your son killed out in that field. He was doing his job, and if it hadn't been for Jones, and Said's niece, he'd still be alive."

"It was a long time ago," Blackwell said.

"Yeah, and you know what I've learned?"

"What?"

"Time doesn't heal all wounds," Cooper said. "I won't find peace until the people I want are dead and gone…just like my son."

"There's more than one way to find peace, Coop."

"Yeah, what's that?"

Blackwell looked over Cooper's shoulder and said, "I was just about to ask you the same thing."

"What the hell are you talking about?" Cooper said.

Blackwell kept his eyes focused over Cooper's shoulder, then pointed behind him. "That thing. What the hell is it?"

Cooper turned, and when he did, Blackwell pulled

out his gun and shot him in the back of his head. Once Cooper was down, Blackwell took a quick look out the front window to make sure no one had heard the shot, but there wasn't anyone in sight. He slipped into a pair of gloves, wiped down the door knob, and when he was sure it was clear, he opened the front door, locked it behind him, and drove away in the van.

BLACKWELL DIDN'T GET AWAY FROM THE SAFE HOUSE as clean as he thought he did. The house itself sat at the end of a cul-de-sac, and while no one had been outside when he fired his gun, the next door neighbor—an elderly widow named Helen Carlisle—heard the shot. The problem was, she had bad hips, needed a walker to get around, and moved with a speed that would make a glacier blush. By the time Helen was able to get out of her chair, she heard an engine start. When she finally made it to the window and pulled the curtains back, Blackwell was just turning out of the cul-de-sac. All she managed to get was a glimpse of a dark-colored van as it went around the corner.

But her husband, Dan, bless his eternal heart, had been a career law enforcement officer, and she knew gunfire when she heard it...mainly because in their younger days her husband would take Helen to the gun range. So, almost definitely a gunshot. And wasn't the van she barely saw as it turned the corner the same kind that had been sitting in the neighbor's driveway? When Helen looked over that way, the van was gone.

She thought of calling the police, but what if she was wrong? Her hearing—while not yet bad—certainly wasn't what it used to be. Maybe the whole thing was nothing more than a loud backfire. And Helen, whose doctor had been encouraging her to move around more, decided she'd go over and knock on the neighbor's door before bothering the police. She knew they had much better things to do than listen to an old woman rattle on about loud noises in the middle of the day.

She went to her bedroom and changed out of her robe and slippers, managed to get her housedress on and her shoes tied—no small task, there—then wrapped her hair in a scarf in case it started to rain, even though there wasn't a cloud in the sky. With that done, she made it to the front door, then had to zig-zag her way down the ramp—the one Medicare refused to help pay for, rotten weasels that they were—and finally reached the end of her driveway. She had to rest for a minute or two, then began the trek up the neighbor's drive. Thankfully, the front porch only had one step up, and while it wasn't easy, Helen managed to get her walker on the stoop and wrapped one wheel around the porch's support post. Then she locked the hand brake and sort of pulled herself up and forward, one bad hip at a time.

She rang the bell twice but no one answered. She put her hand on the knob and discovered the door was locked…not that Helen would have let herself in. It just seemed like checking the door was the right thing to do. But when she put her face close to the door's side window, then brought her hands up to block the glare, she saw something that made her knees feel as weak as her hips.

By the time she made it back home, zig-zagged up the ramp and called the police, nearly half an hour had passed since the sound of gunfire. And Blackwell was long gone by then.

After Becky finished her phone call with Mayo, Virgil looked at her and said, "Mind telling us what that was all about?"

"Mayo says that Henderson dropped the ball."

"How so?"

"He put in a request for prints from all the men out at the compound, but also marked the case as closed."

Virgil couldn't believe it. "That means he'd get those prints back about two weeks from never."

"Don't sweat it, Jonesy," Becky said. "Every scrap of information we have indicates that Jordan and his crew were all pretty tight. I'd bet you anything I'll be able to pull every single one of those guys out of the state database in no time."

Virgil wasn't sure what to believe. "No time, as in a few hours, or no time as in a few days?"

"No more than a couple of hours…if they're in there, that is."

"Let's hope they are," Murton said. "One of those guys was Blackwell's CI, and we need that notebook of his if we're going to find the other men and the drugs."

Virgil stood and looked at Becky. "Make sure the lines of communication stay open between here and the MCU. Sarah said it won't be a problem, but I want access to everyone's reports."

"You got it, Jonesy."

Virgil looked at his brother. "C'mon, Murt. Let's take a little ride. I want to check something out."

"What's that?" Murton said.

"One of the questions Turkis asked us yesterday has been bothering me ever since he said it."

"Said what?"

"He asked if we went back to the compound after everything was over, but we never did."

"There wasn't any reason to, Jonesy," Murton said. "Shelby County handled the crime scene after we got Rosie out."

"I know, but Tony told us they used one of those buildings as a bunkhouse. Henderson wasn't the only one who dropped the ball at the finish line. For all we know, that CI's notebook could still be out there."

BLACKWELL BEAT HIS MEN TO THE OLD SALTER compound located deep in the forest of Shelby County by a little more than twenty minutes. Kevin Crow hopped out of the truck, pointed at the Sprinter van Blackwell was leaning against and said, "What's with the wheels?"

"It's a diversion tactic," Blackwell said. "The buyer is coming up here to do the exchange. He's going to take this vehicle back after we transfer the load."

Crow looked at Blackwell and said, "What's with the gloves?"

Blackwell gave him a smile. "What? You think I'm not a team player? I'm going to help you guys with the transfer, and I don't want my prints on any of the boxes. Where's Jake?"

"Sleeping in the cab of the truck. We were both up pretty late last night."

"Well, wake him the hell up, put some gloves on, and let's get started."

Kevin went back to the truck and repositioned it near the back of the Sprinter van to make the loading and unloading easier. Then he, along with his brother and Blackwell, all worked together and made the transfer from the truck to the van. Once they were finished, Jake looked at Blackwell and said, "When is the buyer showing up, and more importantly, when are we getting our cut?"

Blackwell checked his watch and made a show of calculating an arrival time. "Probably in about six hours. Get the rear doors of the truck closed up. You guys are going to have to get rid of it."

"Where?" Kevin said.

"Doesn't matter," Blackwell said. "Wipe it down, park it at the casino…or hell, park it anywhere you want and walk away. We'll never need it again."

"What about when it's time for the split?" Jake said. "Where are we going to do that?"

"Right here," Blackwell said. "This property, at least for now, is under the control of the DEA. It's the safest place to be. Even the cops aren't allowed in without my permission."

The Crow brothers looked at each other and shrugged. "Sounds good to us," Kevin said.

And Blackwell thought, *What a couple of idiots. Who doesn't think to ask how they're getting back here after they move the truck?*

Those were the thoughts going through Blackwell's head as the Crows turned to close up the truck. When they did, Blackwell took out his gun and shot them both twice to put them down. Then he walked over to the men and shot them again, this time in the backs of their heads, just to make sure they were thoroughly dead.

Blackwell didn't bother to collect the shell casings because he'd worn gloves when he loaded his gun. He hopped in the Sprinter van, drove it outside the compound's entrance, then hit the button on the remote and watched in his rearview mirror as the gate slid shut. When he drove away he didn't look back. Almost home-free now.

VIRGIL AND MURTON ARRIVED AT THE COMPOUND NO more than an hour after Blackwell had left. They came in from the same direction Murton and Tony had the night Rosencrantz was rescued, mainly because it was the route they knew best.

When they got close to the wall, Murton gave Virgil a little play-by-play of what happened, and where he waited as Tony went through the woods and took out the perimeter guards. Then, after they made their way around the side and over to the gate, they discovered a large yellow sticker covering the face of the keypad. The sticker said:

THIS PROPERTY UNDER CONTROL OF THE DRUG ENFORCEMENT AGENCY. ENTRY IS STRICTLY FORBIDDEN. VIOLATORS WILL BE PROSECUTED TO THE FULLEST EXTENT OF THE LAW.

Virgil looked at Murton and said, "Looks like Blackwell isn't fooling around."

Murton was underwhelmed. "Blackwell is a paper pusher, Jones-man. He also thinks he's God's gift to the federal government."

"How are we going to get in?"

"The same way Tony and I did," Murton said. "I'll climb over the wall. There's a push button on the other side of the gate that'll open it up. Once I'm in, I'll hit the button and you can walk right through."

"You want me to do it?" Virgil said.

"Nah, I got it. Take me two seconds." Then, just like he'd done before, Murton reached up, gripped the inner edge of the structure, then pulled himself up and over in one swift, graceful movement. As he was crossing the wall, he remembered his thought process on the night they rescued Rosencrantz. He was worried about the fact that there might have been dogs.

As it turned out, there hadn't been, but when Murton landed on the other side of the wall this time, he discovered they had a problem…and it wasn't dogs.

CHAPTER NINETEEN

When Murton saw the two dead men on the ground behind the truck, he pulled his weapon, then ran over to the gate's control box and pushed the button with his elbow. As soon as the gate started to slide open, Murton looked at Virgil and said, "Weapon out. We've got a situation here."

Virgil saw the two dead men as well, and did what his brother asked. "You check the bodies yet?"

"Nope. Let's clear the place first," Murton said. "It feels like we're alone, but I want to check these buildings just in case."

"All right, c'mon," Virgil said. "Bunkhouse first."

They went through the bunkhouse as fast as possible, checking underneath every bed, the standing closets, the showers, and finally the kitchen. "All clear," Murton said.

When they made their way back outside, the last two structures went very quickly. The Quonset hut, which was nothing more than one big building, was completely empty, as was the smaller concrete block structure where Rosencrantz had been held. Once they were sure they were alone, Virgil and Murton secured their weapons, put gloves on, then took a closer look at the truck.

"Kentucky plates," Virgil said.

Murton took out his phone and grabbed a quick picture of the plate. "Probably stolen."

"Let me check the cab," Virgil said.

"DNA, Jones-man." Murton warned.

"Yeah, yeah, I'll be careful."

Virgil walked over to the truck's cab and opened the passenger-side door. Then, keeping his entire body as far from the interior of the truck as possible, he reached in and opened the glovebox. When he saw what was inside, he closed everything back up and went over to where Murton stood.

"Anything?"

"Piece of junk .38," Virgil said. "No registration for the truck. Did you get the VIN?"

"Yeah, along with head shots of the bodies. I'm going to text everything to Becky."

"Hold off on that," Virgil said.

"Why?"

Despite not wanting to get too close to the victims, Virgil carefully stepped over and placed the back of his hand against the neck of one of the bodies. "Looks like two in the back and one to the head for both of them," Virgil said.

"Yep. And whoever it was didn't bother to pick up their brass."

"Bodies are still warm," Virgil said. "This didn't happen that long ago."

"Good to know," Murton said. "How about you answer my question. Why should I wait to send this info to Becky?"

"Let's get out of here," Virgil said. "I'll explain once we're off this property."

Virgil and Murton double-timed it through the woods, then hopped into the Range Rover to make a quick run back up to Indy and over to the bar. On the way, Murton said, "Now are you going to tell me why I couldn't just email or text those photos?"

Virgil explained why, then made a quick call to Becky to let her know what they'd found. Thirty minutes later they arrived at the bar and found Becky hard at work going through the state's database, pulling out the prints that Henderson had sent to IAFIS.

Virgil looked at his brother and said, "Let me see your phone."

Murton unlocked his phone and handed it to Virgil. Then he looked at Becky, and said, "We've got a plate and a VIN number from a truck that was sitting inside the compound when we arrived," Murton said. "Jonesy wouldn't let me send them to you."

Becky turned to Virgil and said, "You know something, Jonesy? Sometimes you impress the hell out of me." Then to Murton: "He didn't want you to send the photos because of the geo tags that get embedded. It's proof you were there."

"I know," Murton said. "I just thought you could wipe the data once we got back."

"And I would have," Becky said. "But now I only have to wipe it from your phone. If you'd have sent the photos, I would have had to get into the carrier's database and clean that as well. This is easier, and takes less time. Jonesy, I'll need your phone as well."

"Why?"

"To wipe the location data from your history."

Virgil gave up his phone, setting it on Becky's desk next to her computer. Becky printed the photos, then told both men they could have their phones back in twenty minutes or so.

"No problem," Murton said. Then to Virgil: "So, who gets the call? Ed Henderson, or Ross? Because we can't just leave those bodies out there. You know as well as I do that those are probably the other two guys from Jordan's crew."

Virgil was staring down at the bar through the two-way mirror that was centered on the office wall. He half expected to see his father down there again, but didn't. It was just Delroy, working the blender and mixing drinks for a few of the customers.

He turned, looked at Murton and said, "I think our call should be to Ross. The MCU gets to pick its own cases, they're already working this one, and who knows how Ed will handle the whole thing? Besides, if we bring Ross up to speed, there won't be any pushback regarding why we were out there. Ed might have some questions that we're not prepared to answer."

"Here's something else," Becky said. "If you don't tell Ross first, he may end up thinking that you don't have any confidence in him."

Virgil tipped a finger at her. "You're right."

Becky's computer chirped at her, and when she checked the screen, she said, "Oh boy."

"What is it?" Virgil said.

"We just got a request from both the Marion County Sheriff's Office and Indianapolis Metro Homicide."

"Same incident?" Virgil said.

"Yeah, they've got one dead up in Crows Nest inside a residence. According to initial reports, the victim is male, late fifties, and suffered a single gunshot wound to the back of the head. Neighbor lady heard the shot and went to investigate."

Virgil scratched at the back of his head. "I don't want to sound crass, but for both departments to be asking for assistance from the MCU seems a little excessive."

"Maybe not," Becky said. "A tentative ID puts the victim as Paul Cooper."

"Who's he?" Murton said.

"A senior field agent with the DEA," Becky said.

Murton glanced at his brother, and tipped his head just so. Virgil caught the tip…and its meaning. He turned to Becky and said, "Get Sarah on the line, right now."

"Just a second," Becky said. She picked up the phone, put it on speaker and called Sarah. Once she had her on the line, Becky said, "Did you get the notification?"

"Just now," Sarah said. "I was about to call Ross."

"Sarah, it's Jonesy. Don't do that."

"Why not? They're all sitting around down in Shelbyville with nothing to do until Becky is finished pulling the prints from the database."

"I know," Virgil said. "But Murton and I have something else for Ross and Wilson. Send Mayo and Ortiz in their place, will you?"

"I can, but Ross isn't going to like it."

"Don't worry, I'll handle Ross. Besides, he's going to be busy enough that he won't care. Guaranteed."

Sarah didn't sound completely convinced, but she went along with it anyway. "Okay, I'll make the call right now, but if you want my advice, you better do the same, otherwise you're going to have a battle on your hands."

"I'll do that, but give me ten minutes before you call. I need to speak with Ross about something else. Becky will fill you in, but once he hears what I'm about to tell him, he'll send Mayo and Ortiz up to Crows Nest anyway."

Virgil used the office landline, got Ross on the phone and explained what he and Murton had discovered. "It was a complete fluke. We went out there to search for that CI's notebook. We thought maybe Henderson's people dropped the ball with their search, but instead of finding the notebook, we stumbled onto a murder scene. I'm guessing it's the other two guys from Jordan's crew. The truck was empty, so if these are the guys we've been looking for, that means someone else has the drugs."

"Did you contaminate the scene?" Ross said.

"Minimal, if at all," Virgil said. "We checked the bodies for signs of life—they were still warm, by the way—but we did not disturb them in any other way. We cleared the compound, checked the truck, then got the hell out."

"Okay," Ross said. "We're on it. The four of us will head over there right now."

"Yeah, uh, listen, Ross…Maybe it should just be you and Wilson."

Ross let a little of his personality out. "Mind telling me why?"

"Because Becky and Sarah just got a request from both Marion County and Metro Homicide for assistance on a murder up in Crows Nest."

"That sounds like overkill, if you'll pardon the expression."

"I thought the same thing," Virgil said. "Except the victim is a senior field agent with the DEA by the name of Paul Cooper."

"All the more reason I should take the point on that murder, Jonesy."

"Ross, Murt and I are walking a tightrope here. We found those bodies at the compound and can't do anything about it. I need our best over there right now to handle all of it and keep our names out of the record. Eventually you'll have to fill Henderson in, but since neither Murt nor I have any official status, you're going to have to deal with it. We need IDs on those bodies, and that compound needs to be searched from top to bottom."

"I take it Mimi and Chip should head over as well?"

"That'd be a good idea, and I'll let you make the call. Have them handle the scene while you and Wilson do the search. Rip out the flooring of that bunkhouse if you think it's necessary, but find us that notebook. It's the key to getting the DEA out of our lives and off our backs."

"Yet the murder victim up in Crows Nest is with the DEA."

"C'mon, Ross. You know as well as I do that if you

go up there, you're going to do exactly nothing that will help us get to where we need to be. Send Mayo and Ortiz, have them gather any intel they can, pipe it through to Sarah, and we'll go from there. If we can, let's plan on meeting up later to go over everything together…the bodies out at the compound, Cooper, Blackwell, all of it."

"Where do you want to do that?"

"Where else? Rosie's place. He isn't doing anything except sitting around. He'd probably like the company. I'll get in touch and let him know what's going on."

"Yeah, yeah, whatever. You know, for a guy who isn't running the show right now, you sure do sound like you're running the show."

"Force of habit," Virgil said. "I'm really only trying to help. Hello? Ross?"

Virgil looked at Murton and Becky. "I think he hung up on me."

Becky made a very unladylike noise, then said, "You think?"

Virgil gave her a dry look, then asked how much longer on the prints.

"Another hour ought to do it," Becky said. "But here's a question for you: If Mayo and Ortiz are working Cooper's murder, and Ross is out at the compound with Wilson, who's going to look into whoever I find?"

"Who else?" Virgil said. "Murt and I will handle it."

"Fine with me," Becky said. "But why don't you guys go downstairs and get some lunch or something. I can work faster if you leave me alone."

"We can do that," Murton said. "I can always eat."

"One more thing, Becks," Virgil said.

"Really? Just one? Or ten things lumped together to make it sound like it's only one?"

Virgil ignored the comment and said, "Once Nicky and Wu get you into the DEA's system, in addition to Blackwell, take a hard look at Cooper. See if those two guys are connected somehow. I find it hard to believe that Blackwell is sniffing around trying to play both sides of the fence, and meanwhile, a DEA agent is murdered."

"Hang on a second, Jonesy," Murton said. Then he turned to Becky. "How long would it take to do a very basic background check on Cooper?"

"How basic?" Becky asked.

"Credit score, family history, and length of service."

"Heck, I can do that right now," Becky said. "Probably take me ten minutes."

"Do it, will you?" Murton said.

"Sure, but if you don't mind me asking…why?

Once we're in the DEA's system we'll have all we need on the guy anyway."

Murton looked at his brother and said, "When was the last time you heard the name Cooper?"

"Hell, Murt, I don't know. That name is almost as common as mine."

"I know, but for some reason it's ringing my bell."

Murton had no sooner gotten the words out of his mouth when Virgil remembered the little traffic jam that delayed him the day before. The car was a Mini Cooper. He was about to blow the whole thing off as a coincidence, but then he remembered how his father was always telling him that everything is connected. Those were the thoughts going through Virgil's head when his phone buzzed at him. He pulled it out of his pocket, checked the screen and saw it was Patty. And when he punched the Speaker button, the sound of Patty's voice pulled him away again.

CHAPTER TWENTY

Patty's words ran together and she blurted everything out in one long breath.

"Virgil I can't get ahold of my Uncle Rick. His cell is off because he's in a meeting or something and when I called the office where the meeting is being held they wouldn't put him on the phone and when I tried to explain what was going on they hung up on me like I was some sort of crazy woman or something and I need you to get down here right now because I don't know what's happening and I sure as hell don't know what to do next. Sheriff Bolden or what-the-hell-ever his name is, along with the rest of his remaining deputies have got me and Mr. Johnson sitting in the dirt in handcuffs, and one of his deputies was shot in the neck by the semi driver right before the arrow got him. If the driver hadn't shot Deputy Cooper, I think the Indian would have left him alone."

BECKY HATED TO DO IT BECAUSE NO MATTER HOW MUCH grief they were always giving each other, she loved Virgil with her whole heart. But he was clearly in his own world, Murton was just standing there with an expression of disbelief on his face, so Becky did the only thing she could think to do. She punched Virgil on the shoulder…hard.

And it brought him back.

"WHERE WERE YOU JUST NOW?" MURTON SAID. He walked Virgil over to the sofa and had him sit down. "You looked catatonic."

"I was on the phone with Patty," Virgil said. "I put it on speaker so you guys could hear."

Murton leaned sideways and got right in his brother's line of sight. "Virgil, you weren't on the phone. You were staring into the palm of your hand. Your phone is still over on Becky's desk."

Virgil looked over and saw his phone right where

Murton said it was. He turned back, visibly swallowed, then looked his brother in the eye and said, "I don't know what's going on, Murt. I keep having these flashbacks, or whatever you want to call them."

"I'd call them 'episodes,'" Becky said. Then: "What? It's an apt description."

Virgil rubbed his shoulder. "I don't think it was necessary to hit me so hard. You really put your hips into that swing."

"Well, somebody had to do something," Becky said. "Besides, I got you back, didn't I?"

"Yeah, and just in time."

"What do you mean?" Murton said.

Virgil held up a finger. "In a second. Becky, pull up the MCU's file from that time Patty was attacked…the one where we were working the Salter case."

Becky went over to her computer and began typing. Thirty seconds later she had the file. "Okay, I've got it right here. What should I be looking for?"

"Do you guys believe in coincidences?" Virgil said.

Murton shrugged. "I've said it before…they do happen."

Virgil nodded. "You're right. They do. But yesterday when I was headed over here to pick up the beef for our cookout, I got delayed by a little traffic jam, and I'm beginning to think it wasn't a coincidence."

"Why's that?" Murton said.

"Because you said the name Cooper was ringing your bell. I think the traffic jam was trying to ring mine as well, but I had too many other things on my mind to recognize it when it happened."

"In what way?" Becky said.

"In that the car causing the traffic jam was a Mini Cooper."

"What does any of that have to do with the Salter case?"

"Look up the name of the Shelby County deputy who was killed when that semi driver tried to attack Patty."

Murton snapped his fingers and pointed at Virgil. "Don't bother. I just remembered. His last name was Cooper."

Virgil nodded. "That's right." Then to Becky: "Find out if Deputy Cooper and the dead DEA agent are related."

"I'm on it," Becky said.

Virgil and Murton sat quietly and watched as Becky went to work. Less than ten minutes later she had the information.

"Got it. Straight from Deputy Cooper's obituary. It

says his love of law enforcement was inspired by his father, Paul Cooper, a career agent with the DEA."

Murton looked at Virgil and said, "What the hell is going on, Jones-man?"

Blackwell had a problem, and it was a big one. So far, he'd managed to eliminate three men, each of whom would have caused him any number of problems down the road. Cooper had to go because he wanted revenge against Jones and Stronghill, but that was never going to happen. Blackwell had simply been using the man as a means to an end. He'd strung Cooper along just enough to make sure that, as his boss, Cooper wouldn't interfere with his plan, which was to get the drugs…drugs that, once sold, would fund his retirement in style.

And the Crow brothers? Those two idiots would have each taken a third of the cash that was rightfully his, and then his retirement wouldn't have been one of luxury somewhere in the tropics. It would have been one of microwaved dinners in front of a flatscreen TV in a single-wide trailer down by the river.

So, with everyone out of his way, there was only one issue left to resolve, and it wasn't exactly a minor one, either. His own man—the one the Indian had killed out at the compound—was the only person who had access to the buyer. Blackwell knew he was located somewhere in Kentucky, but that was all he had. The buyer's name, location, and contact information was in the notebook, and Blackwell had no idea where it was. He'd searched the compound from top to bottom, and he'd also searched the man's house, but he'd come up dry in both places. And all of that meant one thing: He had to keep stringing Jones along in hopes he might get him the information he needed.

Those were the thoughts going through his head as he backed the Sprinter van into the storage unit he'd rented on the south side of Indy. Once the van was secure, he called for an Uber and got a ride back up to Crows Nest to retrieve his car. He needed to make an appearance at the safe house. Cooper had been his supervisor, after all. They'd once even been friends. But as the saying went, friends are friends and business is business.

And Blackwell needed to take care of business. And the only way to do that was to make Virgil Jones his friend…for now.

Since Ross and Wilson didn't have as far to go, they arrived at the compound well before Mayo and Ortiz made it to the murder scene in Crows Nest. Once they arrived, Ross took out his phone and called Virgil. "Got a few questions for you."

Virgil had a mouthful of Robert's Jamaican jerk chicken, so he tucked it into the side of his cheek and said, "Go ahead."

"What are you doing?" Ross said.

"That's one of your questions?"

"No, but it sounds like you're talking with food in your mouth."

"That's because I am," Virgil said. "Murt and I are having lunch at the bar."

"Must be nice. Maybe I should quit my job too."

"Are you independently wealthy *and* own two other businesses?"

"No," Ross said. He dragged the word out into about four syllables.

"Then I'd keep my job, I was you." Virgil swallowed his bite of chicken and said, "Anyway, what's up?"

"Wilson and I just got to the compound. Here's the first question: How the hell are we supposed to get in? There's a warning sign plastered across the keypad for the gate, and even if there wasn't, I don't have the code."

"Hop the wall. Once you're on the other side, there's a push button on a post that opens the gate. What's your other question?"

"It's a two-parter," Ross said. "This is Henderson's county, as you well know. I'm thinking we should inform him that we're here and that our own crime scene people will be working the area this time."

"That's not really a question, but yes…protocol dictates that the locals be informed that the state is taking the point. As lead detective for the MCU, you should know that. Maybe some remedial training is in order."

"Murton is right. Your sense of humor blows."

"I don't think he's ever used that exact term."

"He does when you're not around," Ross said. "Anyway, I'll give Henderson a call after Chip and Mimi arrive. Here's the other part of the question: Do you have Blackwell's contact information?"

"Yeah, I do."

Ross let out a sigh. "Well, if it's not too much trouble, would you be kind enough to send it to me? I need to inform him that the Major Crimes Unit is working a property that is currently under the control of the federal government."

Before Virgil could answer, Becky slid into the booth next to Murton, handed both men a sheet of paper and said, "The Popes are in the DEA's system."

Into the phone, Virgil said, "Ross, hold on for a second, will you?"

"Yep."

Virgil quickly scanned the document Becky had handed him, then said, "Cooper was Blackwell's supervisor?"

"Sure looks like it," Becky said. She gave Murton a peck on the cheek, then slid back out of the booth. "I'll have more for you later, but I thought you guys would want this right away. Plus, I've got the addresses of everyone else who was killed at the compound. Every single one of them was in the state's database. I'm printing them off for you right now."

"How long until you can tell us if Blackwell's CI is in the DEA's files?" Virgil said. "If we can match that guy up with your list, we won't have to run all over the place knocking on doors."

"Later today. Looks like you're going to have to do a little legwork in the meantime."

Virgil didn't like it, but he knew there wasn't anything he could do or say to change it, so he kept his mouth shut.

As Becky was walking away, Murton looked at

Virgil and said, "At least you're learning. And by the way, you've still got Ross waiting on the phone."

Virgil mentally face-palmed himself, brought the phone back up, and said, "Don't worry about Blackwell. He's going to have his hands full for a while, and I doubt you'll see him out at the compound. I'll make the call for you."

Ross told him that was fine, then he was gone.

Virgil looked at his brother and said, "Ross told me that you've been saying my sense of humor blows."

Murton gave Virgil a wink, then quickly bit into his chicken.

After they'd both put their gloves on, Ross climbed over the wall, then found the button on the post…right where Virgil told him it'd be. He gave it a push and the gate opened right up. Wilson walked through, then they both went over and gave the bodies a quick look.

"Think those are the guys who had the drugs?" Wilson said.

"They must be," Ross said. "There isn't much else that makes any sense. We'll know for sure once Chip and Mimi get them printed."

"Will we, though? Because you're presupposing that we'll find the notebook, and if we don't, those are just two mysterious dead guys."

"We'll find it," Ross said. "One way or another. If it's not out here, Jonesy and Murt will track it down."

"When should we call Henderson?"

"Soon, but not just yet. We need Chip and Mimi's help to ID those bodies, and I want to give the place the once-over before we have anyone else out here. Let's get started, huh?"

Virgil got Blackwell on the line, and said, "I'm afraid I've got some bad news."

"If your bad news is that my friend and supervisor has been murdered in one of our own safe houses, then I'm already aware. I'm on scene now. Look, Detective, I know we got off to a bad start on more than one occasion, but I could really use some help. Both the county and Metro Homicide are here and it's like the circus came to town. No one is listening to me, I have no idea who would want to do this to Paul, or why, but if you could get over here, I'd really appreciate it."

"Agent Blackwell—"

"Please, it's Ethan."

Virgil took a deep breath. "Very well. Ethan, for reasons I can't explain right now, neither myself nor my partner can assist with the murder investigation of your supervisor. But I do have two of my best detectives with the MCU en route to the scene as we speak. Their names are Detectives Mayo and Ortiz. They should be arriving shortly. I'll have them get with you as soon as possible."

"What should I do in the meantime?" Blackwell said. "I don't know about murder. What I told you earlier is true. I may work for the federal government, but I'm essentially a real estate agent with a badge."

"I understand," Virgil said. "I think the best thing you can do right now…in the moment, is to go sit somewhere by yourself and think."

"About what?"

"Think about who would want Agent Cooper dead, and why. Think about the cases he was working. This doesn't sound like a robbery, so there must be something more to the story."

"How do you know it wasn't a robbery?"

"Because we have very good people who know how to handle these types of things. Bottom line, if it had been a robbery, Agent Cooper's wallet and ID would have been taken, but the information we have says they were not. Now, go sit and think. My men will be there shortly."

"Thank you, Detective. I can't begin to tell you how much I appreciate your assistance…especially after the way I've treated you."

"Don't worry about it, Ethan. The MCU will get to the bottom of all this. We always do."

CHAPTER TWENTY-ONE

After Virgil finished the call, Murton looked at his brother and said, "How'd he sound?"

"Genuinely upset. But there was something else, as well. I just can't quite put my finger on it."

"Maybe it has something to do with the fact that he isn't being completely upfront with us."

"In what way?" Virgil said.

"In that Blackwell—by his own admission—was running an off-the-books operation. Tony killed his confidential informant the night we rescued Rosencrantz, and Cooper's kid, the deputy, was killed when we were working the Salter case. Now Agent Cooper is dead as well, along with the two guys we found out at the compound…a compound formerly owned by the Salters, who also happen to be dead."

"What was it you said before? Something about coincidences?"

"They do happen," Murton said. "But usually not like this."

"You're saying Blackwell is playing us?"

"I don't know if I'm ready to make that leap just yet," Murton said. "But if those two guys out at the compound turn out to be the ones who had the drugs, then yeah, I'd say Blackwell is still running his own op and leading us around by the nose." He dropped his napkin on the table and said, "Finish your chicken. I'll be right back."

"Where are you going?"

"Upstairs to get the intel from Becky. I'll be right down."

While Virgil was waiting for Murton, he made a quick call to Mayo and Ortiz and told them to keep an eye out for Blackwell once they arrived on scene. "The information we have right now—which isn't much, by the way—is that Cooper was Blackwell's supervisor."

"Did I just hear something in your voice, there?" Ortiz said. They were in Mayo's squad car and Virgil was on speaker with them both.

"Maybe," Virgil said. "I'm still trying to figure the guy out, but Murton and I are both wondering about how coincidental it is that Blackwell—who specifically asked for our help—didn't want us to contact his supervisor, who, as you know, is now dead. Blackwell somehow already knew of Cooper's death, by the way."

"That is a rather odd contemporaneous alignment of relevant aspects as they relate to the case in question," Mayo said.

Virgil lowered his phone for a second, took a deep breath, then brought it back up to his ear. "Mayo?"

"Yes, Jonesy?"

"Did you renew your subscription of *Thesaurus Monthly* again?"

"Here are two things for you, former boss of mine. One, there is no such publication."

"I know," Virgil said. "I was being facetious. What's the other thing?"

"Murton's right. Your sense of humor blows."

Virgil let that go, mainly because he knew if he didn't, the whole thing would never end. "Listen, I want you guys to do something for me, and it might not be easy."

"We didn't sign up for easy," Ortiz said. "What do you need?"

"Blackwell is already at the scene. Mayo, I want

you to pull him aside and talk to him. Just see if you can get a read on the guy."

"I was going to do that anyway," Mayo said.

"I know. But while you're doing that, I want Ortiz to do something else."

"What's that?"

"Do you guys have any of the new trackers with you?"

"Not our first day, Quitter." Mayo said.

"I'll take that as a yes, and stop calling me that. Ortiz, get a tracker on Blackwell's vehicle, and try not to let anyone see you do it. I'm guessing there are about two hundred cops out there right now, so you'll have to be quick…and a little elusive."

Mayo laughed. "Isn't that what happens late at night when you and Sandy hop into—"

"Mayo?"

"Yeah?"

"Goodbye." Virgil hung up before Mayo could give him any more grief, but he heard both men laughing even as he punched the End button on his phone.

He stuck the phone in his pocket, and thought, *Fuckin' cops.*

Virgil didn't know what was keeping Murton, so he walked upstairs and went into the office. As soon as he entered, the conversation between Murton and Becky stopped. "Why do I get the feeling you guys were just talking about me?"

Becky ignored the question and gave Virgil copies of the files Mayo and Ortiz had gotten from Henderson, along with the list of men who were killed the night Rosencrantz was rescued. When Virgil scanned the list, he felt his shoulders slump. "Becky, these guys have addresses that are spread out all over Shelby County."

Becky turned her palms up. "You asked for the info, and now you have it. I didn't pick where they chose to live."

"Yeah, yeah," Virgil said. Then to Murton: "Let's get moving. I want to check these places out as fast as possible. We might not make it back until midnight."

"Do you want to take the Range Rover, or my squad car?"

"Ah, let's take the Rover. It's more comfortable."

Murton held out his hand and said, "Fine with me. I'll take the keys."

Virgil tucked his chin in slightly and gave his brother a frown. "Why?"

Murton laughed through his nose. "You have to ask? I don't want to be sitting in the passenger seat when you happen to have another one of your episodes."

"First of all, I wish everyone would stop calling them 'episodes.' What I told Bell is true. They're simply very vivid memories."

Becky huffed and said, "Yeah, and that creepy clown from *It* just wanted to be everyone's friend." Then she got serious. "Virgil, Murt is right. You shouldn't be driving until you either figure out what's happening in your head, or it stops. If you won't do it for yourself, do it for your family. That includes me, if you're paying attention." Then she stepped forward, gave Virgil a hug, and held on for a long time. When she let go, a single tear ran down her cheek.

Virgil wiped the tear away with the pad of his thumb, then tossed his keys to Murton.

Mayo and Ortiz arrived at the DEA safe house in Crows Nest, signed in with the Marion County deputy who was keeping the log, then asked for the name of the detective who was running the scene.

"It's Detective Teller," the deputy said.

"Rob Teller?" Mayo said. "I didn't know he got bumped to homicide."

The deputy gave both men a polite little chuckle. "Then you guys need to start paying better attention. He not only got bumped to homicide, he's running the department."

"No shit?" Ortiz said.

The deputy turned the corners of his mouth down and said, "That's the scoop on the local poop." He pointed with his chin and said, "He's over by the crime scene van. My guess is he's trying to talk his way inside the house. Based on the tone and volume of his voice, he isn't having much luck."

Mayo and Ortiz made their way over to where Teller was, and when they got there, Mayo stuck his finger in the center of the man's back and said, "Freeze, I heard you robbed a teller."

The Metro Homicide detective turned around, looked at Mayo and said, "Mayonnaise, you are the last person in the world who should make jokes about someone's name." Then to Ortiz: "What's up, Chipotle? You guys must have really done a number over at the Major Crimes Unit. I heard Jones and Wheeler quit."

"Only because we're so good at our jobs that they couldn't take the embarrassment anymore," Ortiz said. "And speaking of jobs, Metro Homicide must really be scraping the bottom of the barrel if you're running the show. I'm hearing rumors that after your promotion, murderers all across the country are thinking of relocating to Indiana."

Teller gave them a thoughtful nod. "They are. In fact, I've put up a Facebook post saying anyone who caps your sorry asses receives a get out of jail free card...no questions asked."

All three men had known each other for years, so they spent a few more minutes throwing insults at each other…all in good fun, then Teller got serious. "What's the deal with Jones and Wheeler?"

Mayo gave Teller a half-shrug. "Can't really talk about it. There's some political manure floating around the state right now, so they had to take some undertime, if you know what I mean."

Teller waved him off. "If it's political, I don't want to know. I've got enough trouble as it is."

"What's the story here?" Ortiz said. "We got the mini brief, but beyond that, we don't know much."

"Then consider yourself up to speed," Teller said. "Crime scene techs are working the interior right now, so the rest of us are locked out until they're done. You heard who the victim is?"

"Yeah," Mayo said. "DEA guy by the name of Paul Cooper?"

"That's the one."

"Got a preliminary?" Ortiz said.

Teller jerked his thumb at the crime scene van. "You'd think as lead detective with IMH, I might get a little more respect out of these guys, but what do I know?"

"I'll bet you're getting more than Brent Williams ever got," Mayo said.

"Oh, man, Williams…I don't even want to hear that guy's name," Teller said. "Anyway, so far all we have on the interior is there was no forced entry, so the victim either knew who it was, or was tricked into letting them into the house. He took one to the back of the head—a 9mm—from about three to four feet, so it was fairly up-close and personal. No print on the casing, and the door is free of prints as well. They're still working the rest of the house, but it wasn't a robbery."

"Yeah, that's the same basic information we got out of the system before we arrived," Mayo said. "Anything on canvass yet?"

"Not much," Teller said. "The woman who called it in says she heard the shot, but didn't really see anything. She did find the victim, though." Teller pointed at a house with a wheelchair ramp. "Lives right next door. You can speak with her if you want, but we didn't get much out of her."

"She the only one you've talked to?" Ortiz said.

Teller made a half-hearted wave down the street. "No one else along the entire cul-de-sac is home. They're probably all at work."

"Okay," Mayo said. "We're going to nose around a little. There's supposed to be another DEA guy here. Blackwell. Have you seen or spoken with him?"

Teller nodded, then pointed to a government vehicle outside the crime scene tape. "He's sitting in his car right over there. He seems pretty shook up about the whole thing. Says he has no idea who would want to kill his boss."

"Good enough," Mayo said. "If you ever do get in the house, copy me on the report, will you? I'll do the same if we get anything."

"Good luck," Teller said. "We could use it on this one."

Mayo and Ortiz took a few minutes to simply observe the various law enforcement officials doing their jobs. Any number of city and county officers were working the exterior of the house, looking for evidence, but apparently they weren't having much luck because nothing had been flagged yet.

Ortiz turned to his partner and said, "You want to start with the neighbor, or Blackwell?"

"Let's do Blackwell first," Mayo said. "I don't want him to leave, or some damned thing. I'll get him away from his car, and once I do, get that tracker in place."

They both walked over toward Blackwell's vehicle, and along the way, Ortiz pulled out his phone and made a call to Becky. He didn't really need to speak with her, but he did need the diversion. "Hey, Becks. Do me a favor?"

"What do you need?"

"Call me back in exactly two minutes."

"Gonna stick the tracker?"

"That's the plan."

"Two minutes, then," Becky said. She knew the drill.

Mayo rapped his knuckles on Blackwell's window, then wiggled his fingers...an indication for Blackwell to step out.

Once he'd exited his vehicle, Blackwell shook hands with both men and said, "Detective Jones indicated you'd be arriving. This whole thing is beyond me.

Paul was…well, Paul was not only my supervisor, but he was my friend. I'm at a complete loss."

"My partner and I would like to ask you a few questions," Ortiz said. "Have you notified—" Just then Ortiz's phone began to ring. He checked the screen, then let an apologetic look form on his face. "Sorry, Agent Blackwell, but I've got to take this call. Why don't you get started with Detective Mayo and I'll join you as soon as I can." Then without waiting for a reply, he turned away, hit the Answer button and said, "Detective Ortiz."

"How's my timing?" Becky said.

"Perfect." Ortiz turned around and saw Mayo pointing at the house where Cooper had been killed, then both men began walking that way. "I'll only need about five seconds to stick this thing, so we're good."

"I hope you remembered to put a fresh battery in," Becky said.

"They take batteries?" Ortiz said. "I thought they were solar-powered."

Becky gave him a fake laugh and said, "Yeah, lots of sunshine underneath a car, Ortiz. Just about as much that's up your butt. Need anything else?"

Ortiz noticed that absolutely no one was paying him any attention, so he said, "Hang on for a second." He pulled the tracker from his pocket, turned it on, then bent down and stuck it to the frame rail on the passenger side of the vehicle. "Okay, we're good…I think."

"What do you mean, you think?"

"These things don't exactly have the best range."

"They do now," Becky said. "After what happened with Rosencrantz, we upgraded. That thing isn't just a tracker; it's a mini transmitter that works off the cell towers. I can track it from anywhere, and so can you guys."

"Cool. It's almost like we're living in the technological age or something. I'll bet someday we'll—"

"Ortiz?"

"Yeah?"

"I'm busy. I asked if there was anything else."

"Nope. That's all for now. Might need something later."

"Hesitate to call," Becky said. Then she hung up.

CHAPTER TWENTY-TWO

MAYO SPENT SOME TIME WITH BLACKWELL, BUT DIDN'T get much useful information regarding the death of Paul Cooper. They were standing just outside the crime scene tape, close to one of the county squad cars. Mayo parked his butt against the front fender of the vehicle, crossed his arms, and decided to do a little fishing.

"Let me ask you this, Agent Blackwell: How did you come to learn of your supervisor's death?"

"I imagine the same way you did," Blackwell said. "Our agency monitors the local and state authorities, along with the cases they're working. If relevant information pops up, the computer spits it out for us to look into."

Mayo gave him a thoughtful nod. "Yeah, we've got sort of the same system, though not nearly as complex as yours, I'm sure. So, I assume when your agency heard what happened to Agent Cooper they sent you to monitor the progress of the case. Do I have that right?"

"Not exactly," Blackwell said. "They simply knew I was close by and asked that I take the point on behalf of the DEA until the appropriate personnel arrive from Chicago. They should be here anytime, I'm sure."

Mayo wasn't taking notes because he wanted their talk to appear informal. He did have his cell phone recording the entire conversation, though.

"Was he a good guy? Cooper?"

"One of the best. We came up through the ranks together, but his star was a little brighter than mine. That's how he ended up being my supervisor."

"It happens," Mayo said. "How did you feel about that?"

"You're asking if I had any ill will toward my boss and friend of nearly twenty-five years?"

"No. I'm simply asking how you felt about the whole thing."

"There were absolutely no hard feelings between us. To be honest, he got lucky on a couple of big cases. He did some undercover work, the agency knew what they had, so they promoted him over me."

"You never had any big busts yourself?" Mayo said.

"Ah, I had a few, but I realized rather quickly—as

did the agency—that I was more of a desk guy. Undercover work scared the hell out of me."

"It can get your heart rate up," Mayo said. "I've been there myself. Listen, just out of curiosity, a moment ago you mentioned that Agent Cooper was your boss and friend for nearly twenty-five years. Did I hear that right?"

"You did."

"So, I take it you're close to putting in your papers?"

"I am. And now that Paul is gone, I just don't think I can keep doing this job. In fact, I've got enough vacation time and sick days in the bank, I might be ready to go sooner rather than later."

Mayo looked over Blackwell's shoulder and said, "It looks like your people are arriving."

Blackwell turned and saw two government vehicles that were identical to his own pull to a stop about halfway between the safe house and the entrance to the cul-de-sac. Four agents in dark blue windbreakers with DEA printed on the back climbed out of the vehicles and began to head their way. Blackwell looked at Mayo and said, "If there's nothing else, I'll need to bring my people up to speed."

"No problem," Mayo said. "I'll keep you in the loop

with whatever we find." Then he turned and went in search of Ortiz.

Murton had just turned out of the bar's back parking lot to drive them down to Shelby County, and Virgil—who wasn't exactly what anyone would call a good passenger—decided to distract himself by entering the list of addresses Becky had given them into the nav unit of the Range Rover.

"What are you doing?" Murton said.

"Mapping out our route. One of the places we need to check is less than a half mile from the compound. Let's start there."

Murton glanced at the screen, then shook his head. "Are you trying to fool me, or yourself? Because if it's me, your plan isn't working."

Virgil tried to look as innocent as possible. "What plan?"

"The plan that takes us straight to where Ross and Wilson are working a crime scene with Chip and Mimi."

"I thought we'd check in. What's the harm?"

Murton looked at the screen again and said, "We've got a lot of territory to cover, Jones-man. How about we do our jobs, and let everyone else do theirs?"

Virgil wasn't ready to give up. "C'mon, Murt. It's close by and it'd be good to get an update from Ross. And, on the off chance someone discovers we were out there and actually found the bodies, we could use our presence there now as cover."

"That might be true, but it's also the lamest excuse I think I've ever heard you use."

"So you're in?"

"I liked it better when you were really in charge, instead of fake in charge. But yeah, I'm in."

Mayo and Ortiz went to speak with Helen Carlisle, who they found sitting on her front porch watching the police work the area. They introduced themselves, then asked if they could speak with her about what happened.

"I'm happy to help in any way I can, Officers, but I've already given my statement to both the county and the city people."

"That'd be detectives, ma'am," Mayo said. "Not officers." He said it with a smile, and Helen took no offense.

"You'll have to forgive an old lady who has forgotten about rank within the department."

"Forgotten?" Ortiz said.

"Why, oh yes, of course. My husband, Dan, was a police officer. He's since passed, but I used to know a thing or two from all the stories he told me over the years. When I heard that gunshot, I knew what it was right away."

Mayo tipped his head slightly. "If you'll forgive me for asking, why did you wait so long before calling the police?"

Helen looked away for a moment, then said, "Because I didn't want to be a bother. I simply thought if I went next door and rang the bell, I could save everyone a lot of grief."

"Yes, ma'am, that may be true," Mayo said. "But you could have ended up a victim yourself."

"I've made things harder for everyone, haven't I?"

"We don't see it that way," Ortiz said. "Besides, what's done is done. We would like to ask a few things that maybe the other detectives didn't get to just yet."

"Like what?"

"Detective Teller indicated that you saw a van in your neighbor's driveway, and that when you looked out the window, you thought it was the same van that drove away after the gunshot. Do I have that correct?"

"You do," Helen said.

"And what color was it?"

"It was dark blue."

"Do you know what make or model it was?"

"No, I'm afraid I didn't pay much attention. I can tell you this, though. It reminded me of one of those Amazon delivery vans that are always prowling around. Back in my day, if you wanted something, you got in the car and drove to the store. Now all you have to do is get on the computer and, poof, it shows up the next day."

"Did the van have any logos on its sides?"

"It did. But it was rather small, and I'm afraid I didn't pay that much attention. It may have been an L or a I. I'm just not sure. I can tell you it wasn't there very long, though."

"And you're certain you didn't see the man who drove away?"

"Of course I'm certain. I might be old, but I'm still sharp as a tack. By the time I was able to make it to the window, the van was all but gone."

"Did you know the victim?"

"No, but I assume he was with the DEA."

"Why do you assume that?" Ortiz said.

"We had some trouble a few years back, and it all started with that house. People coming and going at all hours of the day and night. It didn't take a rocket doctor to know the people living there were selling drugs. The homeowners association got together behind their backs and went to the police. A week later, the DEA showed up, the druggies went to jail, and they haven't been back since. But every once in a while someone in a government car will show up and stay for a night or two. It's clearly a safe house."

Mayo and Ortiz glanced at each other, and when they turned back to Helen, she said, "Told you I was still sharp."

Ortiz took out a card and handed it to Helen. "If you happen to think of anything else, please call either myself or Detective Mayo anytime."

Both men thanked Helen for her time, then stood and excused themselves. As they were making their way back and forth down the ramp, Ortiz said, "Feels like we're in line at an amusement park."

Mayo looked at his partner. "You mean because of the ramp?"

Ortiz nodded. "Yeah, that too."

Virgil and Murton hadn't yet made it out of the

city when Murton suddenly pulled into a parking lot and placed the Rover in Park.

"What are you doing?" Virgil said.

"My job. Something just occurred to me."

Virgil gave his brother a look. "Well, you know what they say…communication is the key to a happy and long-lasting relationship."

"Your philosophical observations are almost as bad as your humor," Murton said. "But in this case, you happen to be correct. We've got nearly a dozen places to check down there, right?"

Virgil went through the paperwork again. "Yep."

"Except we don't. Turkis said as much in Cora's office during our meeting."

Virgil thought back to the meeting, and after a few seconds, said, "He told us that the man had an arrow sticking out of his back and that according to the Shelby County crime scene technicians, the CI never fired his weapon."

"Exactly," Murton said. "The only people we really need to look at are the guys Tony killed. That narrows the list considerably."

Virgil went through the files one by one, and though it took some time, he managed to pull out the names from Becky's list by cross-referencing them against the Shelby County crime scene report…all based on how they were killed, and whether or not their weapon had been fired.

"Got 'em all right here," Virgil said. "We just increased our chances of finding that notebook by a factor of, uh…well…" Virgil was trying to do the math, but couldn't get the figures straight in his head.

Murton took the file from Virgil, looked at the list, then deleted all the waypoints except the ones they needed from the nav unit in the Rover. "Forget about the math, Jonesy. We increased our chances. That's all that matters."

And they were almost right.

CHAPTER TWENTY-THREE

Ross and Wilson searched the bunkhouse inch by inch, and came up with exactly nothing. Out of sheer desperation, they were going to check the entire grounds inside the compound, but they knew they couldn't do it alone, so Ross made a command decision. He took out his phone and called Mayo.

"You guys done up in Crows Nest?"

"Yeah," Mayo said. "Ortiz and I are at the MCU right now writing it up. We're just about finished."

"Anything to report?"

"Other than the fact that the guy who was killed happened to be a DEA agent, no. There was one witness who saw the van and heard the shot, but unless we can get something from a doorbell cam, we don't have much."

"Okay, forget about the paperwork for now and get back down to Shelby County. I need you both at the compound."

"Sure," Mayo said. "What do you have?"

"Nothing. That's why I need you here. I want you guys to help me and Wilson search the grounds. The buildings are empty."

Mayo told him they were on their way.

CHIP AND MIMI HAD BEEN WORKING THE CRIME SCENE at the compound for nearly an hour. Ross walked over and said, "Do you have anything on these guys yet?"

"No IDs on their person or inside the vehicle," Mimi said. "We've printed them, and sent electronic copies up to Becky. She's running them now."

"Anything out of the truck?"

"A gun in the glove compartment, along with a ton of prints—most of which matched the victims here—but there were a few others as well. I haven't sent those yet because I didn't want to delay the IDs on the bodies. But I'll send them if you want me to."

Ross shook his head. "No, that's good thinking, Meems. But do send them as soon as Becky gets back with you on the victims. They probably won't amount to much, but it might give us a lead on who killed these guys."

"I'll do that," Mimi said. "I take it you haven't found the CI's notebook."

"Not yet," Ross said. "I'm actually beginning to wonder if this is even the best place to look. It seems sort of unlikely that an undercover operative would keep it out here where pretty much anyone could stumble across it."

"Stranger things," Mimi said. "But if you want some help looking, I know a couple of people who could probably assist you."

Ross gave her a smile. "I appreciate your work ethic, Meems, but you've got your hands full as it is."

"I wasn't speaking of me and Chip."

"Then who were you talking about?"

"The two private dicks who are walking through the gate as we speak."

Ross thought Mimi might have placed a little more emphasis on the word 'dick' than necessary as a way to embarrass him…or it could have been his imagination. With Mimi, you never really could tell. But when Ross turned around, he saw Virgil and Murton approaching.

Ross walked over and said, "What are you guys doing here?"

"Hello to you, too," Virgil said. "We were in the area and thought we'd stop by to see what you've found."

"Not a damn thing. I've got Mayo and Ortiz on their way down to help. We're going to cover the entire area inside this compound. You're welcome to stay and help."

Virgil glanced at Murton, who simply shrugged. "I'll tell you something, Jonesy, it might not be a bad idea. If we help here, things will go much quicker."

"We've still got four other places to search," Virgil said.

"That's my point," Murton said. "The lead detective of the MCU just asked for our firm's help. Now we have status, and reason to be here. Besides, once we're done, we can split up the other four places between everyone."

"All right," Virgil said. "Let's do it." Then to Ross: "Did Mayo and Ortiz get anything out of the Cooper murder?"

"Nothing of substance. I understand that you asked them to put a tracker on his vehicle."

"Yes, I did. Is it in place?"

"I didn't ask," Ross said. "But you know those guys. If you told them to do something, they did it."

"Yeah, okay, we can ask them when they arrive. Did you inform Sheriff Henderson of what's going on out here?"

"I did," Ross said. "He came, he saw, and he left. Said he didn't want to get mixed up in violating federal law. Told us to call the coroner when Chip and Mimi are done."

"I can sort of understand his position," Murton said. "The MCU takes the point on the murder of these two guys, the feds are telling everyone to stay out, so it makes sense for the county to wash their hands of the whole mess."

"You get the two victims printed?" Virgil said.

Ross nodded. "Yeah, Mimi sent them up to Becky. Still waiting on the results."

Wilson came out of the Quonset hut and walked over to where everyone stood. His hair was covered with cobwebs. Virgil looked at him and said, "What were you doing?"

"I just finished searching the Quonset hut…again. I got a ladder out and was crawling around up in the rafters."

"I take it you didn't find anything?" Ross said.

"I found out I don't like country spiders that are big enough to smile before they try to bite you."

"Okay, let's get started," Virgil said. "Mayo and Ortiz should be here pretty soon. If we don't find anything, we'll move on to the residences."

Murton cleared his throat, then nudged his brother in the ribs with his elbow. Virgil, nobody's idiot, understood. He looked at Ross and said, "What I meant to say is, uh, I wonder what we should do next."

Ross rolled his eyes, dropped some sarcasm into his voice and said, "Okay everybody, let's get started."

The coroner arrived and did his official duties, then, with the help of his assistants, removed the bodies from the compound. Chip went and found Ross in the woods, told him that they were finished, and were going to head back to the MCU to write up their reports.

"That's fine," Ross said. "Unless you want to stay and help us look under more rocks."

Lawless laughed. "No thanks. Waste of time, you ask me. But have fun."

Ross waved him away, but in the back of his mind, he thought, *Chip's right. This is a waste of time.* He called everyone together and said, "We're done here. Let's close it up and search the residences."

Everyone was so relieved, no one bothered to argue the point. They all walked back to the front of the compound. Murton got the files from the Rover, then handed them to Ross. "We've got it narrowed down to four places."

"How'd you manage that?" Mayo said.

"I deduced it," Virgil said. Then he told everyone his thought process.

"Do we have warrants?" Wilson said.

Ortiz shook his head. "Don't need them. Every single one of the residences were attached as part of the crime scene."

"Who did that?" Murton said.

Mayo chuckled. "Believe it or not, Ed Henderson."

"But they never did the searches?"

Ortiz shrugged. "There really wasn't any reason to, until now."

Ross looked at the files Murton had given him, then they split it all up and left.

Nobody found a thing. Four hours later they ended up at Carla's place, pissed off and tired. Rosencrantz was listening to everyone's report, and he was the only happy guy in the house.

"Why do you look so chipper?" Ross said.

"Because I'm surrounded by friends. But it would be nice if everyone would quit with the bitching."

"It's frustrating as hell, Rosie," Virgil said. "All we need is one piece of information out of that CI's notebook and the whole problem goes away. Except we don't even know if the notebook actually exists."

"It exists," Rosencrantz said. "I'm sure of it."

Murton got interested, mainly because he knew if Rosencrantz had a thought, it was worth hearing. "What makes you so sure?"

"Just a second," Rosencrantz said. Then he grabbed his cane and used it to pull himself off of the sofa. A minute later he was back with Carla's file. He handed it to Murton and said, "No disrespect to the new lead detective of the Major Crimes Unit, but I think I've found something."

Murton tipped his head just so and said, "How does that disrespect Ross?"

"It doesn't," Ross said. "But Rosie showed me that file earlier, and I told him his deductions didn't add up and explained why." Then he turned to Rosencrantz and said, "What'd I miss?"

Instead of answering his partner, Rosencrantz

turned to the group and laid out his thinking for them. "Carla was working this thing all by herself. She had the names of people she'd eliminated, and all the others listed by initials. Becky figured every one of them out, except for one. AB."

Virgil looked at Rosencrantz and said, "Tom, you'd have no way of knowing this—"

Rosencrantz waved him off. "I know what you're going to say, Jonesy. Ross told me all about it…the fact that Ben Clark's father was killed by the Aryan Brotherhood the second they found out you were going to go up there and interview him."

"Not one of my better moments," Virgil said. "They killed the guy because I broadcasted the play before we ever made it."

"That may or may not be true, Jonesy," Rosencrantz said. "But I'd bet you any amount of money you'd care to put on the table that the initials AB don't stand for the Aryan Brotherhood."

"What makes you so sure?" Ross said.

"Basic logic, if nothing else," Rosencrantz said. "Carla had this list, she knew Jordan and his crew were up to something, and she even suspected that one of her own people was in on it."

"And she was right," Murton said.

Rosencrantz nodded. "Yes, she was. But you know

who wasn't on her list? Two of the people who were at the center of the whole thing. Fiona Vale, and Ben Clark."

Murton tipped a finger at Rosencrantz. "And if Carla didn't know about Clark—specifically—she wouldn't have known he had a father in prison."

"Exactly," Rosencrantz said.

Virgil rubbed his face with both hands. "Christ, I really did get a guy killed."

"We were following a trail, Jonesy," Murton said. "Any one of us would have made the same call."

"Still doesn't really help me feel any better," Virgil said. Then to Rosencrantz: "If the initials don't stand for the Aryan Brotherhood, what do they stand for?"

Rosencrantz didn't get a chance to answer because just then Virgil's phone buzzed at him. When he saw it was Becky, he looked at Rosencrantz and said, "Hang on, let me get this real quick. It's Becky, and she might have something for us."

Virgil put the phone on speaker so everyone could hear. "What have you got, Becks? I'm hoping it's something out of the DEA database."

"Not what you'd expect."

"Meaning?"

"Poking around in a federal database isn't exactly child's play. It's proving a little more difficult than I thought it would be. I'm moving very carefully because I don't want any of us to end up in jail."

"What have you found so far?" Virgil said.

"The IDs on your dead guys at the compound. I managed to pull them out of the state's database."

"Who are they?" Virgil said.

"They were brothers…Jake and Kevin Crow."

When Murton saw the look on Virgil's face, he said, "What is it, Jones-man?"

Virgil looked at nothing and said, "A murder of crows."

CHAPTER TWENTY-FOUR

No one actually knew what Virgil meant by his statement, so he decided to tell them.

"I know you guys are aware that I've been having some sort of vivid memories, or waking dreams…"

"I think we've all decided to go with the term, 'episodes,'" Murton said. He made air quotes with his fingers when he spoke.

Virgil gave his brother a look and said, "No, we haven't. Anyway, in one way or another, I think they're connected to this case, because that's when they started."

"Can you tell us about them?" Rosencrantz said.

Virgil nodded. "The first one happened the day I hired Jim." Virgil turned, looked at Wilson and said, "I am sorry about the way I snapped at you."

"Let it go," Wilson said. "I have."

Virgil gave him a grin, then said, "Actually it happened twice in a row when Jim was still in my office." Virgil spent the next twenty minutes telling his men about the memories, giving them as much detail as necessary to help everyone understand.

When he finally finished, Murton stood up and began pacing around the living room. "That's why you reacted the way you did when you heard the Crow brothers' names. You said, 'A murder of crows.' That makes sense. But with the exception of the one episode Becky and I witnessed where you thought you were speaking with Patty, I'm having trouble understanding how the others fit into the equation."

"Well, the one with Patty got us to the connection with Cooper," Virgil said.

Rosencrantz, who was one of the best detectives Virgil had ever worked with, said, "Mind if I ask you and Murt a few questions?"

"Not at all," Virgil said.

Murton sat back down. "Same here."

Rosencrantz started with Virgil. He leaned forward in his seat, let his forearms rest on his thighs and said, "Sandy's father died saving you from that fire. What do you remember about it? Not the funeral, but the fire itself."

Virgil looked down in thought. When he spoke, his words were soft and attenuated. "I remember thinking I was going to die. The whole place was filling up with thick, black smoke. It was getting harder and harder to breathe with every passing second. I could hear the sirens coming from the firetrucks and I remember thinking they weren't going to make it in time."

"You told us that you asked Sandy about her father's funeral and she remembered the same thing you did…a murder of crows. Do I have that right?"

"You do," Virgil said.

Rosencrantz turned to Murton and said, "The night you and Jonesy learned of your grandfather's death, what do you remember about the conversation with Mason?"

"I remember that Virgil and I were both worried it was our mom, but as you know, it wasn't."

"What else?"

Murton thought for a few seconds, then jerked his thumb at Virgil. "I remember Jonesy saying something about how the Iraqis kept cutting the phone lines so we couldn't communicate very easily. He also mentioned the oil well fires and how it was always so dark…even during the day."

Then back to Virgil: "The night Murt shattered your

front window…how did you feel about that? Don't think about it, just give me your knee-jerk answer."

"Confused," Virgil said.

"Murt? Same question."

"Scared," Murton said.

Rosencrantz looked at Virgil and said, "When Ed died, Pate almost killed you when you were standing on Murton's front porch. What was the first thing you saw when you looked inside the house?"

"Pate had a shotgun pressed against the side of Murton's head."

"But that's not entirely accurate, Virgil," Murton said. "It might have been your focus, but I saw your eyes. It happened very fast, but you saw Becky on the couch, didn't you?"

"Yeah, I guess I did," Virgil said.

Rosencrantz jumped back in and retook control of the conversation. "And her teeth were knocked out… just like mine were. Every single one of your, uh, waking dreams has the same common theme. They are all dark memories. Would you agree with that?"

"What are you driving at, Rosie?"

"Just this," Rosencrantz said. "Your brain has been working overtime ever since you guys rescued me, and it seems to me that your subconscious has been trying to tell you something."

"Like what?" Virgil said.

"For starters, the guy who was the mastermind of the entire operation out at that compound. It sure as hell wasn't Theo Jordan, even though everyone thought it was. I'll tell you something else, too. I think it's the same guy who killed Agent Cooper, and the Crow brothers."

"What exactly are you getting at?" Virgil said.

"I've been trying to say it all night. Those initials in Carla's file? AB? That's who's been behind everything right from the beginning."

"Well, who the hell is AB?" Mayo said.

"AB stands for Agent Blackwell," Rosencrantz said. "I should've put it together sooner."

Wilson cleared his throat and said, "Would someone please tell me what the hell is going on?"

Rosencrantz ticked the items off his fingers. "All of Jonesy's memories are connected to either death, or darkness. Look at the murder of crows from the funeral. Crows are black. He learned of his grandfather's passing at night. Murt tossed the rock through the window at night. Becky was brutally attacked and got her teeth knocked out by the same guy who killed my former partner, Ed. I was also brutally attacked and got my teeth knocked out by a guy who worked for someone else named Ed."

Rosencrantz turned and looked directly at Virgil. "Your father has been telling you for years that everything is connected, and that time isn't real. I don't really understand the time part, but all these connections add up to one guy, and I'm telling you, it's Blackwell."

"I believe you," Virgil said. "The problem is, we don't have one single molecule of proof."

Murton barked out a laugh. "When has that ever stopped us?"

———

They all talked it back and forth for nearly an hour, but the bottom line was this: Virgil was right. They didn't have any actionable evidence that Blackwell was the one running the crew at the compound, nor did they have proof that he killed Cooper or the Crow brothers.

"Here's something I don't understand," Ross said. He turned to Virgil and Murton. "You guys stated that in the meeting with Turkis, he told you that the CI's notebook had the names of the two other members of the crew, and possibly the location of the drugs. And not only that, Blackwell has made it clear on more than one occasion that if we can recover that notebook,

Mac's problems, along with Tony's and the state's, all go away. Do I have that right?"

"You do," Virgil said. "What part don't you understand?"

"Well, we're operating from a position of limited information, but we are also in agreement that the Crows were the other two guys."

"What's your point?" Murton said.

"I'll tell you what his point is," Rosencrantz said. "The drugs are gone, and the guys who had them are dead, so there's only one person in the entire fucking world who needs that notebook, because I'm guessing there's another piece of information that the CI had… and Blackwell didn't." He glanced at Ross. "Am I right?"

"You are," Ross said with a smile. "Blackwell wants that notebook because it has the record of who the buyer is."

"How do you make that leap?" Wilson said.

"Exactly this way," Ross said. "Blackwell didn't enter the picture until Jonesy called him that day we were up in Elkhart, and he came screaming over from Chicago. I never could quite figure that out. His reaction to some very basic information on a state case made the guy act like his hair was on fire, and there was absolutely no reason for him to do that…unless he was the one running the entire operation from a distance."

Rosencrantz picked up the file and waved it in the air. "Carla worked for the DEA for years. That's why she had Blackwell listed as AB. Agent Blackwell is exactly how she would have thought about him."

"What are you saying, Rosie?" Murton asked.

"Blackwell is playing both sides of the fence. When he found out the MCU was sniffing around up at the Freedom Pharm facility, he knew he had to do something to cover his own ass. That's why he came rushing into town. He had to protect himself with the DEA, and with Jordan and the rest of the crew."

Virgil bit into his bottom lip. "If that's the case, there never was a CI, and that means Blackwell has been lying through his teeth the entire time."

"That's right," Rosencrantz said. "It's also why he didn't want you to speak with his supervisor…or give you the name of his CI."

"Well, to be fair, I never did ask him," Virgil said.

"Why didn't you?" Rosencrantz said.

"Because I thought there was a possibility that the guy was playing us, but I wasn't sure. That's why I've had Becky digging through the DEA's database."

"He has been playing us," Rosencrantz said. "There never was a CI, but there was a partner."

"Theo Jordan?" Virgil said.

Rosencrantz looked at him and said, "Yup."

"You realize what we've just done, don't you?" Murton said. He was speaking to the entire group.

"What's that?" Wilson said.

"We've taken a very specific set of circumstances and twisted them around until they fit a narrative that works for us. I'm not a lawyer, but I'm pretty sure that's what they like to call circumstantial evidence."

Virgil nodded. "I hate to admit it, but Murt's right."

Rosencrantz wasn't having it. "I'm telling you, Blackwell is the guy. He and Jordan were in on it together, and for whatever reason, Jordan kept the buyer's name to himself, probably as insurance to keep Blackwell in line…if it ever came to that."

"I'm not disagreeing with you, Rosie," Virgil said. "In fact, it's the opposite. Because if you're right—and I believe you are—it explains not only Cooper's murder, but the Crow brothers' as well. Blackwell took out the one guy at the DEA who could pin this thing on him if went south, and he took out the last two remaining members of the crew who knew of his involvement."

"So Blackwell has the drugs, but he doesn't know who the buyer is," Murton said. It wasn't a question.

"It's the most likely explanation," Ross said. "But instead of sitting around talking about it, why don't we just go get the damn notebook? If it's where I think it is, then everything we've just talked about goes from circumstantial to factual."

"You're saying it's at the old Salter residence?" Virgil said.

Ross nodded. "If Jordan was Blackwell's partner, which we've all pretty much convinced ourselves he is, it seems like the best place to look."

"I'm not going to argue your point, Ross, but if Blackwell and Jordan were working this thing together, don't you think he would have already searched the place?"

"Only one way to find out," Ross said.

They all piled into their vehicles and headed for the old Salter residence, now owned by Said, Inc. Rosencrantz stayed behind, still too tired and weak from his surgeries to be of any help with the search. Not that it mattered, because when they got to the gate at the main entrance, it was padlocked and had a placard that was identical to the one out at the compound. It was all full of warnings and threats of prosecution against anyone who entered.

"The DEA does like its signage," Murton said. Then he looked at Virgil. "Got that lock rake?"

Virgil grabbed the rake and had the lock open in about ten seconds. With that done, they all drove up to the main house, and as soon as they saw the front door hanging open, everyone knew they were beat.

"Let's clear it," Ross said. "But we're not going to find anything."

They went in with their weapons drawn, and Virgil and Murton took the upper level, while Ross and Wilson took the basement. Mayo and Ortiz covered the main floor. It took them longer than necessary because the house had been completely trashed. Furniture was overturned, seat cushion stuffing was everywhere, the mattresses were shredded, all the cabinet and closet doors hung open, and even the lids of the toilets had been removed and smashed to pieces.

Once they were all back in the main section of the house, Ross looked at no one and said, "He beat us to it."

"Well, we certainly gave him enough time," Murton said.

"I wonder if he got the notebook." Wilson said.

"My gut says no," Virgil said.

"Why do you think that?" Ortiz said.

"Because if he had, the entire place wouldn't be trashed like it is. This has the look of someone who couldn't find what they wanted."

Mayo holstered his Sig and said, "So either we're wrong about everything we talked about at Carla's place, or we're not and Blackwell may or may not have the notebook…and the drugs."

"That about says it," Murton said. He pulled out his phone and brought the tracker app up. "At least we know where he is. Looks like he's at a hotel near the south side of Indy."

"Okay," Virgil said. "This guy—crook or not—is currently a federal agent. Like Murton said, we know where he is, but there isn't anything we can do about it until we have some solid evidence, and it doesn't look like that's going to happen tonight. Why don't we all head home and start fresh in the morning?"

Everyone said that was fine, and Virgil wrapped it up by saying, "Let's meet at the bar in the morning. Breakfast is on me."

"I hope that means you're buying…not cooking," Ross said.

"Yeah, yeah, I'm buying. I'll let Robert handle the cooking. Eight o'clock work for everyone?"

They all said it did, then got in their cars and left. Nothing seemed to be working.

What they didn't know was how close Ross had been to being right when he suggested they search the Salter residence. His thinking was on track…he'd just picked the wrong place to look.

CHAPTER TWENTY-FIVE

On the drive back home, Virgil called Sandy to let her know that he was on his way.

"I take it Murton is still driving?"

"If that's what you want to call it," Virgil said. "But yes. We're about thirty-five minutes away. The boys okay?"

"They're fine, Virg."

"You sound tired."

"I am," Sandy said. "I was almost asleep when you called. I've got an early meeting tomorrow with Mac and Turkis."

"Ah, I'm sorry. Go back to sleep. I'll see you in just a bit."

"I will, but do you have anything for us yet?"

"We're circling in on it. Wake me in the morning and I'll fill you in."

After Virgil ended the call, Murton glanced over and said, "Woke the missus, did you?"

"She'll forgive me," Virgil said.

"She probably won't even remember you called."

They rode in comfortable silence for a while, the way brothers often do, then Virgil looked over at Murton and said, "When I was telling everyone about these waking dreams, or whatever we're calling them—"

"We're calling them episodes," Murton said. "I'm certain I've made that perfectly clear on multiple occasions."

Virgil laughed, despite himself. "Okay, you win. When I was telling everyone about my episodes, I left out the part about what I told Dad on the phone that night he called us with the news about Grandpa Jack."

"And…"

"And even though it's been decades since that awful night, you filled in the blanks to Rosie's question like it happened only yesterday."

"What's your point?"

"When I'm experiencing these memories, they're more than simple recollections of something meaningful or powerful that happened from my past. I'm actually there in the moment. You saw it in the office when I thought I was on the phone with Patty. Becky did too. I didn't just think I was on the phone with her, Murt. In my mind I actually was, even though I know I wasn't. It's like…"

"Like time isn't real?" Murton said.

"Yeah. But the point I'm trying to make is that you remembered what I told Dad on the phone, almost word for word, even though I left that part out of the discussion."

"It's not something easily forgotten," Murton said. "Sometimes I think about that call more than I care to admit. The man was a big part of our lives and we didn't even get to say goodbye. Other than the years that you and I spent apart from each other, it may be one of my biggest regrets."

"Mine too." Virgil let a few more minutes pass, then said, "I know we've talked about this before, but do you have regrets about what I have with Dad, and the fact that you don't?"

Murton shook his head. "No. Not at all."

"You'd tell me if you did?"

"Of course I would. The fact is, I don't have any regrets because I've experienced it as well."

"You're speaking of the day we helped you move out of his old place?" They passed through a brief rain shower, the water sliding sideways across the windows of the Rover. When Virgil looked at Murton's reflection, the rainwater made it look as if he might be crying. When Murton didn't answer, Virgil said, "Hey, Murt?"

"I'll tell you something, Virgil, and I believe it right down to my core. I think everyone gets exactly what they need out of life. Maybe not always what they want, but definitely what they need, be it good or bad. The hell of it is, I didn't always feel that way. It took me most of my life to learn that lesson, and the truth is I didn't learn it until I was saying goodbye to that house and all the memories it held. And that afternoon, when Mason told me he hears me...that he hears every single word, I realized how lucky I am, and how lucky I've always been."

"I think that's a fine way of looking at things, Murt. But why do I feel like it's not the whole story?"

"Probably because it isn't. I've kept something from you, Virg. In fact, I've kept it from everyone, except Becky."

Virgil was surprised by Murton's statement. "That doesn't sound like you."

Murton let his brother's observation go and said, "Remember the night when Small figured out how she got her kidneys?"

"Yeah, that evening definitely fits into the category of memorable events," Virgil said.

"In more ways than you know."

"What do you mean?"

"She set that recording device on the table, hit the Play button, and walked down to the pond. You wanted to go talk to her, but I convinced you to let me do it instead."

"Murt, I never asked you about the conversation the two of you had because I didn't need to. Sandy told me the whole thing later that night after you and Becky went home."

"I don't doubt it. But she didn't tell you what happened after she walked back up to the deck, because she didn't know."

"What are you talking about?"

Murton smiled in a reflective fashion and said, "I sat there and watched her hug you and Becky, and as that was happening, Mason said, 'Well done, Son. Well done, indeed.' I turned and looked at the cross, but I didn't see him. There was a large butterfly sitting there though, and I knew what I was experiencing right then and there was a gift, just like the night I became part of your family all those years ago. Would I have liked to have seen him? Of course. But the truth is, I never have. Chances are I never will, though I do hope that isn't the case. No matter, the fact remains…just like anyone else, I might not always get what I want, but I do get what I need."

Virgil thought, *Thank you, Dad.* He let it all sink in for a few minutes, and Murton did as well. When they made the final turn down the gravel drive that would take them home, Virgil looked at his brother and said, "Ask you something?"

"Always," Murton said.

"Why did you keep that from me?"

"If you've been listening to everything I just said, I think you already know the answer to that."

"You're saying the visits I have with Dad happen because I need them?"

Murton didn't answer until they were all the way down the road and at the end of Virgil's driveway. He pulled over, put the Range Rover in Park, then said, "No. You've got it backwards, Virg. It's not because you need them…I think it's because Mason does."

Virgil told his brother he'd see him in the morning. "Keep the Rover. I'll walk from here."

"Pick you up around seven or so?" Murton said.

Virgil nodded. "That sounds fine." He popped the passenger door, but didn't get out of his seat.

Murton looked over and said, "What is it?"

"Why'd you do it, Murt?"

Murton thought about the question for a long time before he answered, not because he didn't know what Virgil was referring to…but because he did, and he wanted to frame his answer just so. "What I said earlier is true. We get what we need. I was just a kid…one who had been abused my entire life up until that night when I shattered the window at your house. My response to Rosie's question was as accurate as possible. I was scared out of my mind, but I knew I had to do something to get what I needed. As it turned out, I was lucky enough to get what I wanted as well; a family who not only loved me, but accepted me for who I was. To tell you the truth, as scared as I was when I saw Mason coming around the corner of the house that night, I'd all but given up on life." He pointed his finger at Virgil and continued with, "I was a fuckin' kid, and I'd already given up. So, yeah, I was scared, but in a way I was also testing Mason, and maybe even myself. I needed someone I could trust. I needed to do something drastic to figure it all out. When he saw that front window he could have done about fifty different things—not the least of which was take me out to the woodshed—but he did the one thing that charted a course for the rest of my life. He sat down in the dirt with me and made everything okay simply by being the type of man he was. I sometimes think even you don't realize how much I miss him."

Virgil buzzed the passenger side window down, got out of the Rover, and closed the door. Then he leaned over, looked Murton in the eye and said, "You may be right. But don't forget what he told you, Murt. He hears you. He hears every word." Then he tapped the roof of the vehicle, and said, "See you in the morning, huh?"

"You bet," Murton said. Then he dropped the Rover in gear and drove down the road to his own home.

Virgil walked up his drive, then made his way around toward the back of the house. With the exception of the light over the kitchen sink, the entire place was dark; Virgil's family all in bed and asleep for the night. He wanted to sneak in through the back to make as little noise as possible, and he was getting ready to do just that when he heard Murton lock the Rover with the key fob; the vehicle making a polite little beep.

Virgil naturally turned that way at the sound of the beep, and when he did, he saw Murton go inside his house through the back door, his brother's thought process the same as his own. When he looked at the cross next to the pond, he noticed one of the lawn chairs was turned on its side…probably a result of the boys playing together in the backyard.

He walked down to the pond, set the chair upright, and then, because he knew sleep would be hard to come by, he decided to sit outside for a while. He had no expectations of seeing his father, mainly because whenever he wanted to, he usually didn't. He was thinking that very thought, and as he was, Virgil realized that Murton was probably right when he said it was Mason's need for the visits…and not his own.

The thought made him chuckle aloud, and when he did, Mason said, "Care to let your old man in on the joke?"

Virgil turned in his chair and saw his father standing next to the cross. "It's not a joke, really. Murton told me something tonight that I'd never really considered."

"I'm aware," Mason said. "As a point of fact, he's more right than he realizes."

"You've been spying again?"

"I don't spy on anyone, Virg. But what I told Murton that day is true. I hear every word, Son. Every word that matters, that is."

"I don't doubt it. Mind if I ask you something?"

"Of course not," Mason said.

"Were you at the bar when Sandy and I were there?"

"I'm always with you, Son."

"That doesn't exactly answer my question, though, does it?"

"That's probably a matter of perspective."

The conversations Virgil had with his father were usually frustrating, and this one was proving to be no different. "And that's an evasive response. I'm looking for a yes or no on this one, Dad."

"Then, yes. I was at the bar. I'm always there."

"What do you mean you're always there? You're not there now."

"Aren't I?"

Virgil tried not to shake his head, but failed. "No, you're not. You're right here."

"That's true enough. But I'm at the bar as well. I'm also standing next to Jonas and Wyatt…I'm watching Ellie Rae sleep. I'm with Murton as he's looking out his back window this very moment. He's worried sick about you, Virgil. So is Sandy, and so am I."

"Why?"

"Because you're letting something get the better of you, and you have the power to stop it."

"I don't know how."

"I think you do," Mason said.

Virgil tried to change directions and said, "Were you speaking with Sandy?"

"I speak to Sandy all the time, Virg. Murton, Delroy, Huma, Sarah, Becky, Robert, my grandchildren...all of you."

"Maybe I should be more specific. When I walked inside, Sandy was sitting on a bar stool. I saw her talking to you as you were standing behind the bar. I'm asking if that was real, or if it was all in my head."

"Conceptually speaking, reality has about as much substance as time."

Virgil dropped his head for a moment. When he looked back up, he said, "So now reality is in question as well? Because I'm still having trouble with the whole 'time' concept."

"That's understandable," Mason said. "But reality is what you make it, Virg."

"Why aren't you answering me?"

Mason turned and looked over at Murton's house. "I just did. I think the problem is that you don't want to acknowledge what you're hearing."

Virgil didn't quite understand that, but he let it go. "I've come to accept that we have these conversations from time to time. But something else is happening to me, and I can't seem to make it stop. At first I thought it was lack of sleep, but now I'm not so sure. I'd like to know if you can tell me why it's happening."

"What do you think I've been doing?" Mason said.

"Stop answering my questions with questions."

"Fair enough. Murton's dreams were the driving force behind his past difficulties. You know it, and so do I. Once he figured out what the dream was actually about, his problem went away."

"I know that, Dad. But I'm not having the same sort of problem."

"You're right. As it happens, yours is entirely different."

"What do you mean by that?"

"I mean that the problem you're speaking of…your episodes, as Murton calls them, are symptomatic of a larger issue that's dominating your thought process. The answers, just like the memories you've been reliving, are all in your head, Son. All you have to do is address them."

"Dad, I don't understand any of that."

"Then let me put it this way, Virg: You need to get Blackwell out of your life for good, and you need to do it as soon as possible."

"Why?"

"Because if you don't, it will change the lives of every single person you care about. Is that enough reality for you, Son?"

CHAPTER TWENTY-SIX

THE NEXT MORNING, VIRGIL WAS UP EARLY WITH Sandy, and they had a chance to talk about the case before the rest of the house started to come alive. Once dressed, they snuck out onto the back deck and sat with each other as Virgil filled his wife in on what they'd discovered.

"So, from the looks of things, Blackwell has been running a game on everyone. Jordan wasn't his informant…they were partners."

Sandy, who'd once been a detective herself, listened to everything Virgil told her, then sat quietly for a few minutes and let it all sink in. Virgil watched her wheels turning, and he knew what she was going to say next.

Sandy took a sip of her coffee, then said, "I know you're not going to want to hear this, but it sounds like you're doing everything you can to make the crime fit the evidence."

Virgil nodded rapidly. "I know, I know. Murton said as much, and I'll be the first to admit, on the surface it does sort of look that way. But the fact remains, how we've managed to piece it together is the only real way any of it makes sense."

"Explain that for me."

"Carla had Blackwell on her list; he refused to tell me who his supervisor was; the Salter residence has been torn to shreds; and Cooper, along with the Crow brothers are dead. If Blackwell isn't the one pulling the strings on this whole thing, I don't know who else it would be."

"But nobody can find this notebook?" Sandy said.

"Not yet. If it's out there, we'll find it. We've got a tracker on Blackwell, so even if he finds it, which I'm almost hoping he does, we'll have him."

"How did you get to Jordan and Blackwell being partners?"

"I didn't," Virgil said. "It was Ross and Rosencrantz. Like I said, Rosie got us to Blackwell from Carla's list. But Ross made an observation that no one else had really considered."

"What was it?"

"When we were up in Elkhart working the original case…when this whole thing started, Blackwell was the one who received notification at the DEA about Wilson finding Clark's body at the Freedom Pharm facility. Ross said something to the effect of, 'The guy came screaming over from Chicago like his hair was on fire, and there really wasn't any reason for it.' And I'll tell you something, sweetheart: He's right. The facility might have been under the control of the federal government, but it was a straight-up murder scene. Elkhart County and the state both had jurisdictional authority to investigate, but Blackwell didn't want us anywhere near that place, even though there was a body inside the building."

"I hope Ross's observations are correct," Sandy said. "Because if they are, that means Tony—and by extension, Patty—are off the hook. It also means that Mac, the company, and the state are as well."

"Maybe we shouldn't get too far in front of ourselves," Virgil said. "There's still a bit of work to do before we can accuse a federal agent of being a drug runner."

"I think you're missing my point. Up until last night, everyone was operating under the assumption that there was a federal confidential informant who was killed the night Rosie was rescued. And not only that, the evidence demonstrates that it was Tony who killed him, and the man never got a shot off."

"Where are you going with this?"

"It's simple, Virgil. Tony killed five men who never once fired at him. Was one of those men Theo Jordan?"

"It was."

"Then your theory holds up, and everyone should end up being okay because Jordan might have been running the crew, but it sounds like Blackwell was running the entire operation. And if that's the case, Tony didn't kill a federal informant…he killed a good-old-fashioned drug runner."

Virgil smiled at his wife. "Maybe we should hire you back at the MCU."

Sandy checked her watch, then said, "No thanks. I've been shot at enough for two lifetimes. Maybe more." Then with no segue at all: "Have you heard from Bell?"

Virgil shook his head. "Not yet."

Sandy gave her husband a look and said, "And when you do?"

Virgil turned his response into a question. "I'll go over there screaming like my hair is on fire?"

"That's exactly what you'll do. How much longer is it going to take to get Blackwell in a corner?"

"No more than a day or two. Murt and I are meeting

with everyone in about an hour. We'll probably set up a rotation on the guy." Virgil heard a car turn in and pull up the drive. "Sounds like Arlo is here."

Sandy stood and said, "I've got to run in and tell the boys goodbye. If you guys are going to set up on Blackwell, when will we see you again?"

Virgil shrugged and said, "Next time, I guess." Then he stood and kissed his wife goodbye.

Sandy gave him a gentle rib shot and said, "Next time, he says." Then she kissed him again and went inside.

If Sandy had known what next time actually meant, she would have canceled her entire day and never left Virgil's side.

Twenty minutes later, after Sandy had left with her driver, Virgil said his own goodbyes to the boys, then left them in the capable hands of Huma. Murton pulled up to the front of the house, and Virgil hopped in the passenger seat of his own vehicle, a smile on his face.

"What's with the dopey grin?" Murton said.

Virgil got himself buckled up and said, "It comes with having money."

Murton turned out of the drive and on to the gravel road. "In case you've forgotten, I have money."

Virgil chuckled. "Yeah, but you married into your money. I earned mine."

"You earned yours about as much as I did," Murton said. "The only difference is instead of marrying it, you adopted your way in."

"Can't argue that, I guess."

"Anyway, how about you answer my question?"

"I may have already forgotten what it was," Virgil said.

"Or, you could just tell me."

"Sandy left about twenty minutes before you arrived."

"So what?" Murton said.

"Well, she got picked up by her driver…a nice old guy by the name of Arlo Gonzalez."

Murton shook his head. "At the risk of repeating myself, so what?"

"Don't you get it?" Virgil said. "My wife and I both have our own personal drivers. Believe it or not, I think I could get used to the idea. Now, if you don't mind, step on it, Jeeves. I don't want to be late for our breakfast meeting."

Murton laughed. "Call me Jeeves again, and you'll not only be late, you'll be walking."

Virgil got serious. "What were you thinking about last night when you were watching me through your back window?"

"How did you know I was doing that?" Murton said.

"If you already know the answer, why bother to ask the question?"

"Mason?"

"Yeah." Virgil filled his brother in on almost everything Mason had said, then finished with, "So, I'm wondering…did you feel his presence? Because like I said, he told me he can be in more than one place at a time."

Murton was quiet for a spell, and when he spoke, his tone was full of reservation. "I want to say yes, but then the rational part of my brain decides to get in the game and I manage to talk myself out of it."

"Why?" Virgil said.

"I don't know. That feeling happens with a fair amount of regularity, but then I tend to blow it off."

"Maybe you shouldn't."

Murton audibly exhaled through his nose. "Easier said, Jones-man."

They rode the rest of the way to the bar in silence.

When Murton turned in to the back lot, he shut the Range Rover down, then looked at Virgil and said, "It feels like you didn't give me the whole story."

"That's because I didn't."

"Why not?" Murton said.

"For the same damn reason you're driving and I'm not."

"How about you spell it out for me?"

Virgil unbuckled his seatbelt and said, "He told me that there is a larger issue dominating my thought process, and that the answers, just like the memories I've been reliving, are all in my head. When I told him I didn't know what he meant, he brought up Blackwell."

Murton didn't understand, and said so. "Why?"

"I don't know, but he said if I didn't get him out of my life as soon as possible, it would change the lives of every single person I care about."

Murton thought about that for a full minute, then said, "How can that be? We'll have Blackwell wrapped up one way or another in a matter of days."

"I don't know, Murt. He made it sound like we're running out of time, but I can't figure out how everything is connected." Then, "Hey, where are you going?"

Murton pointed out the side window. "Based on the vehicles in the lot, it looks like everyone is waiting on us. That means I'm going inside the bar to have breakfast. So are you. Then we're going to follow our father's advice and take care of Blackwell as soon as we possibly can, because selfishly, I love my life just the way it is. As a point of fact, yours too. So let's go figure this thing the fuck out, huh?"

Robert had breakfast ready for everyone about five minutes after Virgil and Murton arrived. No one talked about the case while they were eating…Robert's scrambled eggs and bacon among the best any of them had ever had.

When they finished eating, Wilson looked at no one and said, "That might be the single best breakfast I've ever had."

"If you think that was good, you should try the Jamaican Cheerios," Virgil said.

Wilson frowned and tipped his head all at the same time. "What?"

Virgil waved him off. "Ah, it doesn't matter. It was something Jonas told me once. You had to be there to appreciate it, I guess. Anyway, we need to figure out how we're going to handle Blackwell, because the way we left it last night, there is no actual proof of his guilt, even though every single person at this table knows he's our guy." Virgil turned slightly in his seat and said, "Ross? You're in charge of the MCU. How do you want to play it?"

"I was thinking about that earlier this morning on the way over here," Ross said. "We've got a tracker on his vehicle, we know where he's staying, and there are six of us sitting right here. I say we split it up into three eight-hour shifts and wait for him to make a move."

That got a groan from everyone…except Virgil, who already knew it would play out that way. "That's an idea, but it isn't exactly what I'd call a plan."

Ross turned his palms up. "It's a place to start. If we're right about Blackwell—and I think we are—then he's got a ton of pills hidden someplace, a buyer he can't find, and a notebook he needs. The guy isn't going to just sit around and hope someone drops it in his lap. He's going to be looking for it…we discovered that much last night when we were at the Salter residence."

"That's true," Mayo said. "But we're working with a lot of assumptions, chief among them is that he didn't already find the notebook." Then he turned, looked at Virgil and said, "No disrespect to our former fearless leader here, but we don't know for certain that he doesn't have it."

Virgil wasn't buying it. "C'mon Mayo. You saw

that place. There's no way he has the notebook. That house wouldn't have been trashed the way it was if he found it."

Mayo wasn't ready to give in. "That's why I said, 'for certain.' But let me ask you this: When was the last time you were looking for something? I'm serious, here. Name anything at all that you needed, but couldn't find."

Virgil gave Mayo a half-shrug and said, "I needed a set of keys to Sandy's car once and couldn't find them."

"But you eventually did?"

"Yeah, what of it?"

"Did you keep looking after you found them?"

"Of course not," Virgil said.

"So it's possible he did find the notebook, no matter how bad that place was torn up. He could have gotten desperate, started ripping the stuffing out of the couch cushions, or whatever, then stumbled onto its location after the fact."

Virgil held up his hands. "Okay, okay, I'll give you that, but who here thinks he has it?"

When no one responded, Murton looked at Mayo and said, "I don't want to burst your investigative bubble, but Jonesy is right. He doesn't have it. If he did, he'd be on the move, and last I checked, he's still at the hotel."

Mayo shook his head, and Murton caught it. "What?"

"Nothing. Nepotism rears its ugly head once again."

Virgil got them back on track. "Mayo and Ortiz, I've read your report, but I have to ask anyway. Are you guys sure you got everything there was to get from Henderson?"

"Positive, Jonesy," Ortiz said. "Unless he's holding something back. Mayo and I talked about that."

"Nope," Virgil said. "Not Ed. He doesn't have it in him."

Mayo leaned forward slightly and said, "I'll tell you something that wasn't in our report, although in hindsight, maybe it should have been."

"What's that?" Murton said.

"Henderson got a little testy with us regarding Reynolds and how that was handled."

"You're saying you wouldn't have been?" Virgil said.

"No," Mayo said. "But I am saying he was ashamed of the fact that one of his own men was involved in the whole thing, and I'm wondering how hard the Shelby County crime scene technicians went through Reynolds's house."

"You're suggesting that Reynolds may have been in possession of the notebook?" Murton said.

"It's not beyond the realm of possibility. We've been operating under the assumption that Jordan had it because he was the leader of the crew. But what if he wasn't the leader?"

"Ah, it was him, Mayo," Virgil said. "He was the one who was moving the money right under Mac's nose. When was the last time you ever worked something where the guy in charge of the money wasn't in charge of the entire operation?"

Mayo shrugged. "I can't say you're wrong, Jonesy, but I can say this: I think there's a definite possibility that Reynolds was a bigger player than any of us have given him credit for."

"In what way?" Ross said.

Mayo tipped a finger at Ross. "In that out of everyone involved in the whole affair, only two guys had a singular commonality."

Murton laughed without humor. "Blackwell and Reynolds were both in law enforcement."

"I think it's worth a look," Ross said. He was speaking directly to Virgil.

"You're the boss, kid," Virgil said.

"I know. That's why I want you to make the call to Henderson. We'll handle the search, but if you could grease the skids for us, it might make it a little more palatable for Ed."

"Need anything else?" Virgil said. There was no mistaking the sarcasm in his voice.

"Yeah, if you and Murt could take the first shift and sit on Blackwell, that'd be great."

Virgil shook his head. "I liked it better when you worked for me."

Ross popped a last bite of bacon in his mouth and said, "Shouldn't have quit, then. Thanks for breakfast, by the way."

CHAPTER TWENTY-SEVEN

AT THE SAME TIME VIRGIL AND MURTON WERE HAVING breakfast at the bar with everyone else, Rosencrantz was following his doctor's orders and getting a little light exercise in. Nothing strenuous, like weight lifting or any of that nonsense, but the doctors did want him moving. Swimming was their first recommendation, but since Rosencrantz didn't have a pool, aquatics was out…unless he wanted to swim in Virgil's pond, which he absolutely did not. So that left him with walking, which he'd been doing every day since making his great escape from the hospital.

Carla's house was located out in the country and sat quite a ways off the road, which meant she had a moderately long driveway. So, every morning Rosencrantz would get up, do his stretches, then eat a bowl of organic oatmeal that tasted like the manufacturer had managed to leave out both the oat and the meal. After that, he'd walk down to the end of the drive, check the mail, then walk back up to the house.

He'd just reached the road and had gathered the contents from the mailbox when he heard a car approaching. When he turned around, he saw his friend, Ed Henderson, pulling up in his squad car.

Henderson buzzed his window down and said, "Hey, dude. How are you feeling?"

Rosencrantz leaned down—carefully—and said, "Like the doctors might have been blindfolded when they put me back together. I don't think you're supposed to be aware of your liver…only that you have one. Plus, they took my spleen, and I shit you not, I can feel the empty spot where it used to be. Nothing seems like it's in the right place."

Henderson laughed. "Ah, don't be too hard on the docs. I think they did a great job."

"How would you know?" Rosencrantz said.

"Well, they managed to surgically remove your head from your ass, if nothing else."

"I have never had my head up my ass."

Henderson laughed even harder. "Says the guy who once managed to slice open his own nut sack with a metal spatula." Then: "Seriously…are you doing okay, man?"

"Yeah, just trying to get my steps in. They want me to keep moving."

Henderson pointed at the passenger seat. "I've got a bag of sausage McMuffins. Want to watch me eat them?"

Rosencrantz had to swallow to keep from drooling. "Yeah, might as well. Drive on up. I'll be right there."

"Hop in. I'll give you a lift."

"Can't. The up and down is the hardest part. Gotta hoof it."

"You know, with teeth like yours, I don't think you should use the word hoof…"

Once they were finally inside, Henderson looked at Rosencrantz and said, "Man, I've seen turtles cross the road faster than that."

"Yeah, yeah. Give me one of those sandwiches, will you?"

"Nope," Henderson said with a mouth full of McMuffin. "You're not allowed to have this kind of crap. The interweb says it'll kill you."

"That kind of crap is what I've been living on most

of my life. I'm currently experiencing the devastating effects of CWS."

"What the hell is that?"

"Calorie Withdrawal Syndrome," Rosencrantz said. "It's a real phenomenon. Look it up."

"Here's two things," Henderson said. "First, I don't believe you, and second, I brought you something even better." He reached into the bag and handed Rosencrantz a bran muffin.

Rosencrantz gave it a sniff and said, "It smells like squirrel turds. What's in it?"

"Hell if I know. Probably sticks and twigs. I asked for something healthy, and that's what they gave me."

"Thanks, but I think I just lost my appetite."

"How soon before you can transition to real people food?"

"Don't say transition. Some people find it offensive."

Both men spent a few more minutes bullshitting with each other the way cops do, then Henderson got serious. "Mind if I ask you something?"

"Nope. What is it?"

"Jonesy sent a couple of his guys down here to go through my paper on Jordan's crew."

"I'm aware," Rosencrantz said. "Mayo and Ortiz. What of it?"

"How well do you know Mayo?"

"Well enough. He's a solid cop. Why do you ask?"

Henderson bunched up his paper bag and pushed it aside. "Ah, I don't know. The guy sort of rubbed me the wrong way. I pushed back a little, and now it feels like there might be some tension."

"Let me guess," Rosencrantz said. "You said something about how Reynolds went out. Am I right?"

"Yeah, I did. And to tell you the truth, bad cop or not, I'm still a little hot about it."

"I can see that," Rosencrantz said…because he understood. "How would you have done it?"

"Not the way it happened, that's for sure. I probably would have called him into my office and—"

Rosencrantz held up his hand. "Let me stop you right there, Ed. I consider you a good friend, but even so, there's not much I can say about the matter other than this: Reynolds wasn't ever going to make it to your office. That's a known fact."

"And how do you know that?"

"Because the guy tried to kill me. Except he didn't get the job done, and once I woke up and told Jonesy who it was, Reynolds's destiny was practically preordained."

"So the state is sanctioning hits, now?"

"You know better than that," Rosencrantz said.

"Look, here are the facts: Reynolds did what he did, he knew he was going to get caught, and his bags were literally packed when Mok and his crew showed up. The guy came out shooting, and that means he made his own choice. Let me ask you something…why are you so bothered by all of this?"

"Because the county council has me under review for dereliction of duty."

"The state will back your play, Ed. You don't have anything to worry about."

"I think maybe I do, because let's face it…over a dozen people were killed out at that compound, and one of the instigators of the whole mess happened to be working right under my nose. The council is acting like all I do is sit around all day with my hat tipped low and my ankles crossed on top of my desk."

"That's because they're bureaucrats and politicians who don't know dick about police work. Let me get with Jonesy—who I promise you will get with the right people—and the whole thing will go away."

"He has that kind of pull?"

"And then some," Rosencrantz said. "His wife used to be the governor, in case you've forgotten."

Just then Henderson's phone rang. When he pulled it out of his pocket and checked the screen, he glanced at Rosencrantz. "I hope you're right." He hit the

Answer button and said, "Hey, Jonesy. I'm sitting at Rosie's kitchen table. We were just talking about you…"

Virgil heard Henderson's greeting and said, "Well, I hope it was something good."

"In a manner of speaking," Henderson said. "Anyway, what's up?"

"I need a favor. It's not that big of a deal, but it might be a little sensitive."

Henderson, who knew he didn't have any cards to play in the moment, said, "Sure, let's hear it."

"I'd like to have a few of my guys come down and go through Reynolds's place one more time, and I was hoping you wouldn't have any objections."

"I don't, but I have to tell you, our crime scene people gave it more than a casual look."

"I'm sure they did a fine job, Ed. But we've got our own people to answer to as well, and this thing isn't over yet. So…any objections?"

"Can you hang on for just a second?"

"Sure," Virgil said.

Henderson pushed the Mute button on his phone, looked at Rosencrantz and said, "He wants to go through Reynolds's house. Should I make the ask myself?"

"I don't see a downside," Rosencrantz said.

Henderson took the phone off of mute, then said, "Sorry about that. Yeah, send your guys. Let me know when they're coming and I'll meet them there myself."

"Thanks, Ed. They'll be on their way shortly."

"I'll be waiting," Henderson said. "And listen, as long as I've got you on the phone, I need a little favor myself…"

Virgil finished the call with Henderson, looked at Ross and said, "You're all set. I want you guys to go through that place with a fine-toothed comb. If Blackwell makes a move, Murt and I will let you know."

After everyone had left, Murton looked at Virgil and said, "What's going on with Henderson?"

"Nothing we can't handle," Virgil said, as he punched in a number on his phone. "He has a little problem, and I'm hoping to help."

"Who are you calling?"

"A former governor who will make it go away."

"Small?"

"Nope. Someone better."

Murton laughed and said, "I'll be sure and tell her you said so."

Virgil ignored his brother, mainly because Mac had just answered his phone.

"Good morning, Jonesy. I didn't think you usually started this early."

"I try not to, but sometimes duty calls. Sandy told me you guys had a meeting today with Turkis. I hope I'm not interrupting."

"If you were, I wouldn't have answered," Mac said. "As a point of fact, we just finished. Sandy tells us that you're making significant progress regarding everyone's mutual problem."

"We are, and if she's filled you in, you're up to speed. I'm actually calling about something else."

"Let's hear it then, because I've got another meeting in about ten minutes."

"Can you tell me off the top of your head what the royalty percent is for Shelby County regarding the sonic drilling operation?"

Mac snickered into the phone. "You know, for someone who can afford to serve up Wagyu beef like it's buffalo wings down at the local pub, I would think you'd pay better attention to the numbers."

Virgil rolled his eyes. "Says the guy who was—and the key word there is *was*— about to lose an entire company because his own banker had been using said company to launder drug money. Besides, I let my underlings watch the money for me."

"I'm not married, as you well know," Mac said. "But I am heavily involved with a wonderful woman who happens to have a little money herself. Want to know what she's taught me?"

Virgil decided to bite. "Okay, let's hear it."

"I've learned that referring to your significant other as an underling will not get you very far."

Virgil laughed. "I wasn't referring to Sandy, Mac. I was speaking of you."

"Well, it won't get you very far with me, either."

"Are we done playing now?" Virgil said. He was becoming mildly impatient.

"Boy, you private dicks are wound a little tight." Then before Virgil could respond, Mac gave him the number he was looking for.

"Okay," Virgil said. "That's what I thought. As I recall, the contract is open on our end. Do I have that right?"

"If you're asking if we have the power to renegotiate if and when we choose, then yes. May I ask why you're suddenly so interested in all this? Did you misplace a royalty check of your own?"

"You've been hanging out with Murton too much,

and no, I didn't." Then Virgil outlined the problem Henderson was facing, and asked if Mac would make a call on his behalf.

"Sheriff Henderson is one of the good ones, isn't he?" Mac said.

Virgil knew Mac was referring to Henderson's loyalty, and not necessarily his administrative skills. "Yes, he is. He's backed our play any number of times."

"Then no, I won't make the call."

Mac's answer surprised Virgil. "Well, why the hell not?"

"I can see why you only made it as far as First Gentleman of the state. Clearly you don't understand the nuances within the political arena."

"I don't get it."

"I'm delightfully not surprised," Mac said. "There's a better way to handle these types of things, Jonesy. Consider it done."

"What, exactly are you going to do?"

Mac laid it out for Virgil, then said, "Tell Ed he'll be fine. It might not hurt to casually mention that he owes us one."

"Thank you, I will. To tell you the truth, I wouldn't mind witnessing the whole thing."

"Virgil, please, stay away. I've heard the stories about your negotiating skills…"

Murton finished his coffee, then said, "What was all that?"

Virgil narrowed his eyes. "The difference between married money and adopted money. C'mon, let's go sit on Blackwell."

Virgil sent a quick, one-word text to Rosencrantz, then he and Murton headed outside.

Rosencrantz's phone dinged at him, and when he saw the message from Virgil, he smiled.

"What is it?" Henderson said.

Rosencrantz slid his phone across the kitchen table so his friend could read the message. Henderson read the text, which simply said, 'Done.'

"Does that mean what I think it means?"

"Let me give you a known fact about Jonesy, Ed. If he tells you he's going to do something, he does it. I'm not sure how or when it will all play out, but I'd consider the matter handled."

Henderson smiled, then took out his own phone and made a quick call. "Betty, it's me. Get every reserve deputy we have on the roster out to the Reynolds residence. I want them there within the next twenty minutes. No. Not this time, Betty. Just do it." Then he ended the call. He shoved the phone into his pocket and said, "Christ, that woman really knows how to grind my gears sometimes."

"What are you up to?" Rosencrantz said.

"Repaying a favor. I've got at least ten guys who can help the MCU with their search. We'll have it done in no time at all." Henderson stood, clapped Rosencrantz gently on the back and said, "Okay, gotta roll. I'll check back with you when I can."

"Bring me a cheeseburger next time, will you? No joke, man. I don't care what the doctors say. I need some real food."

Henderson laughed. "If Jonesy comes through for me the way you said he's going to, I'll bring you the whole fuckin' cow."

CHAPTER TWENTY-EIGHT

Virgil and Murton found where Blackwell was staying, the tracker leading them straight to his vehicle in the hotel's lot. Murton found a place to park the Rover that would give them a good view of both the main lobby exit and Blackwell's car. Then they settled in to wait.

Murton looked over at his brother and said, "I'll tell you something, Jonesy…Blackwell is our guy. If he wasn't, there'd be no reason for him to be hanging out down here when his office is up in Chicago."

"You think he's sitting on the drugs and simply waiting for us to find the notebook for him?"

"Why else would he be here? He said it himself; he's basically a property manager with a badge."

"And a gun," Virgil said, as he watched the hotel

lobby door. "I guess I can't really argue the point, Murt, but it's no different from anything else we have on the guy. It's another piece of circumstantial evidence that doesn't mean anything unless we can find a way to prove it. For all we know, he's taking vacation time."

"At a Super 8 on the south side of Indy?"

Virgil didn't get a chance to respond because Murton's phone began to ring. He pulled it from his pocket, checked the screen, then answered by saying, "Hello, love of my life. What's shakin'?" He put the phone on speaker so Virgil could hear the conversation.

"I love the way you greet me," Becky said. Then she got right to the point. "I've got good news, bad news, and something that ended up being sort of interesting. Which do you want first?"

Murton, ever the optimist, said, "Let's have the good."

"The safe house up in Crows Nest?"

"What about it?" Virgil said.

"Oh, hey, Jonesy. Didn't know we were on speaker. Anyway, the place where Cooper was killed…it sat right at the very end of the cul-de-sac."

"How is that good news?" Virgil said. He was already losing interest.

"Well, if you'd let a girl finish, I'll happily explain why it's so good."

"Sorry."

"That apology sounded awfully lame, but I accept," Becky said. "The houses on either side of the one where Cooper was killed both sit at an angle in relation to where the van was parked. Sarah just got a report from Teller, the new lead detective for Metro Homicide. The report says that one of the houses had a Ring doorbell, and the angle is good enough to have captured the plate on the van."

"Man, that is good news, Becks," Virgil said. "Tell Sarah to get a BOLO out on that right away."

When Becky didn't respond, Murton said, "This is where the bad news comes into play, isn't it?"

"I'm afraid so," Becky said. "The homeowner wasn't a subscriber to the video capture portion of the system. He used it only for delivery notifications."

"So we don't have any video?"

"Not yet," Becky said. "I may have overstated the bad news part of the equation. We'll have the video by noon at the latest."

"How are you going to manage that?" Virgil said.

"Simple," Becky said. "I'm going to sneak into the doorbell company's system and grab the video. I'm halfway in as we speak. Nicky and Wu are helping."

"How can you grab something that doesn't exist?" Murton said.

"I didn't say it didn't exist. I said the guy doesn't subscribe for that portion of the service. The doorbell company captures the video whether someone subscribes or not. The only difference is, if the homeowner wants to have access to any of their recordings, they have to pay for it. I don't think very many people know that. Anyway, the video exists for every Ring doorbell out there…and that obviously includes the one we need."

"Good," Virgil said. "Get it done, then once you have it, tell Sarah to get that plate out statewide."

"Might want to have her get the paper started on a subpoena for the doorbell company as well," Murton said. "No sense in being over-exposed."

"I'm on it," Becky said.

"What's the news that's sort of interesting?" Virgil said.

"I'll tell you in a second. But first, know this: We've backed out of the DEA's system."

"Why?" Virgil asked.

"Because there was nothing of value we could find to help us. It's like Murton just said…there's no sense in exposing ourselves to that level of scrutiny, especially if there's nothing to gain."

"Okay, fair enough," Virgil said. "So, the interesting news?"

"Something weird is going on in Shelby County."

Virgil laughed without humor. "As many times as we work that area, I'm not surprised. What is it now, and does it have anything to do with what we're up against?"

"I think it does," Becky said. "One of the Shelby County council members—the vice president, no less—is involved in a bit of a flame war on Twitter, or *X*, or whatever they're calling it these days."

"I can't believe I'm about to ask this," Virgil said. "In a flame war with whom?"

Becky let out a little chuckle. "Betty, of all people, which really isn't all that surprising if you've ever met the woman, which I know you have. By the way, if they're now calling the platform *X*, are they still calling the posts tweets?"

Virgil shook his head slightly, even though Becky couldn't see him. "Becky, I don't pay any attention to that social media bullshit. What does any of this have to do with our case?"

"I'm not exactly sure," Becky said. "But I do know they're accusing Ed Henderson of dereliction of duty over what happened with that Reynolds nitwit."

"Yeah, we know all about it," Virgil said. "Didn't know about the war, but I already talked to both Ed and

Mac about the situation. The whole thing is being handled."

"Okay, just thought you should know."

Murton, who could read the tone of his wife's voice said, "It sounds like there might be more to the story."

"In a manner of speaking," Becky said. "I did a little digging, and get this: The vice president of the council—the one who is going back and forth with Betty—is a woman named Stacey Louder."

"So what?" Virgil said.

"I'll give you so what, mister. Care to guess who her husband is?"

"Or you just tell us," Virgil said.

"Boy, somebody sure knows how to take the fun out of everything," Becky said. "Okay, our flame-throwing Stacey clearly wants Ed out of office, and she's doing and saying just about everything she can to make it happen. Betty, on the other hand, is defending her boss like they're the last two standing at the Alamo."

"And this affects us how, exactly?" Virgil said.

"Exactly this way: Stacey married a guy by the name of Mathew Louder, owner and operator of Louder Truck Rentals, right here in Indy. I'm wondering if that's where Cooper got the van that was seen driving away from the safe house in Crows Nest."

"That might be a bit of a stretch, Becks," Virgil

said. "Don't get me wrong, it's a good thought, except it would also be a hell of a coincidence, don't you think?"

"Since you guys are the actual detectives, I'll let you decide. But you might want to keep a couple of things in mind as you do."

"Like what?" Virgil said.

"In their report, Mayo and Ortiz stated their witness told them that the van had either an *L* or an *I* as their logo."

"Okay, that might be something," Murton said. "What else?"

"You mean other than the fact that I'm rather good at what I do? Because I—"

Virgil dropped his chin. "Becky?"

"Yes, Virgie?"

Virgil could practically hear her batting her eyelashes over the phone. "Could you please just tell us?"

"That's what I'm trying to do, but you keep interrupting me. What I was going to say was this: I kept digging until I found something solid on Stacy Louder. As it happens, she's related to your crooked DEA agent."

Virgil couldn't believe it, and said so. "You're kidding."

"Nope. It turns out her maiden name was Blackwell. I looked at their family tree, guys. Stacey Louder and Ethan Blackwell are brother and sister."

When Ross, Wilson, Mayo, and Ortiz arrived at Reynolds's house, they found the sheriff and ten of his men waiting outside. "Didn't think you'd want us to start without you," Henderson said.

"Appreciate it," Ross said. "Tell you the truth, I didn't think we'd have so much help. Not that I'm complaining. You brief your men yet?"

"Just the basics," Henderson said. "It's your show."

Ross turned to the deputies and said, "I know this place has already been searched, but we're going to do it again. We're looking for either a notebook that details the crimes committed out at the old Salter compound, or anything that will help us find the damn thing if it isn't here. We don't know what this notebook looks like, only that it contains the information we need."

One of the men jerked his thumb toward the house and said, "According to that sticker on the front door, if we go inside, the United States Federal Government isn't going to be very happy with us."

Ross smiled and said, "Are they ever? Let's go."

Mayo walked past Henderson, and gave him a friendly clap on the back. "Good to see you again, Sheriff."

Henderson caught the meaning of the gesture and felt the tension slip away. Then he turned to his men and said, "Let's get to it, fellas."

Louder called her brother on the phone and got right to the point. "That woman makes me want to scream. You wouldn't believe the things she's saying about me online."

"I don't know what to tell you," Blackwell said. "Maybe you should drop the whole thing."

"Drop it? Are you kidding me? Bobby and I had a good thing going, and Henderson could have done something to protect him."

"Bobby Reynolds was an idiot, Stacey. I'm surprised he lasted as long as he did. And based on what I've seen, he would have ended up dragging you down with him."

"That is not true. I loved him. We were planning a future together."

"And what about Matt? He's a successful businessman, and has always been good to you."

"Being good to me and being with me are two different things. I never see him, Ethan. Never. He says he's working late nearly every damn night, but who's renting trucks at two in the morning? Don't bother answering. I'll tell you. No one…unless it's one of those bimbos he's got bent over his desk. Bobby was going to take me away from it all, and now he's dead… all because Henderson couldn't keep the state out of county business."

"Look, Stacey, What's done is done. I'm about to make the score of a lifetime, and when I do, you'll be able to live your life however you want. But for now, you've got to let this little war you've got going die down. It's bringing too much attention right where I don't want it."

"Yeah, well, here's some attention for you, Ethan, and I'll let you thank me later. Betty the bitch just posted that Henderson and his men are taking Bobby's house apart…again."

"*What?*"

"That's right. If they find that notebook before you do, I'm guessing the only big score you're going to get is a nice private cell at a super-max prison."

Blackwell didn't bother to answer. He hung up, grabbed his keys, and ran from the room.

CHAPTER TWENTY-NINE

Virgil and Murton were still sitting in the Range Rover watching the hotel parking lot, waiting to see if Blackwell was going to make a move. They were both getting bored, and tired of doing nothing.

Murton looked over at Virgil and said, "I'm wondering if there's some way to force the play."

"What'd you have in mind?"

"We need to put Blackwell with the drugs, right?"

"Yeah," Virgil said. "Except we don't know where they are."

"But if Blackwell thinks we do, he might lead us right to where he has them stashed."

"It's not a bad thought, Murt. But I just said it; we have no idea where the drugs are. I don't see how we can play the guy without that information. All he would have to do is call our bluff, and then we'd have nothing."

"What if we told him we found the notebook?" Murton said.

Virgil shook his head. "Still don't see how it'd work. If that notebook has the kind of information we think it does—like who the buyer is—then we wouldn't have any legitimate reason to keep it from the DEA. That means Blackwell would eventually get his hands on it, and then we've lost control of the entire operation. What we need is for Becky to come through on the doorbell cam."

"And that doesn't really get us anywhere, either, Jones-man. All we'll have is a plate number, which isn't going to help us because if Blackwell has more than two functioning brain cells in his head, that van is stashed somewhere safe until he can make the deal with whoever the buyer is."

"Yeah, yeah, I know," Virgil said. "Not only that, but we can't go to the truck rental place, because Blackwell's brother-in-law owns the joint. For all we know, he's in on it as well."

They spent another few minutes tossing ideas back and forth, looking at all the different angles, when Murton saw Blackwell come out the front door of the hotel. "Here we go."

"Looks like he's in a hurry," Virgil said.

Murton fired up the Rover and got ready to follow.

"Let's give him a few minutes," Virgil said. "I don't want to get too close. We've got the tracker, so we can hang back."

"Believe it or not, I've done this before," Murton said. As Blackwell was turning out of the lot, Murton connected his phone to the Rover's Bluetooth system, then brought up the tracker app. Once that was done, he pushed everything through to the navigation unit so they could follow from a distance.

"Looks like he's going to get on the circle," Virgil said. Indianapolis had a giant 54-mile beltway that circled the city and its outer suburbs. "Let's not let him get too far out in front."

Murton dropped the Rover in gear, and said, "Yes, mother, although I do wish you'd make up your mind." Then he pulled out of the parking area and merged into traffic.

As they were following Blackwell counter-clockwise at the bottom of the loop, Virgil's cell phone buzzed at him. He was focused on the nav unit, so he didn't bother to check the phone's screen before he answered. "Jones."

"Hey, Jonesy. It's Bell. How are you feeling?"

"Hanging in. Sort of in the middle of a moderately slow-speed chase. Can I call you back?"

"No need. Just wanted to let you know that I've got you scheduled for an MRI at Methodist, tomorrow at two. That's the earliest I could get."

Virgil swore under his breath and was about to let Bell know he couldn't make it, then remembered the promise he'd made to Sandy. "Okay, fine, Bell. Waste of time, you ask me, but I'll be there. Just text me the details, will you? I gotta go."

Bell said he would, then ended the call.

Virgil glanced over at his brother, and he knew what was coming. "Don't say it, Murt."

But Murton couldn't help himself. He smiled and said, "Gonna get your head examined, huh?"

"Something like that."

Murton laughed, then said, "Well, like the song says, sometimes you've got to see what condition your condition is in."

Virgil let out a sigh. "Murt…"

"What? All's I'm saying, is all. Besides, there's never anything wrong with a checkup from the neck up." Then he pointed at the nav unit and said, "Looks like our boy is turning south on 74."

"Shelby County?" Virgil said.

"You know what that means, don't you?"

Virgil nodded. "Yeah. He's either headed for where he's got the drugs stashed, or he somehow found out about the search at Reynolds's place."

"My money is on the search."

"Mine too," Virgil said. He punched in Ross's number and got him on the line. "Hey, Boss-man."

"That's my line," Ross said. "But I appreciate the acknowledgment. What's up?"

"I need an update on the search. Have you guys started yet?"

Ross made a motorboat noise, then said, "Started? Hell, we're all but done."

Virgil frowned into the phone. "Little quick, you ask me. This isn't the time to cut any corners, young man."

"We're not. If anything, it's the exact opposite."

"What do you mean?" Virgil said.

"The house—as you know because you've seen it—isn't that big. It's about fifteen-hundred square feet, and it sits on a slab, which means there's no basement."

"I'm not looking for an architectural assessment, Ross. I'm looking for a notebook."

"Then keep looking, because it ain't here."

"How'd you get it done so fast?"

"Easy. Including me, we've got four guys from the MCU, along with Sheriff Henderson and ten of his men. That means there are fifteen guys going through the place. I know you struggle with math sometimes, so let me help you out. Each man only had to search about one hundred square feet. We were practically tripping over each other. I'm telling you, Jonesy…it isn't here."

Virgil swore under his breath again for the second time in as many minutes. "Okay, it was still worth a look. Listen, Murt and I are following Blackwell, and it looks like he's headed your way. Not sure if it's to Reynolds's house, or someplace else. Tell Henderson we appreciate the assist."

"I already did that," Ross said with a bit of a chuckle. "But I'll be sure and let him know that a couple of random private eyes are appreciative of his efforts as well." Then he hung up.

Virgil looked at Murton and said, "I may have created a monster."

Murton shrugged. "It happens. Tell me more about what Bell said."

"There isn't anything else to tell. I'm getting an MRI tomorrow at two."

"And you're going," Murton said. It wasn't a question. "Want to know how I know that?"

"No," Virgil said.

"Too bad, because I'm going to tell you. I'll be the one taking you there."

"Ah, you've got your hands full as it is. Sandy will probably want to take me anyway."

"It's the detectives of the MCU who have their hands full, Jones-man. I'm working on my own schedule. That means I'll be there tomorrow, no matter who takes you."

Virgil looked over at his brother and could feel the love. For some reason, it reminded him of the time Murton had come to his rescue when Pate had him strung up on a beam in an empty warehouse, naked, and close to dying. It had been one of the worst days of Virgil's adult life, but through the bad, he'd gotten exactly what he needed, and what he'd wanted for years: Virgil got his brother back.

Murton felt the stare. "What are you thinking about?"

"The good stuff," Virgil said.

Thirty minutes later, Virgil got Ross back on the phone. "There's no question. He's headed your way. At the rate he's going, you've got about ten minutes before he arrives."

"How do you want to play it?" Ross said.

"I don't want this guy getting suspicious. Close the place up and get out."

"You got it," Ross said. "I take it you're going to hang back?"

"Yeah, we pretty much need to at this point. We'll stay on him for now, but the rest of you guys might as well return to the shop."

"Good enough," Ross said. "I'm going to swing by and check on Rosie before I do."

Virgil told Ross that was fine, then ended the call.

Murton pulled into a gas station about three miles away from Reynolds's place, and he and Virgil simply sat and watched the nav unit. Blackwell made two slow passes by the house, and on the second, he appeared to stop for a few minutes.

"Might be checking the place out," Virgil said.

Murton yawned, then said, "Doesn't really matter at this point."

When Blackwell started moving again, Virgil shook his head, and pointed at the nav unit. "Look at this guy. He's headed back north."

"This is going to get old in a hurry," Murton said.

But then, as if the universe might be listening in on their conversation, Murton's phone rang and the display unit in the Rover showed it was Becky calling.

Murton punched the Answer button on the steering wheel and said, "Yes, M'love?"

When Becky spoke, Virgil and Murton looked at each other and smiled.

"We've got him," Becky said.

Virgil looked at the nav unit display when he spoke, as if Becky could see him. "Tell us."

"Give me thirty seconds and I'll show you. I've already sent the video to both your phones. It should be coming through any time now."

Virgil pulled out his phone and stared at the screen for all of five seconds. "I'm not getting anything, Becks."

"That's because it's a big file. Hold your horses."

Nearly a minute later, Murton said, "I've got it." He brought the video up on the Rover's display.

"That's Blackwell walking up the street toward the house where Cooper was killed," Virgil said.

"Why the hell is he walking?" Murton asked.

"I've got a theory on that," Becky said. "Actually, more than a theory. I'll explain in a second. You're going to lose sight of Blackwell just about the time he's halfway up the drive."

"Yeah, we just did," Virgil said. "What's your theory?"

"Hold on, or you're going to miss something. I had to work the audio a bit, but listen close."

Murton increased the volume a little, then they heard a muffled gunshot. Less than a minute later the van backed down the drive, made a little half-turn that put the license plate in plain view of the camera, then drove out of the cul-de-sac.

"There's more," Becky said. "But I'll let you see that when you get here. It shows the neighbor lady going up to the house, then peeking in the window before hurrying home. Although hurrying is sort of a relative term with her. Anyway, the timing of the call to 9-1-1 matches up with the neighbor, and no other vehicles or people are on camera entering or exiting the house. Bottom line, you've got Blackwell for murder, if nothing else."

"That's great work, Becks" Virgil said. "What's your theory?"

"I got curious when I saw him walking up to the house instead of driving."

"That is odd," Murton said.

"Right? Remember that time I had to get into Uber's system?"

"Let me guess," Murton said. "You never actually got out."

"You got it," Becky said. "I looked at their billing records and Blackwell's credit card was right there no more than an hour after the van left the murder scene. He got dropped off at the Highland Golf and Country Club in Crows Nest, which is only about six blocks from the scene. He needed a ride back to his own car after he stashed the van."

Virgil leaned forward slightly in his seat. "Becky, please tell me you know where he was picked up from."

Becky dropped a little charm into her voice and said, "Well, Virgie, since you said please…"

CHAPTER THIRTY

Ross was sitting at the kitchen table with Rosencrantz and Henderson, and they were all talking about the search that came up empty.

"Bottom line, that was the last place to look," Ross said. "If it's not there—and we know it isn't because we tore the place apart—then I don't have any idea where it is."

"Maybe the damn thing never existed to begin with," Henderson said. He sounded irritated.

"That's always been a possibility," Ross said. "But we're operating under the theory that it must, because Blackwell has the drugs and Jordan had the buyer."

Ross's phone beeped at him, and when he checked the screen, he saw a text from Sarah. A smile began to form on his face, and Rosencrantz caught it. "What's going on?"

"It's Blackwell," Ross said. "We've got him." He gave both men the basic details, then said, "I gotta run. We're all meeting at the MCU in an hour. Rosie, you good?"

Rosencrantz waved him off. "Yeah, I'm fine. Go do your thing, partner. Watch your back."

"Always. I'll be in touch."

Once Ross was gone, Rosencrantz looked at Henderson and said, "Did you go through everything at the bank where Jordan worked?"

"We did. There wasn't anything other than official bank business."

"What about a safe deposit box?" Rosencrantz said.

Henderson shook his head. "This is a waste of time, you ask me."

"That doesn't exactly answer my question," Rosencrantz said.

"Yeah, Jordan had one, but it was empty. I saw it myself. Look, Tom, based on what Ross just said, the notebook probably doesn't matter at this point, right? The MCU will handle Blackwell, and when that happens, the whole thing will be over. I mean, what are they going to do? Chase down a buyer in Kentucky who never got the drugs to begin with? That's why I said it's a waste of time."

"I hear you," Rosencrantz said. "You're probably right. But it's a loose end, and I hate it when that happens."

Henderson stood and said, "Listen, I've got a department to run. That means I've got to go before Betty decides to strap on a six-shooter and bust up a bar fight."

"She probably wouldn't need the gun."

Henderson got a chuckle out of that, but his laughter sounded forced. "Let me know if you need anything else."

Rosencrantz said he would, and walked Henderson to the door. He stood there and watched as his friend got in a county squad car and drove away. Rosencrantz stayed at the front door for a long time, looking at nothing, before he finally decided to walk down the drive and get a little more exercise in. He took his cane with him, and moved slower than normal…not because he wanted to, but because something didn't feel quite right.

———————————

Everyone met at the Major Crimes Unit facility, and they all ended up in the conference room to discuss their next move. Becky brought the doorbell video up on the large wall monitor, and they went through that first, watching the entire sequence in real time.

After the video had played itself out, Ross tapped the tabletop with his index finger, and said, "There's about a thirty minute gap between the time Blackwell drives away and the call comes in to 9-1-1."

"What are you getting at?" Virgil said.

"What if there was someone else in the house? They could have gone out the back, or even been hiding in the van as it left."

Virgil went through his copy of the case notes. "According to the Marion County crime scene report, the back door was locked with a deadbolt, and Cooper still had his keys."

Ross conceded the point, then said, "What about the van? You can't see it in the video until it backs out of the drive. Someone else could have hopped in and hidden in the back."

Virgil knew Ross was doing his best to cover all the angles, and he didn't want to discourage him. He also didn't want to get too far into the weeds over something that probably didn't happen. "It's a possibility, Ross. There's no question about it. But if I've learned anything doing the job you have right now, it's this: Too much information can ruin a perfectly good case. We've got Blackwell dead to rights on Cooper's murder."

"Once we have him, ballistics will probably be able to match up his weapon and pin the Crow brothers on him as well," Wilson said.

Virgil tipped a finger at him and said, "You're right. But what we really need is to get him with the drugs. If we can make that happen, the DEA won't have any other choice…they'll have to drop their asset forfeiture claim against Said, Inc., and then everyone's problems go away."

"How, exactly, are we going to do that?" Mayo said. "Get him with the drugs?"

Everyone turned and looked at Virgil, who said, "Don't ask me. I'm not a member of the MCU. Murton and I are here in an advisory capacity only."

Ross looked down and scratched at the back of his neck. "I appreciate what you're trying to do, Jonesy. Really. I'm also not unaware of the faith and trust you've put in me during your, uh, sabbatical."

"Are you asking for our help?" Virgil said.

"I'm certainly willing to entertain suggestions moving forward," Ross said.

"The mark of any good leader," Murton said. Then he looked around the table until he had everyone's attention. "When Virgil and I were sitting on Blackwell at the hotel, we were tossing ideas back and forth on ways to manipulate him into making a mistake…one that would put him with the drugs. Unfortunately, none of them would work unless we knew where the drugs were actually located. But now that we do…" He spread his hands, and let the statement speak for itself.

"It sounds like you guys have a plan," Ortiz said.

Virgil nodded. "We do. Murton and I talked about it on the drive back up here."

"What'd you come up with?" Ross said.

Virgil stuck his tongue in his cheek, then said, "Well, it involves Betty, of all people."

Ross dropped his chin to his chest. "I'm beginning to have a new appreciation for Cora and the things she has to endure." Then to Virgil and Murton: "Okay, let's hear what you've got."

Like this:

Becky hacked into Betty's X account—a process that took her all of fifteen minutes—then wrote a post that read:

> @stacey_louder: #Shelby-County
> Sheriff H. comes thru again 4 MCU.
> Probable 10-20 on major drug supply.
> #keep-our-sheriff #louder-the-loser
> #stacey-louder-mouthy

Virgil and Murton looked at the post, then back at Becky. "You think that'll do it?" Virgil said. He was a little skeptical.

"If you go back and read through the things those two women have been saying to each other, you'll see. I guarantee it'll work. When should I post it?"

"Where's Blackwell right now?" Ross said.

Becky pulled up the tracker app. "He's back at his hotel."

"Okay," Virgil said. "Once we're in place, go ahead and send it."

"How do you know she'll see it?" Murton said. "The post?"

"I went back and looked at timelines," Becky said. "Every time Betty makes a post directed at Louder, she responds almost immediately."

"I'll bet she doesn't respond to this one," Ross said.

"Doesn't matter," Murton said. "All we need is for her to contact Blackwell."

Virgil looked at Ross. "Got two seconds for me in private?"

"Sure," Ross said. He followed Virgil out of the computer lab and a few feet down the hall. "What's up?"

"Piece of advice?"

"Always."

Virgil looked at nothing for a few seconds, then said, "Situations like this—the ones that seem straightforward and pretty basic on the surface—are the ones that will go sideways on you in a hurry. You get to make your own calls, but I'd put Mayo and Ortiz over at the hotel and have them follow Blackwell when he makes his move. They'll be able to block the exit once he's inside the gate at the storage facility."

"I'll do that," Ross said. "What else?"

"It wouldn't hurt to have Cool overhead in the chopper for aerial support."

Ross squinted an eye at Virgil. "For one guy?"

Virgil tipped his head to the side. "You never know, kid. Better to have him and not need him, than the other way around."

Ross said he'd handle it, and he did. Then thirty minutes later everyone was in place, and Becky made the post on *X*.

After she hit the Send button, she thought, *Betty is going to be pissed.*

STACEY LOUDER WAS SITTING AT HER DESK, GOING over the minutes of the last meeting and attending to other county business, when her phone chirped at her. She picked it up, read the post, then immediately called her brother. "Ethan, it's me. That nasty old crone down here is making waves again."

"Stacey, I don't have time for this right now. I told you to drop it, anyway."

"Well, it's a good thing I didn't because she just posted that Henderson has a probable location on the drugs."

"Jesus, Stacey…not over the phone. These things are like radios."

"Okay, whatever, but how well did you hide them?"

"Well enough. There's no way anyone knows where they are."

"Are you one hundred percent sure, Ethan? Because if you're not, you better go check."

"Stacey, I'm telling you. No one knows. Keep your head down and your mouth shut, and everything will be fine." Then he hung up.

Cool was circling high overhead near the storage facility. He had enough altitude that no one would bother to give him a second look, if they even saw him at all. He called Virgil on the sat phone and said, "I'm on station and I've got you guys turning in right now."

"Good enough, Rich. Probably be a nice boring flight for you."

"Let's hope," Cool said.

Virgil and Murton, along with Ross and Wilson, all walked inside the storage facility's office and found a balding middle-aged man behind the counter, leafing through a car magazine. When everyone walked in, he looked up and said, "Hep ya, fellas?"

Ross pulled out his badge. "I'm Detective Andrew Ross with the state's Major Crimes Unit. Are you the owner?"

The man stood up, visibly swallowed, and said, "Yeah, I am. What's going on?"

"What's going on is we need some information, we need it right now, and we expect you to give it to us."

"What kind of information?"

"We need to see your customer list."

"Mind if I ask why?" the man said.

Ross gave him a flat stare and said, "No." Then he just waited.

"No, you don't mind? Or no, I can't ask?"

Ross kept his stare in place and said, "Yes."

"Look, Officer, you're not being very clear with your answers, and I'm not looking for any trouble, but—"

"I told you, it's detective…not officer. I also told you we need to see your list, and I'm running out of both time and patience. Hand it over."

"Aren't you supposed to have a warrant, or something like that?"

"Only if we're conducting a search," Ross said. "And I don't want to conduct a search. All I want is to see your customer list."

"Why?"

Ross reached over the counter and grabbed the man by his shirt and pulled him forward. "Because I like to read."

The man pulled away, then said, "You can't do that to me. It's against the law."

Ross stepped back and held up his hands. "You're right, of course. My apologies." Then he jerked his thumb at Wilson and said, "This is my partner. He's also a detective with the Major Crimes Unit." Then he pointed at Virgil and Murton. "But these other two guys here? While they are associates of mine, they are not with the state police. They're practically private citizens."

"So what?"

"Well, if you're paying attention, that means they're not bound by the same rules as me and my partner."

"What's your point?"

Ross sighed, like he might be talking to the slow kid in the classroom. "A minute ago you asked if we needed a warrant. The truth is, we probably do, but you know when we wouldn't need a warrant? No, no, shhh…you're going to want to hear this. We don't need a warrant if we discover a crime has been committed on the premises."

"There hasn't been any crime committed," the man said.

"Not yet," Ross said. "But my partner and I are about to step outside. When we do, the guy with the fancy shirt and the big toothy grin standing next to me is going to get that list one way or another. Have a nice day." Then Ross and Wilson headed for the door.

"Hey, now…hold on there, Detectives. Maybe we got off on the wrong foot, if you know what I mean. It happens sometimes, right?"

"I've seen it before," Wilson said. "How about it on the list?"

The man reached under the counter, and before he could get his hands back up he was staring at four guns pointed right at his head.

Murton never let the smile leave his face. "If you even blink, the inside of your eyelids will be the last thing you ever see."

"I'm reaching for the list," the man said without blinking.

"Let me help you," Virgil said. He holstered his weapon and moved behind the counter. When he saw there were no weapons, he nodded at everyone, and all the guns went away.

"Boy, you guys don't fuck around, do you?" the man said.

Virgil scanned the logbook, and after a few seconds, said, "Got it. Unit 241."

"Will one of you guys please tell me what's going on?"

"Isn't it obvious?" Ross said. "We're going to conduct a search of unit 241."

The owner of the storage facility let his shoulders slump. "So where's the warrant?"

"It's on its way," Ross lied. "But let me ask you

something. If someone doesn't pay their bill, what happens to the stuff they've got stored here?"

"We sell it to recoup our costs. It's in the contract."

"So, you effectively take ownership of whatever is in the unit. I mean, you can't sell something that isn't yours, right? That'd be illegal, wouldn't it?"

"Yeah, I guess so."

"Then here's your chance to not go to jail, sir."

"Jail? Why would you take me to jail?"

"Sorry," Ross said. "I misspoke. I meant to say prison, because if our information is good—and I assure you, it is—then you, as the owner of the facility here, are sitting on nearly a half-million pills of illegally manufactured Oxy."

The owner swallowed again, and said, "Let me get the master key for that unit. You know, I tell anyone who asks…I've always been a big supporter of law enforcement."

CHAPTER THIRTY-ONE

BLACKWELL WAS STILL SITTING IN HIS HOTEL ROOM, trying to figure out his next move. The problem was, he couldn't get the sound of his sister's voice out of his head. Had someone seen him leaving the safe house in Crows Nest? Had they heard the shot? Did they get the plate? Even if they had, how could that possibly lead them to the storage unit? And if they had gotten to the facility, did that mean that he no longer had control over the drugs?

Blackwell thought about it until he ended up going around in circles, and finally decided the only way he was going to ease his mind was to drive over to the storage facility and have a look for himself.

He grabbed his keys and headed for his car.

Mayo and Ortiz saw Blackwell get into his car and pull out of the lot. They gave him a few minutes, then began to follow, the tracker keeping them close, but far enough away that they wouldn't be seen.

Ortiz grabbed his phone and, out of pure habit, called Virgil. "Blackwell is headed your way. The navigation unit says, based on traffic, you've got about thirty-five minutes."

"Good enough," Virgil said. "How'd he look?"

"Like his hair was on fire."

The owner of the storage facility got the unit unlocked, then opened the door and stepped back.

"Wait here," Ross said.

The man said he would, and went over and stood next to Virgil and Murton. "This is kinda exciting, ain't it?" he said.

Murton gave him a deadpan stare and said, "Positively titillating." After that, the man didn't speak.

Ross and Wilson slipped into gloves, then walked inside the unit and around to the rear of the van. "Plates are a match," Ross said. When they tried the door handles, they discovered the van was locked up tight.

Wilson reached into his pocket and pulled out a small metal rod with a plastic grip and a pointed end. "Stand back."

Ross turned away, and Wilson put the point of the rod against the glass and began to apply pressure. Two seconds later the glass shattered and fell away.

Ross looked at him and said, "You patrol guys have all the cool toys."

"Says the sniper. And for the record, that's *former* patrol guy." Wilson reached through the side window and hit the button to unlock the doors. When they got the back opened up, a quick check of the boxes revealed more pills than either man had ever seen.

When they walked back out and looked at Virgil and Murton, Ross said, "We've got him."

Virgil checked the time and said, "Okay, we've got about twenty minutes. Ross, take Mr., uh…" He looked at the owner of the storage facility, and finished with, "I don't think we ever got your name, sir."

"It's Perkins. Barry Perkins."

"Ross, take Mr. Perkins back to the office, lock it up, and explain the particulars to him, will you?"

"You got it, Jonesy." Then: "Mr. Perkins, let's take a little walk, huh?"

Once they were back up front, Ross asked Perkins if he had someone manning the office twenty-four hours a day.

"Nope. Not enough money in it. Hell, half the time I ain't even here."

"Good," Ross said. He reached into his pocket, pulled out his card, and handed it to Perkins. "I know you've got questions about all this, and I'll be happy to answer them in a day or two. Right now, I need you to lock your doors and leave. In the meantime, if you have any concerns, you can call the number on that card. A very nice young lady by the name of Sarah Palmer will be happy to assist you. Please do not call anyone else regarding what's happening out here right now."

"I won't," Perkins said. "I'm not looking for trouble."

"I'm serious, sir. If you start to have second thoughts and call the city or county police, it will seriously fuck us up. We don't want that, do we?"

Perkins caught both the tone and the look on Ross's face. "No, we certainly don't."

Ross waited until Perkins had the office locked up, then said, "What's the gate code?"

"One, two, three, four, pound button," Perkins said.

Ross just stared at him until Perkins got in his car and drove away. Then he took out his phone and called Sarah. "Hey gorgeous. Do me a favor?"

"Sure. You guys all okay?"

"Yeah, this one will be a slice of pie, as Wu would say."

"What's the favor?"

"I just ran the landlord of the storage facility off his own property. There's a chance he'll want to put a call in to either the city or the county. Could you let them know we're working one out here and to stay clear?"

"I already did…Boss."

"I like the sound of that."

Sarah laughed. "Just remember…it only applies at work. Be careful, Ross. I love you."

"See you soon," Ross said. Then he ended the call.

What Ross didn't know at the time was this: He'd see Sarah sooner than either of them thought, and for a reason neither of them could have ever imagined.

THE STORAGE FACILITY WAS LAID OUT WITH ROW AFTER row of units all along the interior of the property, the buildings running lengthwise from east to west. A single line of units at the very back ran north to south, perpendicular to the others. When viewed from above, it looked like a giant T with too many stems. Unit 241 was along the back row, centered between two of the east-west buildings, directly in line with the gate. Everyone put their tac comms in, and Ross got them set up.

"Virgil…Murt…I'll want you guys inside with the van. Wilson will take the east side at the corner, and I'll take the west. Mayo and Ortiz will block the exit once Blackwell is in. We've got all the evidence we need, so let's have a nice easy takedown, and everyone goes home tonight. Questions?"

No one had any, so Ross got on his phone, called Mayo and gave him the same briefing. "It's highly unlikely that Blackwell will have a chance to make a break for it, but if he does, I want your squad car blocking that gate entrance."

"You got it," Mayo said. "Is there a code for the gate?"

Ross gave him the code, then said, "Get your tac comms in, and start to tighten up on the guy. I'm looking at my phone right now, and he's less than a mile out."

Mayo told him they'd be ready, then ended the call.

Ross pulled Virgil aside and said, "What am I missing?"

Virgil looked at his detective and said, "Have Cool drop down close enough to get on the tac comms. Other than that, you're good. I'm proud of you, young man. Let's do this, huh?" Then Virgil and Murton stepped inside the storage unit and parked their butts against the front of the van's grill, their weapons out and held casually at their sides.

Murton looked at Ross and said, "If Blackwell doesn't show, don't forget to unlock the door and let us out."

Ross gave him a wicked grin and said, "I'll try to remember."

Then the door went down, and Virgil and Murton were in the dark.

Murton looked over toward Virgil, and even though it was difficult to see him, he said, "When Blackwell opens the door, do you think we should say something like, 'Surprise,' or 'Ta-da?'"

"No, I don't. I think we should—"

"Off the comms unless it's tactical," Ross said.

"Yes, sir," Murton said. And he meant it.

Then Ortiz was in everyone's ear. "We may have a problem. He drove right past the entrance. We're hanging back just a bit."

"Did he spot you?" Ross said.

"Negative," Mayo said. "I think he's just being cautious. Looks like we'll be going around the block."

"Stay off of him," Ross said. "There's a gas station right across the street. All our other vehicles are parked behind that building. If he's going around the block, pull over on the west side of the station and he'll never see you. Once he's through the gate, Cool will give you the signal to pull up and block it."

"Roger that," Ortiz said.

"Cool?" Ross said.

"Copy. I'm in position."

BLACKWELL FELT LIKE SOMETHING WAS OFF. He couldn't quite put his finger on it, but just as he was getting ready to turn into the storage facility, he had the feeling he was being followed. He drove on past the entrance and decided to go around the block to see if anyone was on his tail. He kept a close eye on his rearview mirror, but after three turns he didn't notice anything out of the ordinary.

Still, it never hurt to be careful. He pulled over to the curb and parked his car, watching the mirror for a few minutes. When Blackwell finally decided that he was letting his imagination get the better of him, he put his car in gear and pulled away. Less than a minute later, he made the final turn, then pulled into the storage unit facility.

Mayo and Ortiz were directly across the street, and Blackwell never saw them. Mayo said, "Headed your way. He's at the gate now."

Ross got on the comms: "Mayo, Ortiz, wait until he's all the way through the gate and it closes up on him. His unit has a clear view of the entrance, so I don't want to spook him before he has a chance to open the overhead door. Break. Cool, are you with me?"

"Loud and clear, Ross," Cool said. "I'll let them know."

BLACKWELL PUNCHED IN THE CODE, THEN DROVE through the gate and straight over to where the van was stashed. Once he was out of his car, he walked over to the unit, stuck the key in the lock and gave it a twist.

When he raised the door, Virgil and Murton were right there and waiting.

Virgil was standing with his back against the van, his arms crossed casually over his chest, his Sig P226 resting comfortably in the crook of his elbow. When Blackwell opened the door, Virgil gave him a humorless smile and said, "Hello, Ethan. You're under arrest for murder, possession of drugs with intent to distribute, and a bunch of other stuff we'll think up later."

Blackwell started to reach for his gun, but when Virgil pulled the hammer back on his Sig, Blackwell froze.

"That would be a mistake, Blackwell," Murton said. "On the ground…right now. This isn't the time to think. It's time to do what you're told." Murton took a step forward, and when he did, Blackwell turned and started running for the gate.

Virgil let his shoulders slump, looked at Murton and said, "I hate it when they run." Then into the comms… rather dully: "Mayo, Ortiz, he's headed your way."

"We see him," Ortiz said.

Blackwell was running hard, looking over his

shoulder at Virgil and Murton. In the back of his mind, he thought he heard himself wonder why they weren't chasing him. He was halfway to the gate before he looked forward and saw Mayo and Ortiz. He skidded to a stop, turned around, and started running back toward Virgil and Murton, who were simply standing there watching the whole thing play out. Blackwell ran right past them, and as he did, he looked over at both men and shot them the bone.

But Ross and Wilson had moved up, and were both closing in on Blackwell. Once he was close enough, Blackwell tried to do a little juke to get past them, but he never had a chance. Wilson held his ground, balled up his fist and hit Blackwell—hard—right in the center of his face.

Blackwell dropped, and when he did, Wilson leaned down, took the man's weapon, and said, "Stop resisting." Then together, Ross and Wilson rolled him over, got the cuffs on him, and did a quick but thorough search for other weapons. After they had that done, Ross read Blackwell his rights, then told Mayo and Ortiz to bring their squad car over for transport.

Everyone thought it was over…until they heard Cool screaming at them over the tac comms.

———

Everything was happening at the same time:

Mayo and Ortiz were walking back to their squad car to bring it over like Ross had asked.

Murton had stepped into the storage unit to examine the van and the drugs.

Ross was making Blackwell's gun safe for transport by stripping it down to its basic components.

Wilson was guarding their prisoner, his knee on Blackwell's back, facing away from everyone else.

And Cool was the only one who saw it.

Virgil was still leaning against the side of Blackwell's car, watching everyone work the scene. Murton clapped him on the back and said, "I'm going to check out the van."

"You bet," Virgil said. "I'll be right there. Gonna call Sandy and let her know that we're wrapping it up."

"Might want to mention that Mac is out of the woods as well," Murton said over his shoulder.

"I will." Virgil pulled out his phone, hip-checked himself off of Blackwell's car, then brought up Sandy's number and hit the Call button. Virgil wasn't walking anywhere in particular…he was simply moving around the way people do when waiting for a call to go through.

He'd taken no more than two or three steps when the thing no one really understood had its way with him once and for all. And this time when Virgil went away, it wasn't just for a few minutes.

It was for good.

CHAPTER THIRTY-TWO

From Cool's perspective, if only for a moment, time slowed to a crawl. He had the helicopter on autopilot and was flying in a lazy circle overhead, watching everyone through a pair of image-stabilizing binoculars. Mayo and Ortiz were headed toward the front gate, Murton had just walked inside the storage unit, and Ross and Wilson both had their backs turned, taking care of Blackwell and his weapon.

When Virgil went down, he collapsed like someone had just flipped his switch to the off position. He didn't trip or stumble or take a misstep. He simply dropped straight down. His phone skittered away a few feet from his hand, and the side of his head hit the pavement…the impact slightly lessened by the fact that his shoulder hit first. Cool was looking right at him when it happened, and when he went to grab the stick to disconnect the autopilot, his hand seemed to be moving much slower than it should have been. It looked like the rotor blades of the helicopter were moving so slowly he could see their reflection in the windshield as they made sluggish, lethargic passes right above his head.

Then, in an instant, everything went back to normal. Cool would later tell everyone that even though he knew it was all in his head, time seemed to have almost stopped. But in the moment, when Virgil went down, he got on the tac comms and began shouting at the other members of the MCU.

"Virgil is down. *Virgil is down!* Clear me a spot, right now. I'm coming in hot." He pointed the nose of the helicopter dangerously low toward the ground, reduced the power, and let gravity have its way, the altitude bleeding off so fast the altimeter was having trouble keeping up with the rate of descent.

Murton came running out of the storage unit, looked both ways, but couldn't see his brother anywhere. Ross and Wilson were running toward the opposite side of Blackwell's car, and Murton leapt over the hood, stumbled the landing, then got back up and was right there at Virgil's side. "Don't move him. Don't touch him. What the hell happened?"

Ross and Wilson didn't answer because they had no

idea what was going on. Mayo and Ortiz jumped in their squad car and came racing over.

"I need a spot," Cool said. "Somebody talk to me."

Ross knew it would be close, but he said, "I think you've got room right between the rows of buildings, Cool, but it's going to be tight. I mean really tight, man." Then he turned and said, "Mayo, get over by the building on the left. Ortiz, take the right. Watch the rotors and guide him in."

Murton took both sides of Virgil's head in his hands and kept his neck straight. "Ross, get down here and help me roll him. Easy now. Take his arms and gently roll him on his back. Ready? One, two, three…"

Once they had Virgil on his back, Ross said, "What the fuck happened? Nobody fired."

Murton's voice was tight…running right on the edge of panic. "I don't know. I don't fucking know."

Cool was hovering almost right above them, and then Mayo and Ortiz both began waving their arms back and forth. There wasn't enough room for Cool to land where they needed.

Murton put his ear to Virgil's chest and listened for a heartbeat, but he couldn't hear one because of the noise from the helicopter. The rotor wash made it impossible to even feel if his heart was beating or not.

Then Mayo said, "Cool, take it back up and spin

around the other way. There's more room at the junction between the buildings on the back row."

Cool did what Mayo said, and as soon as the helicopter had backed off, Murton could both hear and feel Virgil's heart beating. "His heart is pumping, and he's still breathing. He's not bleeding anywhere that I can see. I don't know what the hell is going on."

Wilson saw Blackwell trying to get up, so he ran over and clubbed him on the back of his neck, dragged him over to the storage unit, rolled him inside, then closed and locked the overhead door. Then he ran back to where Virgil was.

"Rich, we're going to need your help over here, but keep it wound up," Murton said. He was running his fingers along the back and both sides of Virgil's neck, trying to tell if he had a spinal injury.

"On my way," Cool said. He locked the collective in place, set the engine at fifty percent power, then jumped out and ran over to help.

Murton looked at everyone and said, "We gotta get him on board that chopper, but we don't have a backboard or a C-collar. I've got his head and neck. It's vital that we keep them as steady as possible. Wilson, take his ankles. Ross and Cool, I want each of you to get under his shoulders as best you can. Mayo and Ortiz, I need one of you on each side, right at his waist-line.

Let's keep him level and straight all the way to the chopper. We're not trying to run. Slow and steady wins this race."

"Watch the tail rotor when we get close," Cool said.

Everyone gave Cool a sharp nod, then Murton said, "Okay, here we go. Steady now…"

Sandy's phone rang, and when she checked the screen, she saw it was Virgil calling. She hit the Answer button and said, "Hey, boyfriend. Since you're calling me, this must be next time. Did you get your man?" Then she heard a crackling noise when Virgil's phone slipped from his hand, though Sandy didn't realize what had just happened. "Hey, Virg? Are you there? Virgil?"

Then, in the background, Sandy could hear someone shouting, and then a few seconds later what sounded like the noise of a helicopter. "Virgil?"

When she didn't get an answer, she kept the line open, picked up the receiver of her desk phone and called Murton. When the call went to voicemail, she hung up and quickly tried Becky, who answered on the first ring.

"Hey Sandy. What's up?"

"I just got a call from Virgil. When I answered the

phone it sounded like chaos on the other end. I think something is wrong. I can't reach Virgil or Murton."

"They're tracking Blackwell. Unless the guy did something weird, they should be wrapping him up right about now."

"Becky, listen to me. If you heard what I did on the phone, you'd know something is wrong."

"Hang on for a second. I know they had Cool for aerial support. Let me try him on the sat phone."

"Hurry, will you?"

Becky didn't bother to answer. She hit the Hold button, then made a call to Cool. When she got him on the line, Becky listened as Cool told her what he knew, which, by his own admission, wasn't much.

"That's all I've got," Cool said. "I'm seven minutes out from Methodist. Tell Sandy she better get over here as quick as she can. He didn't look good, Becky. He didn't look good at all."

AFTER COOL WAS DONE WITH BECKY, HE CALLED HIS girlfriend, Dr. Julia Evans, and explained what was happening. Evans told him they'd be ready, and when Cool touched down six minutes later, Julia was waiting, along with a trauma doc, a general surgeon, and the hospital's top neurologist.

They got Virgil off the helicopter and onto a gurney, then rushed him straight to the Emergency Department, each of the doctors peppering Murton with questions along the way.

Most of Murton's answers were exactly alike. He just kept saying the same thing over and over. "I don't know. I don't know."

There hadn't been room on the helicopter for Mayo, Ortiz, or Wilson because they had to put Virgil on the floor of the aircraft. So the three men got Blackwell out of the storage unit, read him his rights again, then took him down to Central Booking.

As all that was happening, the doctors got Virgil into the exam room, and Murton, Ross, and Cool ended up in the waiting area, staring at the walls. Murton called Becky and asked her to find Sandy.

"I already did," Becky said. "She's on her way, and I am too. What the hell happened, Murt?"

Murton shook his head. "Nobody knows." He told Becky to be careful, and he'd see her soon. Once he was off the phone, Murton looked over at Ross and said, "What the fuck happened?"

Ross said the same thing everyone else had been saying for the past hour. "I don't know."

"I saw the whole thing," Cool said. "I was looking right at him, and I don't know either. He took out his phone, made a call, and had just brought the thing up to his ear when he went down. He just…dropped."

Evans came out to the waiting area, then asked for Cool, Murton and Ross to follow her. Murton looked at her, and said, "Julia…?"

She shook her head. "Not out here, Murt. Follow me."

Doctor Evans unlocked a door just down the hall from the waiting area, then held the door as Cool and Ross went in, and as Murton followed, he caught the look on Julia's face…and the tear that hung in her eyelashes. When he glanced over her shoulder, he saw Sandy running toward him.

When Sandy saw her brother-in-law, she screamed. "Murton…"

Murton wrapped her up in a hug, then led Sandy into the room where Evans was waiting.

Once everyone was seated, Julia said, "First of all, he's alive. I want everyone to take a second and hear me on that. Virgil is alive. They're doing an MRI on him right now. The neurologist thinks it's either a brain bleed or a tumor. We won't know until they're done with the scan."

Sandy bent forward and buried her face in her hands. Everyone gave her a minute, and after she gathered herself together, Sandy looked at Evans and said, "Are there any other possibilities?"

The tear that had been caught in Julia's eyelashes finally let go, and that was an answer all in itself.

Nearly an hour later, the neurologist walked into the room and discovered it so crammed full of people, he didn't know who was who. The doctor looked around, and said, "If you'll forgive me, I'd like to have a moment with family only, if you please."

"Then speak up," Ross said. "Because that's what you've got."

Sandy stood and said, "My name is Sandy Jones. I'm Virgil's wife. These people are all part of my family. Please tell us what's going on."

The doctor looked around the room like he wasn't sure if he should continue, or not. Ultimately, he decided that since his patient's wife had given him permission, it didn't matter. He took a breath, looked directly at Sandy, and said, "Your husband is still in the MRI, but I've seen the initial scans. He's concussed, obviously, but that is the least of his problems."

"If you've seen the scans, why is he still in the MRI?" Sandy said.

"We're doing another one, this time with contrast to get the best look we can. Your husband is a lucky man."

"Explain that." Ross said. There was some bite in his voice.

The doctor turned to Ross. "And you are?"

"He's with me," Sandy said with a little bite of her own. "Answer the question, please."

"In all likelihood, the fall saved his life. He has a mass on his right temporal lobe, and we'll talk about that in a moment, but first I need someone to answer a few questions for me. Has Mr. Jones been—"

"That's Detective Jones," Cora said.

"Yes, of course," the doctor said. "Has Detective Jones demonstrated any unusual behaviors of late?"

"A *mass*?" Sandy said.

Murton took hold of her hand and said, "Hang in there, Small." Then to the doctor: "Define unusual."

"It varies from patient to patient, so it's rather hard for me to say. In a general sense, has he acted strangely in any way whatsoever?"

Sandy wiped her nose with the back of her wrist.

"He has. It's like he's been having…" Sandy shook her head and turned her palms up. "I'm not sure how to describe it."

"We've been calling them episodes," Murton said, and this time he wasn't trying to be funny.

"What do these episodes look like?" the doctor asked.

"Virgil calls them waking dreams," Murton said. "He sort of goes away for a few seconds. Maybe as long as a full minute. But he told me that when he does, it feels like time isn't real. He's reliving old memories…ones that in actuality would add up to much longer than the amount of time he's, uh, lost within himself. I don't know if that makes any sense or not, but that's my take on it. I've personally witnessed it."

The doctor nodded. "Yes, that's exactly the kind of thing I'm speaking of. How many times has this happened, and when?"

"It happened twice in a row with me," Wilson said. "This was about a week and a half ago."

The rest of them took a few minutes and told the doctor of the other episodes they'd witnessed with Virgil, and when.

The doctor gave them all a thoughtful nod and said, "The mass is affecting his cognitive abilities. Hallucinations of that sort are very common in situations like these."

"What about the mass?" Sandy said. She could barely get the words out. "Is it brain cancer?"

"We can't be sure until we're done with the scans," the doctor said. "And I don't want to get your hopes up, but I think not. The first look showed what we typically see with something called meningiomas. That's a very scary-sounding name for a benign tumor that originates from the meninges, the membrane-like structures that surround the brain."

"If he has a brain tumor, how does that make him lucky?" Sandy said.

"I may have misspoken," the doctor said. "I was referring to the fact that he's here right now, and that we caught it in time."

"Then he's not very lucky at all," Sandy said. "He had an MRI scheduled for tomorrow anyway."

"I'm afraid you're wrong about that, ma'am," the doctor said. "The fall was caused by a very minor blockage of one of the blood vessels near the tumor. The tumor itself had put enough pressure on the vessel to cause your husband to pass out. If he hadn't fallen when he did, it's very likely he would have died in his sleep this evening from a stroke." He held his thumb and forefinger about a quarter-inch apart. "It was this close. With your permission, we'll be operating as soon as possible."

"Yes, of course you have my permission. When will you start?"

"As soon as the second scan is complete. No more than thirty minutes from now."

"I'd like to see him," Sandy said. "Is that possible?"

The doctor shook his head. "I'm afraid not. The truth is, he won't be coming out of the MRI machine for more than a few minutes before he goes right back in."

"Why?"

"We'll be doing an MRI-guided LiTT."

"I don't know what that means," Sandy said.

The doctor nodded like he'd heard the statement a thousand times. "Yes, of course. My apologies. Okay: The LiTT device. That stands for laser interstitial thermal therapy. Essentially, the LiTT uses a probe inserted through a very small hole in the skull. We'll use the MRI to guide the probe to the problem area. Once in position, a laser beam is directed through the probe to heat up the tip and destroy the tumor. The entire procedure takes about three hours."

Murton stood up and looked the doctor directly in

the eye. "Your patient is my brother. So, let me ask you the one question everyone in this room is dancing around: Is he going to make it, or not?"

EPILOGUE

ONE WEEK AGO:

AFTER HENDERSON LEFT, ROSENCRANTZ STAYED AT THE front door for a long time, looking at nothing, before he finally decided to walk down the drive and get a little more exercise in for the day. He took his cane with him, and moved slower than normal…not because he wanted to, but because something didn't feel quite right. By the time he got to the end of the drive, turned around and made it back to the house, he thought he knew what was bothering him, and it had nothing to do with his injuries.

He pulled out copies of all the case notes he'd printed from everyone's files, then got on the computer and logged into the MCU's system. Once in, he downloaded the most current version of every piece of available information, then spent the next four hours going through it all, comparing everyone's notes with what he suspected.

When he was sure he was right, he walked outside and sat down on the back porch and stared at the spot where he'd planned to put up a swing set for his unborn child. Then he called his friend, Wu, in Jamaica, and asked for a favor.

Virgil was certain he was going to die. He knew it the way someone does in that split second right before the pall of death takes them away from everyone they'd ever known and loved. Virgil tried to call out to his brother, but the words wouldn't come and there was pain...as hot and intense as anything he'd ever experienced. He couldn't move, and in his mind, Virgil knew he was at his own end and there was nothing he could do to prevent it, his fate in the hands of those who'd gone before him.

When Murton cut the ties that held him against the steel beam and lowered him to the floor, Virgil was sure he saw his mother. She stood behind them, her face radiant, the room somehow brighter with her presence.

She shadowed Murton's efforts, her hands over the top of his as she directed his movements, and though he tried to reach out to them both, Virgil was unable to move, and then there was an eternity of nothingness, as if time wasn't real at all.

NEARLY A WEEK HAD PASSED SINCE THE SURGERY, AND still, Virgil didn't wake up. Sandy was beside herself with worry and fear. Delroy sat in the hospital room near the window, watching her pace back and forth.

Finally he stood, walked over to Sandy and wrapped her up in a hug. "Virgil going to be okay, him. You wait, you see. Jamaicans have a saying, us."

"What is it?" Sandy said.

Delroy smiled, and said, "Time soon come, mon. Time soon come."

AND THEN...THIS:

The room, and everything in it, seemed alive somehow...the furniture, the walls, the curtains, even the window glass. Virgil could see colors he never knew existed, and everything appeared to be vibrating with a frequency all its own. Sandy had a glow around her entire body—a beautiful white aura that clung to her like a second skin.

"There you are," Sandy said. She barely got the words out before she started crying.

Virgil, who could still feel the effects of the surgery, looked at his wife and said, "What time is it?"

Then, even though she was crying, Sandy began to laugh as well. When she could finally speak, she wiped the tears from her face, looked at her husband and said, "It's next time, Virg."

Virgil reached up and touched the bandage that was wrapped around his head. "What happened?"

"What's the last thing you remember?"

"I was tied to a beam. Murton saved me. I think I saw my mom."

Virgil saw a look of panic start to form on Sandy's face. He closed his eyes for a moment, then said, "Wait, that was...I was...it was a memory. Things are mixed up. I think I was dreaming." He opened his eyes and asked, "I'm okay?"

Sandy covered her mouth and the end of her nose with the tips of her fingers, her brows knitted together. "You tell me, Virg."

Virgil looked away for a few seconds, then said, "You're my wife. We have two boys...Jonas and Wyatt.

Murton and Becky live across the pond from us. Where are they? The boys."

And that's when Sandy knew her husband was okay. "Huma took them down to the cafeteria. They'll be back up shortly. Let me go find the doctor."

"Don't leave me just yet," Virgil said.

Sandy pushed the call button for the nurse. Then with a bit of wifely sarcasm, said, "Look who's talking."

MURTON DROVE DOWN TO SHELBY COUNTY AND PICKED up Patty. "I'd like to make this quick, if you don't mind, Pickle Chick. Don't want to be away from Virgil too long."

"I told Mac I could handle it myself, Murt."

"And I have all the faith in the world that you can," Murton said. "But I might have to lean on her a little."

They talked about Virgil on the drive over, and Patty asked if he was really okay.

"Yeah, I think so…other than being a little empty-headed, that is. He's really rockin' that lopsided mullet too."

"Murton Wheeler, that's terrible," Patty said, though she was laughing when she spoke.

"Brotherly love," Murton said. "There's nothing quite like it." Then he got serious. "He had us all pretty scared there, for a minute, anyway. The doc said it was close."

"I'm going to come up and see him once he's home. I didn't want to intrude at the hospital."

"I don't think Virgil would ever consider your presence an intrusion."

They rode the rest of the way in comfortable silence, then, when they arrived at the county's administrative offices, Patty puffed her cheeks, and said, "Let's get this over with."

Murton badged them through security, and Patty noticed a few DEA agents milling about. "What are they doing here?"

Murton looked away and said, "Beats me. Not my department."

They went straight to Stacey Louder's office, then walked in and closed the door behind them like it might have been their own place of employment.

"Who the hell are you two?" Louder said.

Murton pulled out his badge and said, "I'm Detective Murton Wheeler with the state's Major Crimes Unit." He placed his hand on Patty's shoulder. "And if you don't know who this woman is, you don't deserve to be sitting in that chair."

Louder stood from her seat and tried to live up to her name. She pointed a finger at Murton and said, "Are you one of the people who framed my brother and arrested him on those bogus drug charges?"

Murton leaned forward, kept his voice low and said, "First of all, volume doesn't work with me, so dial it back, sister. And secondly, the only three factual words in your last sentence happen to be 'people,' 'brother,' and 'arrested.' Now sit down, shut up, and listen to what Mrs. Stronghill has to say, or I'll perp-walk you out of your own office as an accessory."

"Accessory to what?" Louder said.

"Possession of an illegal substance with the intent to distribute. Murder wouldn't be out of the question, either."

"Prove it, dickhead."

"I don't have to prove anything, Stacey." Murton tipped his head at Patty and said, "Do you know how much money the county receives annually, thanks to this woman's company?"

"Of course I do. The county is very grateful. What does that have to do with me?"

Patty looked at Louder and said, "Sit down, Stacey." She said it so calmly and professionally that Louder sat down like it was her own idea. Once Louder was seated, Patty said, "If you don't want to be responsible for those funds being redirected right out of your county's budget, you will drop your ridiculous campaign to get rid of Sheriff Ed Henderson."

"I will not. That man is a disgrace to the uniform. He even got one of his own deputies killed. A man I cared for very much."

Murton shook his head. "The man you're talking about was a crooked cop who nearly killed my friend and fellow detective."

"Too bad," Louder said. "Now get the fuck out."

Murton put his hand over his chest. "Stacey, the language, please. But, whatever you say. I'm sure Said, Inc. won't have any trouble renegotiating the contract with the county once you're gone."

"I'm not going anywhere, asshole. Now, get out. I won't say it again."

Murton gave Louder a wink and said, "You won't have to. Have a nice life, Stacey."

He and Patty walked out of the office and over to the elevator. While they were waiting, Patty looked at Murton and said, "So, should I have Mac cancel the contract?"

Just then the elevator dinged and the doors opened up. Three DEA agents stepped off, and Murton said, "Thanks for waiting. Two doors down on the right."

"Thank you, Detective," one of the agents said.

Murton gave the man a nod, then got on the elevator with Patty. As the doors were closing, he said, "I'd leave the contract in place. Why punish the whole county over one bad apple? Some people, huh?"

Patty gave him a friendly little shove and started laughing.

Rosencrantz spent the week trying to decide what to do. Once he finally made his decision, he got in his squad car and drove over to Henderson's office. When he walked in he was pleasantly surprised to discover Betty was nowhere in sight, mainly because he didn't yet have the strength to fight her off.

He stuck his head around the corner and into Henderson's office. "Got a second?"

Henderson looked up in surprise. "Hey, Tom. Jesus, what the heck are you doing here? You shouldn't be driving yet."

"Ah, I can drive," Rosencrantz said. "Getting in and out of the car is sort of a challenge, but other than that it's two pedals and a steering wheel."

"Yeah, but if you got hit or something…"

"I'm good, Ed. Really. Can we sit?"

"Sure." Henderson got up and pulled a chair over.

"Get the door, will you?" Rosencrantz said.

"You bet. Say, did you hear the news?"

"I guess not. What is it?"

Henderson took a seat behind his desk, smiled, then said, "The county is dropping their dereliction of duty claim."

"Is that right?" Rosencrantz said.

"Yep. Looks like everything is back to normal around here."

Rosencrantz turned and looked out the window. "Good to know."

"So, I don't think you answered me. What brings you by?"

"I needed to ask you something, Ed."

"Sure. Anything."

"You know that notebook everyone was looking for?"

"Of course. What about it?"

Rosencrantz finally turned away from the window and looked right at his friend. "Where is it?"

"Tom, I don't—"

Rosencrantz held up his hand, palm out. "Stop. You

and I are friends. At least I thought we were. Don't you dare lie to me."

Henderson took a deep breath, then said, "How did you know?"

Rosencrantz pulled out his phone and brought up a video. He hit the Play button then turned it around so Henderson could watch. "I had a friend get this for me. That's you taking the notebook out of Jordan's safe deposit box during the search. The camera doesn't lie, Ed, so I'll ask you again. Where is it?"

"What tipped you off?" Henderson said.

"You did. You kept trying to get everyone to think it didn't exist, or it would never be found, and every time you said something, you sounded awfully sure of yourself."

"That's a little thin."

"Maybe, but you asked a question you shouldn't have. You said, 'What are they going to do? Chase down a buyer in Kentucky who never got the drugs to begin with?'"

"So what?"

"Nobody ever told you about the buyer being in Kentucky, Ed. Hell, we weren't even sure there *was* a buyer."

"I was trying to look out for you, man."

"Me?" Rosencrantz said. "What does it have to do with me?"

"You're the best friend I've ever had. I didn't want to add to your grief."

"What the hell are you talking about?" Rosencrantz said.

"It was Carla, Tom. She was sick. That's why she left the DEA. It was either quit, or get forced out. Blackwell gave the information to Jordan. I only discovered that after I found the notebook."

"You're saying the whole time Carla and I were together she was lying to me?"

Henderson pointed a finger at his friend. "No. Do not go down that road. Carla loved you…heart and soul, Tom. You're all she ever talked about around here. She wasn't lying to you. She was trying to protect you."

"Sick how?"

"She was dying from the same thing that killed my mom. It's called motor neuron disease. It's a terrible way to die. Believe me, I know. I watched it happen to someone I love. I'm sure she would have told you eventually, but after she was killed, and I found the notebook, I didn't want to make her death worse for you."

Rosencrantz sat quietly for a few minutes, then said, "Where is it? The notebook."

Henderson unlocked his top desk drawer and pulled

out a thick, three-ring binder. Rosencrantz reached over and picked it up, then carefully stood and headed for the door.

"Where are you going?"

Rosencrantz wiggled the notebook in the air. "I'm going home to do a little reading. I'll probably have a bonfire later tonight. Care to join me?"

"Yeah, of course," Henderson said. "I'll be there. Then, "Are we okay?"

Rosencrantz stopped and turned back. "Yeah, we are. Congratulations on getting the dereliction of duty charge dropped. You owe me a fuckin' cow."

Virgil spent two more days in the hospital before the doctors gave him the news he wanted to hear more than anything.

"Your tumor was completely benign, we got it all, and other than the fact that you now have another hole in your head, you're as good as new and free to go home. In a few more days you'll be feeling like your old self, and due to the type of procedure we used, a week after that you'll be cleared to go back to work. How are you feeling? Any headaches, nausea, or dizziness?"

Virgil shook his head. "Nope." He reached up and touched the bandage that covered his scalp. "The incision is still kind of sore, but other than that, I feel fine."

"Good. That's exactly what I want to hear. The soreness will fade with time. That's the good news."

Virgil gave the doctor the brow. "That implies that there might be bad news."

"As your hair continues to grow back around the incision, it's going to itch like mad, if it doesn't already. It'll drive you crazy." The doctor pointed his finger at Virgil and said, "Take a Benadryl if you need to, but whatever you do, leave it be. That is not a scab you want to pick at."

Virgil was sitting on the side of his hospital bed, and Sandy was right next to him. He assured the doctor he'd leave it alone, then said, "I can't begin to tell you how much I appreciate what you did for me…and my family."

"All in a day's work, Detective."

Virgil gave the doctor a sheepish grin, and said, "I'm not a detective anymore. I quit a couple of weeks ago."

"Well, I heard you tried to," the doctor said with a grin of his own.

"What are you talking about?"

"The governor came by yesterday to visit. You were

sleeping and she didn't want to disturb you, so she entrusted me with this." The doctor reached into his lab coat, pulled out Virgil's badge, and handed it to him. "She said if you didn't want it, you'd know what to do. Then she mentioned something about pond scum. I didn't know what she meant by any of that. Do you?"

Virgil took the badge and slipped the chain around his neck. After he had it tucked inside his shirt, he took Sandy's hand in his own, looked at the doctor, and said, "Yeah. A story from another time."

Thank you for reading State of Time. If you're enjoying the series, then there's good news: Virgil and the gang will be back soon in **State of Unity.**

Visit ThomasScottBooks.com for further information regarding the Virgil Jones Mystery Thriller Series, release dates, and more.

— **Also by Thomas Scott** —

The Virgil Jones Series In Order

State of Anger - Book 1
State of Betrayal - Book 2
State of Control - Book 3
State of Deception - Book 4
State of Exile - Book 5
State of Freedom - Book 6
State of Genesis - Book 7
State of Humanity - Book 8
State of Impact - Book 9
State of Justice - Book 10
State of Killers - Book 11
State of Life - Book 12
State of Mind - Book 13
State of Need - Book 14
State of One - Book 15
State of Play - Book 16
State of Qualms - Book 17
State of Remains - Book 18
State of Suspense - Book 19
State of Time - Book 20
State of Unity - Book 21

The Jack Bellows Series In Order

Wayward Strangers - Book 1
Brave Strangers - Book 2

Visit ThomasScottBooks.com for further information regarding future release dates, and more.

ABOUT THE AUTHOR

Thomas Scott is the author of the **Virgil Jones** Mystery Thriller series, and the **Jack Bellows** series of novels. He lives in northern Indiana with his lovely wife, Debra, and his trusty sidekicks and writing buddies, Lucy, the cat, and Buster, the dog.

You may contact Thomas anytime via his website ThomasScottBooks.com where he personally answers every single email he receives. Be sure to sign up to be notified of the latest release information.

Also, if you enjoy the Virgil Jones series of books, leaving an honest review on Amazon.com helps others decide if a book is right for them. Just a sentence or two makes all the difference in the world. Plus, rumor has it that it's good for the soul.

For information on future books in the Virgil Jones series, or to connect with the author, please visit:
ThomasScottBooks.com

And remember:

Virgil and the gang will return soon in State of Unity!

Scan me with your Smart phone!

Made in United States
Orlando, FL
31 August 2024